Wrapped

ALSO BY
JENNIFER BRADBURY

SHIFT

Wrapped

Jennifer Bradbury

Atheneum Books for Young Readers
New York * London * Toronto * Sydney

Acknowledgments

Thanks to Mom for all the *Masterpiece Theatre*, even when I pretended to think it was lame. Thanks to Jana and Katy for all the stories we loved and the ones we made up. Thanks to June for the steady diet of Elizabeth Gaskell and Jane Austen DVDs, and for being such a cheerleader. Thanks to Marissa Doyle and Regina Scott for their expertise and the warm welcome to Regency world. Thanks to Pat Taylor for introducing me to Jane Austen—*Persuasion* remains my favorite. Thanks to Robin Rue, for telling me the truth and for making this whole writing thing so much more fun. Thanks to Beth Miller for talking me off the ledge, and to Kiley Frank for the encouraging notes that show up with every reprint, rewrite, or editorial letter. Thanks to Angie Wright for the faithful readings (I owe you lunch forever). Thanks to the staffs of the Burlington Public Library and the Mount Vernon City Library for never minding when I request more YA titles. Thanks to Caitlyn Dlouhy, for always seeing the possibilities, and for her unerring eye in guiding me to the best version of any story. And thanks to Jimmy, for loving the book before I even wrote it, pulling me through every revision, and putting up with me. I promise there will be dancing in the next one.

ATHENEUM BOOKS FOR YOUNG READERS * An imprint of Simon & Schuster Children's Publishing Division * 1230 Avenue of the Americas, New York, New York 10020 * This book is a work of fiction. Any references to historical events, real people, or real locales are used fictitiously. Other names, characters, places, and incidents are products of the author's imagination, and any resemblance to actual events or locales or persons, living or dead, is entirely coincidental. * Copyright © 2011 by Jennifer Bradbury * All rights reserved, including the right of reproduction in whole or in part in any form. * ATHENEUM BOOKS FOR YOUNG READERS is a registered trademark of Simon & Schuster, Inc. * For information about special discounts for bulk purchases, please contact Simon & Schuster Special Sales at 1-866-506-1949 or business@simonandschuster.com. * The Simon & Schuster Speakers Bureau can bring authors to your live event. For more information or to book an event, contact the Simon & Schuster Speakers Bureau at 1-866-248-3049 or visit our website at www.simonspeakers.com. * The text for this book is set in Minister. * Manufactured in the United States of America * First Edition * 10 9 8 7 6 5 4 3 2 1 * CIP data for this book is available from the Library of Congress. * ISBN 978-1-4169-9007-9 (hardcover) * ISBN 978-1-4391-5902-6 (eBook)

To Evie June and Arun Saroj,
and all the adventures that await you both

London

June 1815

Chapter One

"Put the book down, darling," my mother said from her chair beside the mirror.

"The chapter's end is only a short way off," I replied, reaching out with my other hand to flip the page. Despite the ache in my shoulder from holding the book at arm's length so the dressmakers could work on my gown, I didn't want to give it up.

"For heaven's sake, you've read it a dozen times," Mother said, rising to snatch the book from my hand. I half lunged for it, an action answered by the jabs of a dozen pins in places sensitive enough to ensure the book was lost to me for now.

"It improves each time," I told her, letting my arms fall, the sensation of the blood rushing back into my fingertips too brief before the dressmaker nudged one elbow upward again.

"Please, miss," the woman said, gesturing at the bodice, managing to sound even more exasperated with me than Mother had.

I lifted my arms again, posing as if I were about to take

flight. According to some, I was. My debut had come, bringing with it Mother's long-awaited opportunity to parade me about in front of all of London. The dress wrapped itself around me in tucks and folds of silk the color of cream as it stands on the top of a cup of tea, waiting to be stirred in. The trim at the neckline was exquisitely wrought in lace Mother had warned me more than once not to tell Father the price of. I'd pleaded unsuccessfully to have this particular dress made from a shimmering red sari fabric my brother had sent home to me from India. Mother was firm that red was perfectly unsuitable.

She was right, of course, as she was about most everything. She was right that this color was far more appropriate for a girl making a debut, that it would allow me to fit and stand out at the same time. I wasn't sure I was ready to do either yet. And I was relatively certain I wasn't prepared to step into society as Mother's protégée. I adored my mother, but I didn't want to be her. Not yet, anyway.

"You really might at least pretend to be more diverted by all of this," she complained, turning down a corner of the page of my book before placing it on the dressing table. I fought the urge to beg her to use the scrap of lace I'd employed as a bookmark. I didn't want creases in that particular copy of *Mansfield Park*. But the damage was done. And Mother was incensed enough with me already.

"On the contrary, Mother," I said, balancing on my left foot just long enough to scratch the back of my right knee with my toe, "I find the prospect of this evening's entertainment so over-whelming that it helps to have something to occupy my mind." Mother almost smiled. "It does promise to be an affair. I'm sure I've waited long enough before agreeing to be seen at one of these events, don't you think?"

"Never be the first or the last to adopt fashion," I said, echoing her words dutifully.

"But you *must* be the first to make an impression on our host this evening," she said, a smile beginning at the corner of her mouth. Mother had declined two earlier invitations for parties of this sort. But when this one from Lord Thomas Showalter came so fortuitously timed with my debut, Mother accepted with haste. I couldn't blame her, exactly. Lord Showalter was exactly the kind of man she or any other eager mother wanted for her daughter. He might have been the most sought-after man in all of Hyde Park, if not all of London itself. He was charming, handsome, and rich.

I rolled my eyes, whispered, *"E 'una verità universalmente riconosciuta che un uomo solo in possesso di una fortuna deve essere in mancanza di una moglie."*

"Don't mumble, dear," she ordered.

This time I slipped from Italian to Russian and spoke a bit louder. *"Все знают, что молодой человек, располагающий средствами, должен подыскивать себе жену."* I loved the way Russian insisted on tickling the back of my throat.

"Agnes." Mother's tone carried the warning for her.

I translated the line again, this time to German, so Mother might recognize it at last. *"Es ist eine allgemein anerkannte Wahrheit, daß ein Junggeselle im Besitz eines schönen Vermögens nichts dringender braucht als eine Frau."*

She stiffened, crossed her arms. "You know how it vexes me when you show off—what man will stand for that, I wonder?"

Finally, I all but shouted at her in French. *"C'est une vérité universellement reconnue, qu'un seul homme en possession d'une bonne fortune doit être dans le besoin d'une femme."*

She took a moment, narrowing her eyes to tiny slits. "It's not enough that you must cavort about in tongues that no respectable girl has any business speaking, but you must quote those books in the bargain? Honestly, Agnes."

I smiled sweetly. "I was agreeing with you," I said, "or at the very least A Lady was." I looked down at the younger of the two dressmakers. "It's from *Pride and Prejudice*," I said. "'It is a truth universally acknowledged, that a single man in possession of a good fortune, must be in want of a wife.' Have you read it?"

The girl's eyes lit up and she began to nod, but Mother cut short her reply. "Of course she's read it. Half of England has read it, which is why it's vulgar to quote it."

"Half the world has read the Bible and we quote it all the time," I teased.

"I'll pretend you didn't just compare the scribbling of a female novelist to the words of our Lord," she said. "Whatever will I do with you?"

I sighed. "Marry me off to a rich man before he sees how clever I am. And with me in this gown at this evening's most romantic of events, it appears your task is half done already."

Mother sat again, placated a bit by my apparent acquiescence to her plan. "The entertainment he has chosen is gruesome, but it will provide a stunning foil for your beauty."

We'd agreed that we would both politely decline actively participating this evening if pressed to do so. But Mother would not risk staying clear of the party outright. She was sure that Showalter was finally ready to seek a wife after several years in our London society and that if I weren't there to be seen as a candidate, my chance would be lost.

I didn't have the stomach to tell her that part of me wanted to stay here in my room and reread an A Lady novel or continue working on my Hebrew translations.

"Lady Ershing told me they do this sort of thing all the time in France. But so many of the fancies out of Europe have to be weighed against good English judgment and civility, I always say," my mother mused.

"They trim their gowns in red lace in Paris, ma'am," one of the seamstresses offered. Mother had brought the dressmakers here in order to preserve the secrecy of my gown. She couldn't bear the thought of my first debut gown being copied or seen by anyone before I'd had a chance to wear it. Her paranoia knew no bounds on this score. Already she'd been favoring the shop far from Bond Street and the prying eyes of her friends and neighbors. But bringing the dressmakers to our home was extreme even for her. She'd already arranged to do the same with the final fittings for my presentation gown, but that dress was still being pieced at the shop.

Mother jabbed a finger at the girl. "How dreadful. Just because the French do it doesn't mean we should. England is her own sovereign sensible state."

"And may we stay that way for eternity, God save the King and damn Napoleon!" I said.

Mother's gaze darkened. The two dressmakers pretended to be fascinated with the pleats. "Take care to find a way to voice your patriotism more appropriately," my mother warned.

"Yes, Mother." I sighed. But I felt the same about the mad little man across the Channel as anyone in England. Napoleon had more lives than a cat, had been the villain of the newspapers and in our household since I was a child. Before I even properly understood that he aimed for nothing less than ruling the world—and England with it—I used to spy on my brothers as they staged reenactments of the Battle of Trafalgar in the nursery.

Ten years Napoleon had haunted us. And with his most recent return from exile, the threat had gained strength anew. It was enough to make me wonder if debuting under such a shadow was at all sensible. I'd tried once to persuade Mother on this point. Her reply had been swift and certain: The very best affront we could offer the French would be to continue on with our lives as if Napoleon and his ambitions worried us not at

WRAPPED   9

all. Solid English tradition scoffing in the face of danger. She'd sounded as though she belonged on the floor of the House of Lords at Father's side.

Mother seemed to read my thoughts. "It is so important that you debut now, Agnes," she affirmed. "It is your duty. Our duty. To David and his compatriots, that they may know we have confidence enough in them to protect us. To those of the lower classes who need to see their betters continuing with the important traditions and rites that make ours a great nation . . . and to flout Napoleon, the little cockroach!"

I rolled my eyes. "I can hardly see how my debut will cause old Boney to flinch, Mother."

She sat up straighter, her chin lifting. "Principle, Agnes," she said gravely. "It's the principle of the matter."

"To say nothing of *your* principles," I teased. Mother had waited longer than she wished for my debut season to arrive. Her own season had resulted in a triumphant match with my father. I suppose I couldn't hold it against her that she was eager for me to find such happiness.

Mother hesitated, softened a bit, and then spoke. "Well, I have been very patient, haven't I?"

"Mother, I'm barely seventeen!" I said, falling as easily into the argument we'd been having for the last two years as I might into my own bed.

"*I* debuted at sixteen," she replied, on script. "And married your father at seventeen. Of course custom dictates a longer engagement these days. Though I think anything longer than two years is a bit absurd. . . ."

Mother suddenly sprang to her feet and worked her way in between the two dressmakers. "This pleat does not lie properly. It will not do."

"You're not so eager to marry David or Rupert off," I complained.

"David is years from being a suitable husband. And Rupert . . ." She paused, shook her head. "Even with your father's fortune, I do not know that he will have the same sense to marry so well."

"No one could marry as well as Father," I said sweetly, even meaning it.

Mother smiled, swatted at my hand. "You're a good girl, Agnes," she said. "And you'll make an excellent wife. Though I shudder to think what kind of home you'll keep." She nodded to the wallpaper. "I still can't account for those."

I smiled at the golden walls, flecked with shimmering pink cherry blossoms and snaky green dragons peeking through the branches. I'd begged Father to bring me something special when he'd gone as part of a delegation to Japan when I was nine or so. He'd brought the paper, telling Mother that the empress herself had it hanging on the walls of the throne room and that it was perfect for his dear princess.

The dull floral that had been on my wall since my grandmother's time gave way.

"I'm sure you'll be at hand to advise me," I said quietly, looking about the room at the other objects that Father had brought home during his years of travel, or that David had sent from various ports while at sea. The pointy little slippers from Turkey, the delicate toy drum from the Indies, and the dozens of books in various languages, some of which I'd managed to read, others still waiting to be unlocked.

Mother looked at me. "Lord Showalter's tastes do run quite the same direction as yours."

It was true. I'd been to Showalter's twice before, and the house was chockablock with curiosities, the bulk of which had been ferried over from Egypt. Nothing went together. Strolling through his sitting room was like rummaging through the world's attic, so varied and odd was the collection of items he possessed and displayed. He even had a small golden idol shaped like a bird on his mantelpiece.

"Perhaps you'll even be so kind as to decorate our entire house so that I might have time to concentrate on my studies?"

Mother shook her head. "Education is for children. And you've already had far more than your share. I let your father keep finding those language tutors for you, but there comes a time when every girl must step out of the schoolroom and into the life that awaits her." She held my eye. "And that time for you is come at last!"

At this, the seamstresses stepped away and looked to

Mother. She circled round me, studying every stitch and hem and pleat and ruffle and fall of fabric.

"Very good," she said finally.

I looked at myself in the mirror. Still a girl in a lovely dress, my auburn hair pinned back, waiting for Clarisse to do with it what only she could.

But what that girl in the mirror felt surprised me. I'd spent months arguing with Mother about allowing me to continue my studies, pleading with Father to convince her to delay my debut. And yet, in this dress . . .

I looked beautiful. How odd a sensation. Mother was beautiful. I was not. And yet in the dress I looked like a girl ready to make her debut, a girl who belonged at a party, or a coronation or something important. And then an even odder shiver ran through me: I wanted to see what could happen at parties and dinners for a girl dressed like I was. At least it would be something new, possibly exciting, even if it was a quick step into the rest of my life.

Suddenly all of me couldn't wait to wear this dress tonight.

Mother must have noticed the change.

"You wear it well," she said.

And for once I could not argue.

Chapter Two

❧

That night we found ourselves in a corner of Lord Showalter's gardens, four houses east of our own residence. Summer cottons and silks billowed on the warm breeze as a few dozen guests glided across a lawn so perfectly trimmed I was almost sorry to walk on it. Nervous whispers rippled through the crowd around me as we followed our host through an ivy-covered archway and onto a broad stone patio. A hedge of oily torches spat plumes of smoke, beckoning us closer to the object we'd all been invited to see. Amid the ring of firelight sat a table draped in scarlet velvet.

A mummy lay upon it.

Lord Showalter, resplendent in a waistcoat of blue the color of the night sky above us, opened his arms as we crowded onto the pavers. It was clear he could sense the same unease and curiosity that ran through us all, though he seemed to relish it, letting the silence build as he surveyed our faces.

His eyes landed on me, seemed to hold there a bit longer,

and I was reminded of how Mother and half the women of the Park described him. *Magnetic*. Showalter could hold an entire room in his gaze at once but still make each person feel as if he or she were its most important occupant. Mother explained it was a gift, the talent of a natural-born host and leader, the type of man who inspired loyalty and ardor in equal measure.

But I was a girl in a beautiful dress, a girl capable enough of giving back as good as she got. I nodded, smiled demurely, and held his stare.

His eyes never strayed from mine as he smiled mysteriously, then asked, "Who will be the first to dare upset our Egyptian guest on his journey through the underworld?" He looked at each of us, even though I was quite sure he'd determined who'd be first even before sending out the invitations. But I wasn't expecting what he said next.

"Agnes Wilkins! *You* must take the first pass," Showalter boomed, beckoning me forward.

"Me?" I asked in alarm. Whispers rippled through the crowd.

My boldness of a moment before retreated as I flushed. Showalter was showing me some preference.

"Of course," he said. "In honor of your pending debut, Miss Wilkins."

I waited for Mother to intervene, to tell Showalter that I couldn't possibly—we'd *agreed*—but the expression she wore when I glanced her way told me I was on my own. Had Showalter's choice outweighed all her opinions about how lurid this affair was? Was the whim of a would-be suitor already overriding her *principles*? Finding no help in Mother, I looked back to Showalter. He was waiting, his stare so loaded with expectation that I found myself taken aback again. Was I imagining that there was an invitation to more lurking beneath that sly grin?

Finally I found my voice. "Your kindness is most generous, but I could not presume—"

"I insist," he said, taking my elbow and steering me to the foot of the mummy. I could imagine the eyebrows rising behind me and felt my throat tighten. I expected Mother was by now beaming triumphantly, scheming about how best to announce an engagement that apparently she'd been plotting for months.

I was not the only girl at the party who was meant to enjoy her first season this summer. I knew Julia Overton was supposed to be here. Dr. Clerval, the physician to half the residents of the Park, had brought his daughters. There was another girl, the niece of one of the new families at the south end of the Park, here as well. We were all in new gowns, all novices at social events like this, all fresh from the schoolrooms or tutors.

But Showalter had singled me out.

"Just there, Miss Wilkins," he said, his breath warm on my shoulder.

"Lord Showalter—"

"Just take the blade here"—he slipped a small silver knife

under a band of the linen—"and slide upward. Then you peel
the wrappings back a layer at a time."

"Sir," I began to protest, but he'd already disappeared back
into the crowd of his guests to fetch others to join me for the
entertainment.

But there's a person in there, I thought, trying not to wince. At
least the remains of one. Someone who'd been folded carefully
up inside those layers of fabric, someone who hadn't meant to
be seen again at all.

Someone who hadn't expected to be put on display, ogled
by curious eyes.

Someone a little like me.

As oddly flattering as it felt to have caught the eye of
Showalter, here was one feeling I was certain I would never
enjoy: the sensation of all these eyes staring at me, appraising
me, sizing up what my future was meant to be.

I sought Father's face in the crowd, and found him eyeing
me from the periphery, an unreadable smile on his lips. The one
that walked so fine a line between mockery and contentment.

"Don't look so frightened, Agnes," my brother Rupert whispered as he joined me at the body, proud to be among those
chosen to cut first. "It's just some old bones and linen."

"I'm not scared of the mummy," I returned.

"You and your nonsense talk about women being the equal
of men." My oldest brother shook his head. He reached for his
own knife and a handful of the linen.

"Lord Showalter didn't say we could begin," I pointed out, though etiquette concerning affairs of this sort was a bit muddled. Even Mother had been unsure of the protocol. "Didn't say we couldn't. Trust me, Agnes. Fellow from down at the club"—he paused briefly to saw through a bit of the linen—"he told me all about these things. He's got an uncle worth sixty thousand a year who's already hosted one unwrapping. He said you just grab a knife and start digging away. There's all sorts of little things the old natives used to wrap up in the cloths—trinkets mostly, items they reasoned the body would need in the next world."

"I'm familiar with the purposes of mummification," I said.

"But the good bit," Rupert continued, ignoring my jab as he hacked away, "is that sometimes they would hide some valuable items. And not just old things that are valuable because some museum might want them. Jewels and precious stones and so forth."

"It just doesn't seem right somehow," I said, "disregarding the last wishes of a human being."

He shrugged. "Just a body, Agnes. Don't let your imagination get the better of you. Though I fear those novels you are so fond of have made you afraid of the real world."

I felt it unwise to point out that a horde of London's wealthiest and most fashionable citizens preparing to pillage a centuries-old Egyptian mummy like a Christmas pudding was perhaps as far from the real world as I could imagine.

But to Rupert, past twenty but with no more sense than he'd had at fourteen, this was real.

Our host placed a third and final guest at the body, Lady Kensington. Showalter stared at us gravely, but the volume of his voice carried out to the thirty or so other faces watching eagerly in the firelight. "Begin! But beware awakening the mummy and rousing its curse!" He managed to keep his stony expression for a few seconds before he collapsed into a giggle, and motioned to the sitar player who had followed us outside from the dining room to offer some musical accompaniment to our macabre task.

What a sitar had to do with Egypt, I couldn't tell, except that Showalter and many of his guests seemed content to lump all things exotic and foreign into one tidy category.

I realized sadly that this might be the closest I ever came to glimpsing the wonders of the world beyond England. How I longed to board a frigate to Egypt—or anywhere, for that matter—wander through a bazaar, ride a camel to the pyramids and the Valley of the Kings with a veil pulled across my face. I'd rather hear street musicians plink away at odd instruments than listen to a sitar player and a string quartet fail to reproduce the mystery of North Africa. I looked at the mummy then for what it truly was—an emissary from the world I would likely never know or taste or feel—and it nearly broke my heart.

Rupert had already dug a swath a few inches wide, revealing only more wrappings. Lady Kensington swallowed hard and picked up her own knife, delicately sliding it under an edge. I steeled myself to my task, reasoning that the sooner I began, the sooner I'd be excused. But my eye fell on a living person as out of place here as the mummy. A young man sat perched on a stool just outside the firelight. He suddenly rose to his feet, balancing a great ledger book across one arm, a grease pencil waiting in his other hand.

He was no guest. His coat was too shabby and his shoes too low at the heel to merit an invitation. But his height, his intent brown eyes, and the square shape of his jaw more than made up for any indignity in his dress. He rivaled even my imagined picture of Mr. Darcy. I forced my eyes away, afraid of being caught staring by the mysterious young man or anyone else.

"Agnes," came Lord Showalter's voice at my ear. "Others are waiting. You must take your pass and find what you will."

I understood why it mattered to him that I enjoy this. That others see me enjoying it. He'd made that clear when he called me out first.

But I didn't understand why I felt both flattered *and* annoyed by his attention.

I picked up my own small, sharp knife, but still I hesitated. I studied the bundle that sat before me, wondering if it was a trick of the torchlight that made the wrappings where I stood seem a bit lighter in color. I was about to ask Showalter if he noticed it as well, when he spoke again.

"Please, Miss Wilkins," he said. "If you are uncomfortable—"

"I'm not," I said quickly. But now I was irritated and wanted only to get this over with.

"What is that young man doing?" I asked him as I felt the first bit of linen give way under the knife. The stranger hovered near the head of the body now, furiously jotting notes into his ledger as Rupert and Lady Kensington hacked away.

Showalter followed my gaze. "He's someone from the museum. They like to catalog the bodies, describe the remains and the condition of the wrappings. Claim it helps to document every specimen, even ones for private parties. I don't even know this fellow's name, but Banehart at the museum sent him over."

"Hmm," I said, cutting through more of the layers, the dust of the linen making my fingers slippery.

"Don't worry, my dear, he can't take any of the things we find. I paid for this mummy—and half the ones in that museum. So what's here is ours to keep. Certainly if something is precious enough we might choose to donate it to the collection, but it is my greatest wish that you'll return home tonight with a lovely memento of this auspicious evening."

"Aha!" my brother cried, chest thrust out, golden hair falling into his eyes as he extracted a small ankh from the furrow of linen he'd plowed. The trinket was lovely, burnished gold crested with a dark green stone. My brother, however, seemed to think that he was the one worth admiring. Rupert held the ankh above his head for the crowd to see, grinning as if he'd just rescued it from a pit of hissing asps.

As the guests surged forward to inspect this prize, I continued in my course, determined to find something and have done with my part in desecrating the grave of a fellow human—be it male, female, pharaoh or merchant. Blessedly, we were still nowhere near the actual remains. But the pile of linen already unwound from the body seemed impossibly large, spilling off my narrow end of the table, coiling about my feet, as if I were the next in line to be immobilized and preserved for all eternity. I glanced at Showalter. Perhaps I was.

"A fine discovery," Lord Showalter said to my brother, holding the ankh up to catch the torchlight. If Showalter had a natural gift for commanding an audience, he was equally adept at keeping one enthralled. He appeared to enjoy this role immensely, particularly when he could pontificate on a subject he knew as well as Egypt. "The cut and color of the stone are consistent with artifacts from a certain Theban dynasty."

Then a metal edge emerged from the cloth in front of me, like a scallop shell half buried in the sand. My pulse raced as the undeniable excitement of the moment took hold. I glanced up to see if anyone else had seen it yet, but they were all still attending carefully to Showalter's impromptu lecture about Rupert's ankh. So no one noticed as I pulled the item from the wrapping. No one but me saw the object breathe fresh air for the first time in a thousand years. The feeling was unexpectedly thrilling, and I could only imagine what it might feel like to unearth whole temples forgotten to time, like that Swiss man had found at Abu Simbel a couple of years ago.

I started to call to the others, but they were listening raptly as our host delivered a detailed description of a small scroll found by Lady Kensington at the shoulder of the corpse.

I left them to Showalter's performance and studied the treasure I'd unwrapped. It was an intricately carved outline, shaped like a dog's head, made of what appeared to be iron owing to the rust flaking from the corners. It fit perfectly in the palm of my hand, the snout tipping out at the first knuckle of my ring finger, its ears extending to the base of my thumb. The detail along the edges was extraordinarily precise, each tooth in the parted muzzle sharp, the ruff at the back of the neck bristling. A small scrap of linen clung to the rim, secured with a knot too tight for me to work out easily. The characters printed upon the linen there were even more impenetrable. A different sort of hieroglyph, I reasoned, but just as unreadable as those on Lady Kensington's scroll.

Showalter was concluding his lecture, and I knew my discovery and I would next be on display. I stared at the sad little dog's head.

And I felt pity for it in a way that surprised me. Pity that it had been plucked from its own quiet life inside the wrappings, would now be subject to scrutiny, have its value and utility assessed.

It wasn't fair. Any of it.

I checked the crowd again, especially the young scribe from the museum. He was frantically jotting notes, straining to get a closer glimpse of the ankh.

Showalter had said we could keep what we found, hadn't he?

And hadn't our friends and neighbors seen enough of Showalter standing over me this evening to keep tongues wagging and minds whirling for weeks?

And hadn't I had as much attention as I could endure for one evening?

Yes, yes, and yes.

Satisfied, I closed my palm around the trinket and tucked it into the bodice of my dress.

Chapter Three

❦

I'd only ever stolen biscuits from the kitchen at home, so I was surprised that I felt as cool in that moment as the bit of ironwork hiding in my dress.

And it was this realization that thrilled me even more than the act itself.

To stand amid a throng of people and have a secret. To have done something just beneath their very noses was simply the most delicious feeling.

Not that I had in the strictest sense actually stolen it. If I was guilty of any theft, it was merely that I robbed the other partygoers of a glimpse of the little object.

I slipped nearer the knot of admirers poring over the scroll. Lord Showalter, brow furrowed, announced, "No, the hieroglyphs are unfamiliar."

"Has the Crown made any progress in that area?" Lady Marbury, the oldest and most respected member of the Park's grand society, asked gravely. Britain had recovered the Rosetta

Stone from Napoleon's troops after his defeat at the Nile some
ten years ago. I'd seen it at the museum and knew like the
rest of the world that it represented the best hope for eventually unlocking the hieroglyphics adorning the many artifacts
now populating London, that it might hold the keys to unlock
the secrets of ancient Egypt.

"No, my lady, but my people at the museum assure me we
are making progress."

Lord Showalter was as avid a collector of experts as he
was of Egyptian antiquities. He'd brought dozens of scientists and historians to London from the Continent and Egypt,
several of whom were installed as employees at the British
Museum.

Showalter himself had only been living in London for the
last five or six years. Mother said he'd inherited his title and a
stunning manor somewhere near York but hadn't lived there,
taking degrees from Cambridge and then spending a few
years on the Continent, where he'd increased an already sizable
fortune by buying shares in a shipping company. But then he
moved to London to indulge his passion for Egyptology, to be
at the heart of the world's greatest collection of artifacts, and to
oversee developments and steward the considerable funds he'd
endowed the museum with.

Showalter's valet—a man I knew only as Tanner—suddenly
broke through the crowd in great agitation and whispered in
his master's ear. I could not hear what was said, but I could see

Showalter's face transform from contented self-importance to something altogether grim.

"When?" he barked, glaring at the valet in a rare display of temper. I blanched, half-worried that my theft had been seen, that I was about to be exposed. . . .

"Just received the message, sir," said the valet, his voice rising to match Showalter's. The light caught the rest of his face now, revealing the oddity that made him seem at home among Showalter's collection of curious objects. One of his eyes had a misshapen pupil, the black dot spilling out into the gray-brown iris like the cracked yolk of an egg.

"I beg your pardon," said Showalter, pushing his way free of his guests. "I've urgent business to attend to. I'm sure Mrs. Blalock and the Wilkins family will continue events in my absence." He left without another word, striding hurriedly back to the house, Tanner scurrying behind.

My brother immediately took charge. "Right, then. Who's next? Agnes obviously hasn't the nerve for all this. Who will take her place?" I gladly surrendered my knife, slipping away as Rupert installed three new treasure seekers.

I felt a hand on my arm. "You can't think I didn't notice that!"

Julia Overton stared at me, her eyes imploring. We'd been friends since we were small, having resided three doors down from each other for much of our lives. Julia's family usually summered in the Lakes, and even took me with them one year, and we'd shared tutors in music and painting.

"Notice what?" I asked her, my cheeks growing hot. My hand flew instinctively to the bodice of my dress as if to make sure the dog's head wasn't peeking out. At the last moment, I let my fingers rest on the jade pendant I had insisted Mother allow me to wear this evening. It was another of the baubles Father had brought me from his travels. This one came from China, the sea green stone shaped into a delicate little butterfly. I'd worn it faithfully since he presented it to me on my eleventh birthday. I rubbed the wing as if it were a talisman.

"Don't play coy, Agnes Wilkins, everyone saw it!"

Suddenly my palms and forehead felt damp. The small iron dog's head in my dress seemed to burn against my skin.

"I don't"—I cast about desperately for a lie—"know what you mean."

"Truly? You didn't notice that Showalter as good as declared himself right there?"

I breathed, smiling with relief. But Julia misinterpreted the reason.

"I expect you'd be pleased. He's only the man half of London's matchmakers are gunning for this season. And he fancies *you*!" she said, her own smile just a little too perfect, the slightest hint of bitterness in her voice. Julia was my friend, but I was reminded of a painful truth: During our debut, others would pit us as rivals for the affections of London's wealthiest and most weddable men.

"I don't know that I'd say that," I protested.

"Of course you wouldn't, but you don't have to," she said, adding, "*He* did. And he's so young—"

"He's twenty-six, Julia, near ten years older than the both of us."

"I'll be fortunate to land one only twenty years my senior. And not half so handsome in the bargain."

Handsome? Showalter was tall and lean, no hint of a belly beneath his waistcoat. He had all his hair, and everyone spoke highly of his fine teeth and easy smile.

But did I find him handsome?

He wasn't awful. But he certainly wasn't a Mr. Darcy. There was nothing brooding or mysterious about Showalter. Still, perhaps a Darcy in fiction was better than one in reality. Because life with such a man as that could be hard, despite its pleasures. Maybe Mother and Rupert were right: A Lady *had* poisoned me. Perhaps what I really needed was a kind, simple fellow—a Bingley—rather than one who incensed me to passion or anger by turns like Mr. Darcy had Elizabeth.

I didn't want to think of it any longer. "Have you been here all evening? I didn't see you arrive."

She nodded. "Yes, well, my chaperone put us a bit late arriving because she couldn't find her shawl, but I've been here. Was it awful, by the way?"

"I've not seen your chaperone or her shawl," I offered lamely.

"The *mummy*, Agnes. It looks ghastly."

"Not as ghastly as using it for entertainment," I said under my breath, eliciting a snort from Julia.

"Well, when you're mistress of this place, you can insist on croquet or lawn bowling—something less sinister."

I didn't want to insist on anything as mistress of this house. I tried to wrest the subject away once more.

"Where is your chaperone now?" I asked.

She glanced round. "Talking to your father."

I looked and saw Emmaline Perkins, a stylish widow, bending Father's ear. He listened politely, but I could tell by his expression that his mind was elsewhere.

"And yours?" Julia asked me.

"Napping inside, perhaps," I said.

Father abhorred the practice of hiring chaperones to arrange matches and generally keep girls like Julia and me in check. But Mother—and custom—dictated I have one. Father managed to persuade her that his ancient aunt Rachel would be just the person. Aunt Rachel wouldn't do much to secure a match, but she also hadn't gotten in the way of my studies. Mother had worried that a less vivacious chaperone might place me at some disadvantage, but Father teased that his money and title were enough to draw interest.

I just hadn't counted on them drawing interest so quickly.

"Lucky," Julia said, shaking her head lightly. "Oh, Agnes, I envy you."

"Well, she's *still* a chaperone," I said. "I'm supposed to drag her around with me during the day. And by God she moves slowly."

"It isn't only that your chaperone is so easy to evade," Julia interrupted. "You *belong* here. I feel utterly out of place in all this." She cast her eyes on her own new dress—a perfectly nice frock of pink silk—and waved her glass of sherry toward the crowd.

"I assure you I don't fit at all," I said. "And you look ravishing, by the way."

She smiled. "As ravishing as I can when I weigh a stone under what I ought. Mother swears she'll have me eating nothing but honey and goose fat if I don't have my court dress filled out by next week's fitting."

"She's mad," I said. "You're perfect."

"I'm far from that, but I'll do fine. Still, I'm glad you'll be clearing off so soon. The rest of us will have a hard time finding husbands until the men are all convinced you're spoken for."

"Really, Julia—"

"Stop being modest. It merely adds to your already lengthy list of things I wish I were." She shook her head gently, the smile on her face shifting a little.

"I feel about as natural here as a pig in church."

"Well it doesn't show. And I've never seen so many men staring at a pig." She nodded to the guests.

I was having difficulty breathing.

"At least there's one eligible young man who doesn't fancy

you," she added, nodding toward the mummy, where Rupert presided over the extraction of a small figurine from the body, something looking like actual flesh now peeking from the wrappings at the feet.

"Quite right about that," I said. "Though I can't imagine anyone fancying *him*." I huddled close to Julia to share Rupert's latest misadventure, one involving a goat and a statue in Covent Garden. "Did you hear—," I began, but stopped when I saw her expression.

She was looking at me wide-eyed, expectant, but more than that, a little caught out. "Oh," was all I managed.

Julia nodded, this time her cheeks growing pink. "Mother's convinced he's a good match for me. Lady Perkins is working toward it already."

"Oh," I repeated. Julia was a lovely girl. Smart and genuine and kind.

Everything Rupert wasn't. I couldn't make myself imagine them together.

But I knew the rules, and imagination rarely entered into things. Julia's father was a successful merchant and manufacturer, and though they had money, they had no title. Father had lands and a title and a seat in the House of Lords, all making Rupert something of the best-case scenario for someone like Julia.

"He's a decent sort of man," she said, though I could tell she was fishing for reassurance.

I hesitated. "He is," I said carefully. "Mother always says

he possesses enough of my father's good attributes to make her hopeful. She seems to think he needs only the right sort of woman to refine those qualities."

Mrs. Perkins appeared suddenly at our sides. "Miss Wilkins, always stealing the show, aren't we?"

"I've done nothing like," I said to the woman, whose husband's death had left her with just enough to be independent, but not enough to live in style.

"Come along, Julia," she ordered. "I've arranged for you to take a turn next at the body."

"Mrs. Perkins is only nervous because next to you, I make a poor comparison," Julia said with mock sincerity. "She knows that next to a corpse I shall fare much better."

"Stop it, Julia!" I pleaded, but Mrs. Perkins whisked her away, her shawl a storm cloud of gray silk.

Before anyone else could waylay me with gossip or questions about my dress, I headed into the gardens.

A waiter—not one I recognized—intercepted me as I sought refuge in the cooler region of the shrubbery, far from the party.

"Champagne, miss?" he asked me, eyeing my chest and bodice in a manner I'd have thought bold in one above his station, much less a servant borrowed from another household to cover the party. They must have scrambled to find him, as his coat sleeves were shamefully short, even for a servant. I waved him off and continued walking.

A few minutes' stroll brought me to the center of the

gardens. I leaned against another of Showalter's acquisitions. In the moonlight, it looked like little more than the stump of a large, squarish tree. But the granite surface was dimpled with carvings, all radiating the remains of the sun's heat. More hieroglyphics, as unintelligible as the scroll they'd pored over back at the party. The granite pedestal now sported a mirrored gazing ball.

In the borrowed light, I studied my own reflection. I saw a version of my mother, the arched brow vaulting over each green eye, the nose I thought too sharp on me, but elegant on her. Even my mouth was hers, the upper lip somehow off balance with the lower, a perpetual pout. Only my hair was different: Mother's was fine and blond, mine halfway between David's brown and Father's red, a handful of my curls already springing free from the small golden circlet Clarisse had pinned there a few hours ago.

I did look the part. And in a sense Julia was right. It was my birthright to marry well and fall easily into the life my mother had lived before me, that she'd been planning for me since the cradle.

Would it be with Showalter?

Was the unrest stirring in my belly now a product of my nerves at so imminent and likely a match? Or was it the first fluttering of something more like affection?

Did it matter?

I traced the reflection of an oak behind me in the orb's

shining surface. Its limbs were elongated and distorted by the curve of the ball. I ran my finger down the straight trunk as it sank into the ground.

Finding no answer to my question, or fearing the answer I might settle on, I resolved to return to the party and hoped Mother hadn't noticed my absence. But as I pushed off the pedestal, I caught movement.

Before I had a chance to decide it was just a bird or a squirrel skulking in the brush, I caught the unmistakable reflection of someone in a red frock coat stepping quietly from the oak's shadow to crouch behind an overgrown hydrangea in full blossom.

I froze. Terror born of the realization that I was not alone, had not been for some time, overrode every thought.

And then my mind began to race, keeping time with my pounding heart. That coat was the uniform of the serving staff. I realized that it was likely the very waiter who'd eyed me so lasciviously as I fled the party.

Why had I wandered so far?

The music from the party would surely drown my scream. I'd only succeed in signaling to this man that I was aware of his presence, possibly forcing him to act more rashly and quickly than he already intended.

And if I turned around and ran back to the party, he would easily intercept me.

Which left me only one option.

Chapter Four

Long before Showalter had come to London and made the Park his home, I'd spent hours straying from my own gardens through gaps in the hedgerows to those of our neighbors. I'd explored the wilds of these gardens, dodging the torments of a governess or my brothers. If I could get far enough away from my pursuer, I was sure I could disappear into the tangle nearer the river.

But I'd have no chance to hide if I couldn't convince my pursuer that I wasn't fleeing from him. So instead of sprinting away, I let my hand linger on the warm glass of the ball, then walked past it, farther into the garden.

I placed each footfall deliberately, slowly, my beaded slippers crunching politely on the groomed pathway as I fought the urge to look behind me. Around the first bend in the path, I stepped casually onto the mossy shoulder. Faintly behind me, I heard the careful placement of boots as their wearer tried vainly to step without dislodging the loose gravel.

As I rounded another twist in the path, I sidestepped from the shoulder, picked my way over a bed of ferns, and ducked behind a boulder so massive that the gardeners had been forced to landscape around it.

Moments later I saw the waiter slipping from tree to tree on the opposite side of the path. He was indeed the man who'd eyed me so boldly.

I let thirty feet or so unspool between us before even allowing myself to breathe. When he disappeared around a bend in the path, heading for the river, I realized I was shaking.

I began to move again, angling back toward the path and the pillar where I'd first discovered him, trying to slow the racing of my heart. Once within sight of the party, and back on the main pathway, I allowed myself a glance back. The moonlight shone full on the groomed landscape, no trace of the man anywhere.

I paused at the hedge and peered through the lattice of leaves. The other guests were still clustered around the mummy. I patted my hair, winced as I flicked away a thorn embedded in my arm, and smoothed the front of my dress.

The greater problem of what and whom to tell of my misadventure in the garden remained. Mother would be embarrassed enough that I'd slipped away unchaperoned, and the notion of a strange man following me in the bargain might be more than she could bear. And Father would certainly gather men to find the waiter, to make him explain himself. I imagined the scene that might result, the shadow that would descend over the party, and it would be all my fault. Even worse, I'd once again be the center of attention when all I'd wanted was a moment to go unnoticed.

On top of it all, it was *possible* that the man in the red coat wasn't even following me, had meant me no ill. Maybe he was simply going into the garden to meet a serving girl. Rupert would certainly chastise me for my vivid imagination. And if Showalter caught wind of one of his staff shirking duty, then he'd have even more reason to speak to me.

But for all the good reasons I gave myself not to tell someone, my nerves would not quiet themselves. I would tell Father, but in the morning.

As I drew closer to the fire-lit circle, I realized that people were gathered not around the mummy, but rather Showalter.

Mother intercepted me as she saw me approach. The edge of her gown bore a silk brocade featuring—of all things— the silhouettes of tiny Egyptian figures, their angular bodies perched on straight-backed thrones, pointing flattened hands from the ends of arms bent in impossible directions. Her hair, shot through at the temples with the faintest ribbons of silver, remained as expertly arranged as Clarisse had left it, her matching golden circlet like a halo. I brushed my skirts and pretended to see the wrinkle or spot my mother had surely already observed.

"We've *discussed* this behavior," she whispered as she eyed my dress before taking my arm. "Skulking away . . . where is the book?"

"Book? I wasn't reading, Mother! I just went for a short walk—"

"Whatever you're doing, you're neglecting your duty."

"What's happening?" I asked, noticing that the music had ceased.

"Something is wrong," she said. "Showalter has just returned. Come!" She dragged me by the hand toward the crowd.

"I'm sorry I cannot tell you more," Showalter was saying as he tugged at his cravat. "But I've just received word that this particular mummy is in fact a *very* important find."

Thrilled gasps rippled out from the partygoers as they surged closer to the body. The leathery skin of the mummy's stomach now peeked through the linen wrappings, and one eye peered out emptily at the sky. Despite the warm summer air, the flesh of my bare arms prickled.

"The specimen my colleagues at the British Museum received this afternoon was the one that was to have been delivered here. There has been a terrible confusion."

I searched the crowd for the waiter from the garden. He was not among the faces gathered around the table.

Showalter allowed us all a moment to enjoy our proximity to so valuable an artifact. "As you all are no doubt aware, I take my patronage of the British Museum as both a patriotic and a scientific duty, and it grieves me that we may have disturbed a mummy that bears so much"—he paused here, to scan our faces and smile weakly—"*significance.*"

I looked around at the crowd of friends and neighbors, some of whom were speculating that a pharaoh could be in their midst. What could be more significant than that? But still they stared in amazement at our host, and I wondered if they might look to me with the same eager fascination that they bestowed on Showalter if he indeed offered for me. But the thought was cut short when I caught sight of a flash of red and the profile of the very waiter who'd been following me. My heart quickened anew as I watched him slip around to the front of the house. I turned back quickly and willed Showalter to finish so that I might convince Father to take us home.

But Showalter loved little more than an audience. As he went on, I noticed his valet, Tanner, staring toward the corner of the house where my pursuer had just disappeared. He kept his eyes fixed on the spot as he stepped quietly from his master's side and stalked away.

"So if you will all be so kind as to return any discoveries you may have found in the wrappings to the table, I'll have them delivered to the museum with haste. I'm terribly sorry, and I assure you we will have a second gathering with a more appropriate specimen later this summer."

Sir Joseph Cargill—who was reliably drunk hours before anyone ever caught up to him at parties—applauded awkwardly at Showalter's speech. But Lord Showalter didn't look the part he usually played. He glanced around nervously, then asked with absolute agitation in his voice, "Where on earth is that whelp who was meant to be cataloging these things?"

"I'm here, sir," came a voice from below the table on the opposite side. He rose, a pile of linen folded as carefully as he could manage in his hands. "The linen, sir," he began, "we use it to verify locations and cond—"

"I know what you use it for," Showalter snapped. "Make yourself useful and scurry on back to the museum to prepare—"

"But Lord Showalter, procedure . . . you see . . . science even . . . dictates that—"

"I've given you instructions simple enough for even you to follow," Showalter said. "Do not embarrass yourself further in front of your betters."

The boy's face fell as the linen spilled from his hands. He turned, retrieved his ledger, and began his retreat from the garden.

I was shocked at this manifestation of Showalter's temper. Without thinking, I whispered under my breath, *"Il est un brute."*

Showalter looked up and fixed a bemused smile on me. "He is a rough beast of a thing, is he not?"

Now I found myself surprised at both the strength of his hearing and his facility with French. The young man paused, turned, and looked even more humiliated than he had before. I was desperate to explain myself, eager to make sure the kind-faced young man understood that my insult had been directed at Showalter's treatment of him.

But he disappeared before I had a chance to speak.

Showalter had already forgotten him as he addressed us once again. "I'm most disappointed that our evening must end prematurely. I've sent my footman round to gather your coachmen and ready the carriages." He sounded once again like himself, but there was something else there behind the swagger.

Fear.

I'd never seen the man nervous before. Even when he first made my father's acquaintance (Father inspired many men to new depths of self-doubt, so quiet and confident was he), he seemed as sure of himself as he did when relaying the history of some urn on his mantel. Now I recognized an apprehension that was almost startling. The crowd around him began to disperse, some coming forward to return just-acquired trinkets back to the mummy, others scattering for hats and shawls.

Showalter caught me studying him. I straightened, suddenly nervous again. Guests flowed past, offering hands and thanks, but our host seemed to have eyes for me only as he wove his way through the crowd to stand before me.

"A most exciting evening, sir," I managed.

He nodded gravely. "Though not for the reasons I'd anticipated," he admitted. "I was so looking forward to this evening— to celebrating the advent of your debut. I had it all planned perfectly. . . ."

Planned? Was he trying to tell me he'd arranged the party for me? That he knew Mother would accept the invitation? And how, I wondered, was the process of disturbing the carefully preserved remains of a thousand-year-old pharaoh the perfect way to commemorate my introduction into society? Or better still, to signal his intentions to offer for me? If a courtship began this way, I could not imagine what we might do to celebrate an engagement.

I smiled and said, "But how fortunate the error was discovered before the remains had been further compromised."

"Yes, I think we were in time." He reached down and took my hand, giving it a light pat as if it settled the entire matter.

I looked around to see if anyone else had caught the gesture. Mother was beaming at me from a few feet away. Yet it took all my will to keep from snatching my hand from his grasp.

"Thank you, Lord Showalter, I'm sure all the residents of the Park will look forward to—" But I was interrupted by a scream piercing the air.

Showalter dropped my hand and ran for the front of the house. I followed him through the open garden doors, through the ballroom, the great hall and foyer to the front drive where the carriages stood waiting. A knot of partygoers buzzed about a small black coach with a door hanging open, horses idle in the traces.

"He's dead!" I heard the voice of Dr. Clerval call out.

The crowd launched a fresh round of gasps into the air.

Husbands and fathers clutched wives and daughters gallantly, and Showalter tossed me a look that made me wonder if he intended to go all in then and there and draw me to him. I looked quickly away and slipped closer toward the body.

It wasn't merely retreat from his affection that pushed me away from Showalter. I had never seen a dead body before—at least not one presumably so freshly dead.

"It's the mummy's curse," I heard more than one voice whisper.

The man's body looked to have fallen from the carriage; one leg still dangled from the step below the door. I could see no mark upon him. No wound or cut or spot of blood to match the scarlet serving coat he wore. But his head did seem to be turned a bit too far to the left. It appeared unlikely that he'd so contorted himself in his fall from the carriage. Unlikely that he was meant to be in that carriage at all. And unlikely now that I'd ever know for certain who had been stalking me in the garden. Because the corpse that lay before us now was the very man I'd fled not a quarter of an hour ago.

Chapter Five

Rupert collapsed into his chair at breakfast, reaching for his cup, complaining that the tea had gone cold before he even touched the pot. My brother might have been easier to love if he appreciated how ridiculously advantageous his life was, if he had the good grace to be a *little* humble. I wondered if any girl—Julia included—could inspire him in this direction.

"Some excitement last night, Aggie?" he asked, using the pet name given me by my other brother, David. David was at sea, a lieutenant on a sixty-four gunner. I loved to hear *him* call me Aggie, but from Rupert's mouth it sounded as insulting as he no doubt meant it to.

"Quite," I said after sipping from my own cup, trying to mask my curiosity. Upon returning home last night, I knew I should have been upset by the evening's events. Mother had been so agitated that Father dosed her with a drop of laudanum and sent her to bed.

But a dozen drops from Mother's small amber vial wouldn't have made me even drowsy.

Before falling asleep, I resolved to tell Father my tale at the first opportunity. But when I awoke just after dawn and hurried downstairs after dressing, I learned from Mrs. Brewster, our housekeeper, that Father had risen earlier and ridden into town on urgent business.

So I would wait. Father would know what to do, who to tell about what I'd seen, or if it even might be of importance. He might have been handed his title and place in the House of Lords by an accident of birth, but if any man could earn it, I'd no doubt it would have been him. His intelligence and integrity were the favorite topic of my friends' parents when Father was not around.

The door from the front hall opened as Mrs. Brewster glided into the room. Her long gray summer dress was starch-stiff, pleats in the sleeves that would have wilted by midday in the summer heat on anyone but her. She stared proudly over our heads at the portrait of my grandfather as she announced, "Lord Showalter to see you, Miss Wilkins."

"So early?" I muttered, tossing my napkin to the table and rising from my chair.

"Come to see if you're all right, I'd wager," my brother said.

"Or perhaps he has no tea and toast at home."

Rupert looked positively confused. "Of course he has tea and toast. He has twenty thousand pounds a year, you git."

Rupert's obsession with the wealth of others was not among his better qualities. He'd memorized the incomes and assets of virtually every one of his peers in London society. It was the closest he came to any true talent.

I glared at him, noticing for the first time the outlandish neck scarf he wore. The print looked almost like animal skin— or maybe peacock feathers. Rupert's attire was usually carefully thought out to avoid drawing attention to anything except how expensively tailored his jackets were. Bright colors and patterns, he once told me, stole the eye away from the invisible seams and perfect lines.

"What on earth is that?" I asked, nodding at the garish addition.

He looked down at his chest, and then back at me, his cheeks tingeing pink.

"Just . . . something. That is—"

He was saved further explanation by Showalter's entrance. Rupert also rose from his seat.

Showalter still wore last night's suit, and the expression to match. He crossed the room to the table, bowed like a duck diving underwater, and motioned for me to sit down.

"Miss Wilkins," he said, nodding. "Rupert," he said, turning to my brother.

"Will you sit, sir?" I asked.

"Thank you," he said, folding himself into Mother's chair.

"Will you take tea?"

He nodded again, then reached for the teapot and my mother's waiting cup. "Are you quite recovered?" he asked as he poured, dropped in two lumps of sugar, and tipped the milk pitcher slightly into the steaming liquid.

"From last night? I assure you I've almost completely forgotten it," I lied.

He gulped at the tea. "Very well. It is easy for the ladies to move on, is it not, Rupert?"

Rupert nodded knowingly. "Certainly. They are accustomed to allowing the stronger sex to handle matters, and this is a matter far too indelicate for women to bear."

Only my brother could make concern sound so insulting. I resisted the urge to fling the toast platter at his head. It would have been empty at any rate, as Showalter had removed the last two slices and was slathering butter and preserves across them with my knife. I raised an eyebrow at Rupert.

"Make yourself at ease, Lord Showalter," I said, adding, "I'm sure your night was even longer and more exhausting than ours was."

He nodded his head. Between sips of tea, he told us that the dead man bore no identification. No other household claimed him as an employee, though several of the staff had seen him serving at the party and assumed he was simply one of the many members of neighboring households loaned out to Showalter's for the evening. And more than once he made mention of the pall it might cast on his household, his good name even, to have a murdered stranger tumbling from a coach on one's drive.

It was ridiculous that anyone would associate the death with Lord Showalter or his household, but gossip would link his name with the unidentified dead man for a few weeks at least.

"It will be forgotten in a fortnight," I consoled him.

"Yes, but now with the other attacks—"

"Other attacks?" my brother asked as the hairs on my neck bristled.

Showalter gulped down a bite. "You haven't heard, then?"

Now I grew impatient. "Please enlighten us."

"I thought it would be the talk of London by now," he said. "Early this morning, two more of my guests from the party were attacked!"

My hand rose to my mouth. "You don't mean—"

"Murdered?" Rupert offered.

Showalter shook his head vigorously. "Heavens, no! I meant to say their *homes* had been attacked. Lady Kensington awoke to find the bureau and closets of her dressing room ransacked."

"Ransacked!" I repeated.

"Yes. And a choice jewel or two missing from the chest."

"Is she all right?" I asked.

"Better than Mr. Squires," he said solemnly.

"Not poor Squires," I whispered. Squires was solicitor to my father and half of this side of London. He loved A Lady's novels almost as much as I did, though I suspected I was the only one who knew it.

"He's not dead either, but he has a nasty headache. Seems last night he heard a noise in the parlor, went downstairs to investigate, and that was that. Awoke with a knot the size of an apple on his temple."

"Anything taken?" Rupert asked.

"Not that they can see, but he's uncertain that his memory is as reliable as it should be owing to the force of the blow."

"Oh dear," I said, relaxing back in my chair. "Terrible luck for our neighbors."

"But already people are saying it's more than that. Servants are whispering, vendors are talking. I have it on good authority that the evening newspapers will lead with the story," Showalter said as he licked jam from his thumb.

"A slow news day indeed if a pair of simple burglaries take precedence over news of the war—," I began, before he interrupted.

"But they've blown it all up into something else entirely, of course. One man murdered and two homes vandalized suddenly becomes proof of a mummy's curse! The Curse of the Hyde Park Mummy, they're calling it!"

"Nonsense!" I said, leaning forward in my chair. "The paper can say anything it wants, but it's simple bad, coincidental luck, isn't it?"

Showalter hesitated, scanning the table for more food. On finding he'd cleared it, he reached for the teapot and poured another cup. "Certainly . . . I suppose . . ."

I was stunned that one who'd invested a fortune in Egypt and its treasures had not developed a thicker skin on this point. "Do you mean to say there is something to this?"

Sensing my disbelief, he backed away. "No. But the power of these stories and rumors of happenings with other mummies and tombs and so forth . . . they can stoke the imagination in a powerful way."

"Certainly—but those are merely myths, are they not? Is there any validity to them?" The pharaohs were merely kings who got salted and wrapped after they died. They weren't superhuman. They couldn't curse us from beyond the grave, could they?

"I've never experienced any of it firsthand," he said carefully, "but there have been many reports of strange doings associated with the opening of tombs, or the removal of artifacts. . . ."

A chill seized me. "What kind of strange doings?"

He swallowed hard. "Unpleasant things . . . things far too upsetting to worry you about, much less discuss over breakfast."

I'd heard snatches of tales where people involved in digs or removal of artifacts met with calamitous circumstances shortly after. But those were over in Egypt when the items were removed . . . this was *England*.

"Could it be true?" I asked. "You said yourself that the mummy was an important one—"

Showalter held up a hand. "I've said too much already, and upset you in the bargain," he began. "We must leave the topic at once. Here I came to make sure you were all right, and I've

only upset you even more. Pray, do not think on this any longer."
He bit his thumb. "I do hope these events don't cast a pall over
the remainder of the season's parties."

"No," I said, but I was still thinking about the possibility of
curses.

He looked at me anew, his expression softening. "You're a
great comfort to me," he said, his gaze lingering a second longer
than was proper before realizing Rupert was still at the table
with us. "And you as well, Rupert. Steady heads, the both of
you. I'm grateful for your friendship."

"Not at all," Rupert said.

"We are glad to be of any help," I said. Showalter smiled.
The silence lasted just long enough to foretell he had more to say.

"Miss Wilkins," he began at last, "I noticed how very curious you were about the specimen from last night's unwrapping.
And I was wondering—"

He paused, looked to my brother, and smiled sheepishly.
Rupert reached for his own cup, shrugging.

"I was hoping, rather," Showalter went on, "that you might
allow me to escort you to the museum one morning. I'm sure
the curator would be most willing to offer us a private tour, and
I'd very much like to afford you an opportunity to have your
questions handled by one so peerless in his knowledge as Mr.
Banehart."

I froze. Last night's performance was more than just a
celebration of my debut, then. Julia had been right. Mother

had been right. Showalter was making overtures to court me. I found the confirmation of this more overwhelming than I expected.

"I—"

His words came in a tumble. "You probably think me brash for inviting you under such a cloud as the one that has settled on our street, but I confess that I'm afraid that if I do not move swiftly, I may not have another opportunity."

Now my head positively swam. Showalter, it appeared, was in even more of a hurry than Mother.

"She'll have to speak with Mother," Rupert broke in. I was grateful for his intrusion, grateful that it gave me a moment to think.

Showalter turned toward him. "Of course. I would expect nothing less. And we would bring her along, or some other suitable chaperone. You, perhaps?" he asked Rupert.

Rupert snorted. "No, thank you. I'm afraid the museum bores me. Dreadful stuff."

"Your aunt, then?" Showalter returned to me. His smile was eager, his words kind. It was all as simple and as easy as I could have hoped for. Put on a lovely dress, go to a party, and catch a man. I should have been delighted, but I couldn't help feeling as if it had all been too easy, too pat. As if I'd been robbed of the opportunity to struggle for a match, for love, as a character in a novel might.

"I will speak with Mother," I managed to say.

He nodded, satisfied, and stood. "Well, I'm sure your day is bound to be as busy as my own."

Showalter had a day of meetings with inspectors from Scotland Yard or with museum officials to look forward to. I anticipated little more than calling on Julia to see if she might have heard something more, or perhaps even enduring a visit with the Hallishaws, as they always could be relied on for the choicest gossip.

Showalter paused at the door. "By the way, are you both certain that all the items removed from the wrappings last night were returned to the table?"

I felt the heat rise through my chest and neck; the tips of my ears seemed to glow like a coal drawn from the grate. My brother—always eager to take charge in situations he knew nothing about—provided a welcome distraction. "Positive. I was at the table the entire time, even when you were called away by your manservant. All four of the items found were back on the table at the end of the evening when we left the body."

"You're certain?" Showalter asked.

"Yes," my brother said.

"Agnes?" he asked me.

I thought of the little dog's head hidden in the black velvet hatbox that I kept in the bottom of my wardrobe. I'd put it there the moment I'd returned from the party. I knew I should retrieve it. But again, Showalter's attentions muddled things. How embarrassing now to own to my deviance, in front of

Rupert no less, and on the heels of Showalter inviting me on an outing. How disastrous might it be for a potential match if he discovered too early in our courtship my imperfections, my attachments to silly objects.

My independence.

And what of the curse? What if it were true? If an evil had visited people who'd merely attended the party, what might it mean for a girl who was so foolish as to keep something from the body?

I thought quickly. It would be much better if I returned it later, when things had calmed down. Or if I managed to leave it secretly behind in the museum when Showalter escorted me there.

I sighed and spoke. "You said yourself, we women have no head for these things. I confess I was lost in the excitement of the unwrapping and paid no attention. Why?"

He eyed me with—what? Suspicion, perhaps? He stopped, shook his head.

"Don't trouble yourself any more with this, Miss Wilkins," he said, smiling. "Promise me you'll go read one of those books you like so much, take your mind off the unpleasantness."

I curtsied and thanked him for the suggestion. He nodded at Rupert and ducked out the door.

But reading was the last thing I wanted to do. I had so many questions, so many possibilities, that I felt a story was unfolding around me at this moment.

Chapter Six

❧

I returned home that afternoon with Aunt Rachel in tow. I'd been wholly unsuccessful in persuading her that she'd be wiser to nap while I called on Julia. As a result, I'd learned nothing new by day's end except that local gossip had the mummy rising off the table last night to strike white the hair of one of the party guests. And Julia was no help in piecing together last night's mysteries, especially as we had both our chaperones with us, which meant our conversation was confined to dresses and the weather.

Aunt Rachel retired to her rooms. I was meant to be reading in the library.

But I still needed to speak with Father.

His study door was shut, a whisper of voices carrying through the panels.

Telling Father about my experiences last night would have to wait. Instead I raced to my bedroom, tossed my bonnet onto the bed, and hurried to my chair by the fireplace—the very one that shared a chimney with the hearth in Father's study.

"—should he succeed in the Channel, we're done for!" my father was saying as I heard the creaking lid of the rosewood box in which he stored his tobacco insert itself into the conversation. The lid fell shut again. I knew from watching him a hundred times that he was now adding a pinch of cardamom (a habit he'd acquired while in India).

"He does seem to have more lives than a cat," admitted a voice I recognized as belonging to the Earl of Bathurst, the secretary of war. I felt truly sorry for Mr. Bathurst. He probably hadn't anticipated actually administering the cabinet in a time of conflict. His predecessor had retired barely six months ago when we thought that the greatest of the danger had passed. But that was before Napoleon came back.

The greatest enemy of all Britain and her holdings had been defeated—*soundly*—last winter.

But he returned. Like always.

For over a decade, he'd terrorized all of Europe and even gone so far as Africa and the Americas in his quest to extend his influence and power. Bonaparte had come terribly close to overtaking the Continent completely.

Only the ships that patrolled the narrow channel between Normandy and Dover protected us, and they were spread dangerously thin dealing with the emperor's forces all over the Atlantic. All England lived in fear of what might happen if he ever succeeded in breaking through our naval blockades and bringing his Grande Armée to our shores.

Since I'd discovered that when the fires were unlit I could listen in on Father below, Napoleon had been the favored topic. At first it had merely been a game, but as I grew and understood more—and after David took to sea—my eavesdropping took on greater purpose.

And it wasn't simply Father or Parliament members who could seem to talk of little else. Bonaparte's infamy and the latest drama on the Continent found its way to the ladies at cards after dinners when the men had all retired to billiards and cigars, where they also offered undoubtedly sage advice on what to do about the tiny Frenchman. The newspapers carried daily war news, but it was nothing like as accurate as what I could glean here by the fireplace. And by the time what my father knew made it out to the general papers, I'd often known about it for several days.

I knew the situation at present was perhaps as dire as it could be. Napoleon had only a month ago been rescued from his exile on Elba and reinstalled as emperor. France was mad for him, his power and popularity even greater now, after he'd been absent from leadership for so long. In his last letter, David said he'd seen men taken prisoner after battles at sea who prayed to Napoleon before they prayed to God. The villain had, after all, resurrected himself from the dead (politically and militarally speaking, of course) not once but *twice* since he first ascended.

And now he'd done it again. His armies were gaining strength and zeal each day, and our navy and shipbuilders were preparing for the inevitable moment when Napoleon did overtake the rest of Europe and made to cross the Channel and come for us.

It seemed inescapable that he—the man who'd survived for eleven years as the most feared in all the world—would one day march on British soil. It seemed almost as inescapable as my future.

Almost.

"What of our recent attempts to . . . eliminate him?" my father asked Bathurst.

The earl sighed. "Our spies cannot get close. His return was unexpected enough that the assets we had in place have not had sufficient time to reintegrate themselves into his household."

"When I think of last spring . . . the coach driver . . ." My father paused to draw on his pipe.

"We lost a good man and made the monster more cautious in the bargain," Bathurst lamented.

These were the pieces of conversation that set my heart racing. I had overheard planned assassination attempts, reports on secret military missions, summaries regarding suspected persons in the service of a foreign, malevolent power.

But it was the careful mentions of the shadowy souls carrying out these orders that stirred me most. There were hundreds of patriots—French and British—working secretly within France to advance Britain's cause. The man who'd posed as the coach driver was one of these. But Napoleon had his spies as well—most of them working between London and the coast, gleaning information about naval deployments, defensive strategies, or what we knew of Napoleon's plans.

But I wasn't even supposed to know any of this, so I could never ask questions. I'd understood the assassin had been unsuccessful, but it was the first I'd heard that he had been so unfortunate as to be killed.

I was still pondering his sad fate when inside the study, my father rang the bell to summon the parlor maid. The sound made me jump, my movement dislodging the rack of pokers and shovels and the small broom used to clean the ashes from the grate in winter. The clatter echoed down into the chimney, and I knew into Father's ears.

Silence fell within the room. I dashed for the door and down the steps, willing my feet to fall silently on the treads. Before Father could puzzle together that I'd been listening from my room, I'd appear at his door.

I knocked and swept in without waiting for an answer.

"Hello, Father!" I sang. "I'm just back from my errands and hadn't seen you since last night. Though I didn't know you were engaged! I'm terribly sorry to have interrupted what must be very important to bring Mr. Bathurst"—here I paused, turned to my father's guest, curtsied slightly, and slipped a *"how do you do*" into the middle of my lie—"all the way to the Park in the middle of the afternoon."

I uttered all this in one breathless burst, hoping the flush in my cheeks would register as excitement rather than guilt. Father eyed me skeptically. Bathurst merely smiled and sat straighter in his chair, something most of my father's friends and associates had begun to do since my season began. Granted, my gowns had been let out a bit in spots, but certainly not enough to warrant such gestures of respect from men who'd known me from my infancy. It unnerved me.

I felt Father's eyes on me as I tugged off my gloves. Father knew. He *always* knew.

"Hello, Agnes," he said dryly, motioning me to his side. I took his hand.

"I've not yet had opportunity to congratulate you on your debut, Miss Wilkins," Mr. Bathurst said, after a moment during which I was sure my father would scold me for my skulking and spying.

I turned to him, smiling as best I could after what I'd heard. "Yes. Thank you, sir."

"You must be pleased, Sir Hugh," Mr. Bathurst said to my father, "such a fine girl. And already snagging the interest of a very prominent neighbor, I understand."

My father patted my hand and smiled, staring at the pile of papers and the inkwell littering his desktop. "I suppose." He turned his gaze to me, his gray-green eyes mirrors of my own. "Yet

I cannot help but feel much the same way as I do when I argue on the floor that we must send more ships or troops off to war."

My breath caught in my throat. I fought tears. Lucky for us, Mr. Bathurst did not catch the significance of the moment.

"My dear Hugh! She is merely free now to secure her place in society. She is not off to fight!"

My father released my hand and busied himself with breaking the wax seal on a letter that lay on his desk. The downstairs maid appeared at the door and inquired as to the reason for her summons.

"We'll take some refreshment, please, before we go," my father ordered.

"Go?" I asked, alarmed.

He nodded. "Bathurst has come to fetch me down to Tilbury. There's a man there we need to speak with."

"How long will you stay?" I asked.

"I hope we will return evening after next," Father said, adding, "and I'll be bringing with me a surprise."

I looked at the smile on his face and wondered what he could be bringing home from a port town half a day's ride east to compete with the exotic gifts he'd brought me in the past.

I wondered how he could see me as a girl about to make her debut, as the same girl he was loath to let Mother send out into the world of matchmaking, and still see me as the girl who grew giddy at the prospect of some trinket brought home hidden in his traveling case.

He leaned forward and caught my eye. "Is something the matter?" he asked, stymied by my reaction to his promised surprise. I forced a smile. My father had enough to worry about, with a war brewing and a son at sea. He didn't need to know I'd outgrown his little gifts. And he certainly didn't need my silly fancies and petty larcenies to distract him from whatever part he was meant to play in thwarting Napoleon's plans. At least not until his return.

"Nothing that won't keep."

"You're sure?" he pressed.

I set my shoulders and smiled. "Quite."

"Will the young miss be joining you, then?" Caroline inquired impatiently from the doorway.

"No, thank you, Caroline," I said, stepping away from the desk. She nodded and withdrew.

"Are you off, then?" my father asked me, though I could hear in his voice an admonition to make as hasty a departure as was polite.

"I'm quite tired. I've been calling on Julia, and with last night's late evening—"

"You're all right, though?"

"Of course, Father."

"A gossip with a friend is good medicine, I daresay," said Mr. Bathurst.

"Truly. Of course we were a bit preoccupied with last night's events."

Father nodded. "More curse of the mummy nonsense, I suppose?"

"Something of an epidemic," I said. "Not only were Lady Kensington and Mr. Squires attacked last night, but also Lord Morgan's home was burglarized this morning in the broad light of day! Really, it seems awfully convenient to blame some otherworldly entity—"

"And no doubt whoever is perpetrating these crimes has thought of that very thing," my father agreed.

"Certainly. That brings the total to three persons who've suffered since the party—of course, not counting the fellow with the broken neck—"

"Agnes!" my father said sharply. "Take care!"

I nodded. My face reddened now from legitimate shame. It was worse than unladylike to speak of the misfortunes of others so coldly: It was inhumane. "Of course, Father."

I stood waiting for him to dismiss me, but Bathurst spoke first. "Did you say three, Miss Wilkins?"

I turned to our guest. "Yes, sir. Lady Kensington, Mr. Squires, and Lord Morgan."

"Then you haven't heard about Mrs. Blalock?" As a particular friend of Lord Showalter, Mrs. Blalock had been at the party with us. When Showalter had been almost a stranger to our London circle, she threw a ball to welcome him.

"Mrs. Blalock?" I asked.

Bathurst looked to my father before continuing. Father

gave him a wave of his hand as if authorizing him to proceed and feed my strange fancies.

Bathurst explained that Mrs. Blalock had returned home this morning after a couple of hours at the shops to find her lady's maid lying unconscious on the carpet of her bedroom.

"Oh!" I said, my hand flying to my mouth.

Mr. Bathurst nodded gravely. "They fetched some smelling salts, and then a doctor, but it took her hours to come around. She appears to have had some sort of fit."

Or some new manifestation of the mummy's curse? I wondered.

"I will send Mrs. Blalock a note and ask if there is anything we can do."

"Your mother has already called on Mrs. Blalock. I think she is there still."

"Very good, Father."

"Now, go translate something," he said with a grin. "Anything more lively than listening to a couple of old men talk about Napoleon, or imagining sinister goings-on in your neighborhood." His attempt at a smile was only marginally successful.

I nodded and headed out the study door as Caroline returned with the tray, laden with a plate of sandwiches and a steaming pot. I made for the stairs and began to ascend toward my room. Try as I might, I could not follow my father's advice and think on lighter matters.

Could it really be a curse? Could the awakened spirit of an Egyptian king be exacting vengeance for our disrespectful curiosity?

Possibly.

But something about that list of names troubled me. That something teased my mind as I topped the staircase and turned toward my door.

Kensington.

Squires.

Blalock.

Morgan.

Certainly they were all neighbors to a degree—almost everyone at the party had been. There were but a handful of guests who did not have homes within a mile of our own.

But they were not the wealthiest guests at the party. Certainly Lady Kensington and Lady Blalock both had more money than the king, but Squires was only a solicitor, letting rooms from a wealthy client during the summer to be near his employers. And it was well known that Lord Morgan's assets were tied up in speculation—a scandal that had befallen him and that the rest of the neighborhood pretended not to know about.

If I were a burglar, these certainly would not have been the people I'd have chosen to victimize—particularly at such great risk. Two in the middle of the morning, all during the height of suspicion after last night's events.

I passed into my room through the salon, securing that door shut after I entered. Everything was as I'd left it. I fished a key from the bowl on my desk, inserted it into the lock of the wardrobe I'd locked this morning as a precaution, and twisted. My dresses spilled out, crowded with the few new arrivals. I pulled out the hatbox and removed the lid.

Inside lay my secrets. A broken quill I'd liberated from the library one afternoon, the plume at its top too pretty to let it end its life in a rubbish bin. The playbill from the first time Mother took me to the opera. The band from David's midshipman's hat. He'd searched the entire house for it last time he'd been here, but I couldn't bear to let him leave again without keeping some part of him where I knew it was safe. A seashell I'd saved from a trip to Brighton, the closest I'd come yet to leaving England. And beneath them all, the little dog's head. I withdrew it and the little strip of linen still dangling from it. It was exactly as I'd left it.

No one had seen me remove it, had they?

Unless . . .

The waiter. His eyes on my bodice. What if it wasn't my décolletage that had captured his notice?

I fingered the cool iron shape and the scrap of linen. Had he been chasing this?

Last night's scene sprang back into my mind. The flickering of the torchlight, the oddly incongruous music, the mummy lying on the table—the faces of the guests crowding around. The sight in my mind's eye jolted me.

When I'd returned from the garden, Lady Blalock, Mr. Squires, and Lord Morgan held in hand the cutting tools, even as Showalter rushed back into their midst and declared an end to the unwrapping. Before I'd left, it had been Lady Kensington with Rupert and me at the body.

Kensington, Blalock, Squires, and Morgan.

That meant that if the curse—be it supernatural or man-made—was real, there would certainly be one more name soon added to the list of victims.

Wilkins.

Chapter Seven

❧

I slept very little that night, puzzling over the "curse" and half fearing someone would come creeping through my window (though it was twenty feet to the garden below).

But that was only one source of my anxiety.

If the only other persons subject to the curse—whatever it might be—had been those who'd actually participated in the actual unwrapping, it seemed that either some vengeful spirit was exacting punishment . . . or someone was looking for something that was supposed to have been on the body.

I scrambled out of bed, reached beneath my mattress, and plucked out the dog's head. I'd grown frightened enough that it no longer seemed sensible to leave it in the wardrobe.

No one else could possibly have been as deviant as I. Six people had had a chance at the mummy. Five items were found, four returned. I stared at the dog's head, my heart pounding.

This was what the perpetrator—supernatural or not—was after. This was causing all the trouble.

I was the cause of all the trouble.

What to do about it had haunted me throughout the sleepless night. If it wasn't a curse, whoever or whatever was looking for the dog's head was up to nothing good, I reasoned. Why else would all our neighbors have been harmed? The violence brought about by the search for this object was surely evidence enough that something sinister was going on. So simply waiting for it to find me, to find the dog's head, seemed foolish in the extreme.

And if it was a curse, then it seemed even more foolish to wait.

I needed help.

But the question of who to seek help from was far more difficult. The police? They'd dismiss me as a silly young woman caught up in the romance of the curse. Certainly Lord Showalter would take a similar approach. And there was still the possibility of a match to consider, and still the inconvenience of confessing to him, the potential for jeopardizing what Mother had worked so hard to achieve.

There was also the danger of it all to consider. There was no guarantee that by simply surrendering all to Showalter or some other authority, I wouldn't transfer the same sort of bad luck that was lying in wait for me. No, my recklessness had resulted in this mess, and I must do what I could to atone for my error.

And perhaps it was a product of listening to sensitive

conversations in Father's study for all these years, but something else told me that if the burglar would go to such extremes to track down this object, then it was of some great importance. And objects of great importance were not the kind of thing to go crying from the rooftops about.

How I wished Father were home. Not only would he know what to do, whom to tell, how to let the sting of my embarrassment do its work and then ebb away without shaming me further, but his steady hand and sensible presence would allow me to do what I felt most tempted to. Panic. I was terrified, and the fear that our house, that my room, might be next threatened to swallow me whole. The fact that I might have jeopardized both my own future and the safety of my good neighbors made me queasy. And in truth, the only thing that would keep me from succumbing to the wave of guilt and fear was doing *something*.

I consoled myself that Father would appreciate the delicacy of my situation. I hoped that he would credit my seeking information as making the best of a bad situation. And I knew that the more I could share with him when the time came, the easier it would go for both of us.

And there was but one place in London where I might seek information about an important Egyptian relic. A place where I was not known. A place where I could ask my questions, gain what intelligence I could, and still be home in time to watch from the front window for Father in the event that he returned early from Tilbury.

The British Museum.

When morning finally broke and I heard the household stirring below stairs, I was already up and dressed. I checked my reflection in the glass and reached for my bonnet just as the knock came at my door.

"Enter," I called.

Clarisse crept into the room, looking sheepish. "You have dressed your own hair this morning, Miss Wilkins?"

"Yes, Clarisse. I decided to make an early start of it today," I replied in French. Though she was my mother's lady's maid, Clarisse had been sent to me each morning since my nurse was discharged three years ago. I already planned to persuade Mother to allow Clarisse to come with me after I married. Mother knew we'd have a hard time finding one so gifted as Clarisse in subduing my hair. But more to the point, Clarisse was dear to me. She was only a few years older than I was, and I'd come to think of her as a friend.

"You will have some breakfast before you go, mademoiselle?" she asked me, this time slipping into her native tongue.

I shook my head. "I rang for tea an hour ago."

She looked toward the tray still bearing the nibbled crumpet I had been far too agitated to eat. "Then I will go and see if Madame Rachel is ready," she said, taking a step toward the door.

"Don't trouble yourself," I said. "Aunt Rachel needs her rest. And besides, I'm only out to take the air this morning."

"But your mother—"

"Won't even know," I said, turning and smiling. "I just need a few moments to myself—what with all the excitement of the past few days—"

She grinned. "And a certain man declaring himself . . ."

"*Assez*, Clarisse," I said. "No one's declared. He's merely invited me—"

She shook her head. "It is there," she said, smiling and lifting one shoulder. "I am French, after all. We know these things better than you English."

I rolled my eyes. "Of course you do. But you must trust me when I tell you I need some time away this morning. And trust me that I won't get into any mischief."

Clarisse didn't exactly nod, but she moved to help me with my bonnet all the same. She held the light summer cap, meant to keep the sun from adding any more freckles to my nose, and stared woefully at my hair. I'd managed to apply a bit of pomade to the curls meant to frame my face, but they'd already unraveled.

"I really must go if I'm to get back before I'm missed," I pleaded before she could offer to repair my handiwork. She smiled and tucked my head into the fabric of my bonnet, tying the ribbon as expertly as she might dress a lock of my hair.

"Perhaps you are not telling me the complete truth?" she said slyly.

I started. "What?"

"Perhaps you are off to a secret meeting with your intended?" she teased.

"Clarisse!"

"You *are* hiding something!" She laughed. "Though why you dare let him see you with your hair in such a state—"

I shook free of her hands. "Take that as your proof that I am not off to a tryst," I said, and hastened from the room, her laughter trailing after me.

"But why so early?" she asked as she followed me to the top of the stairs. "Moonlight is far more . . . *romantique.*"

"You're being ridiculous," I said weakly.

Clarisse eyed me doubtfully. The bell from within my mother's room chimed—her signal to Clarisse that she was ready to be dressed and coiffed.

"You'd better go," I said. "Mother won't want to be kept waiting."

"Nor will your beau!" she whispered. "You must tell me—"

I didn't let her finish. "Tell Mother I've merely gone to take the air, but only if she asks."

Before she could reply, I hurried down the stairs, through the front hall, and out the door into the bright morning sunshine of London. Time did seem of the essence; if my home was going to be broken into, I wanted to find out why before the moment came.

But before I reached our gate, I encountered an unexpected sight. Rupert was reaching for the trellis leading up to his window.

"Good morning, brother," I called.

He turned and faced me, his back pressed to the sandstone wall. "Ah, hello."

His hair was even more a fright than my own, his eyes swollen in their sockets, rimmed by an angry pink. He still wore that ridiculous neckscarf from the day before, but he was missing several buttons from his coat.

"Long night or early morning?" I asked brightly, pleased that the volume of my voice caused him to wince.

"None of your concern," he mumbled, reaching back for the trellis and his room above.

"Perhaps Father's or Mother's, then?"

"I'm a grown man," he said.

"Grown men use the front door after long nights at the club. Or wherever you were drinking last night," I said, adding, "Though I'd wager it's with *whom* that might be of greater interest. At any rate, *boys* climb into windows to avoid their fathers."

"Then what do you call a girl walking out early in the morning without her chaperone?"

"Lucky," I replied, "to be on her own . . . and seen only by her brother, who cannot reveal that he saw his sister leave without revealing that *he* had been out all night."

Rupert considered for a moment. I wondered what had him so ashamed that he would rather let me go than risk trouble for himself. He was certainly old enough to carouse at any hour he wished. Young men were expected to drink too much, to enjoy the company of their fellows before settling on wives. But I could tell Rupert was hiding something.

He shook his head, tossed a choice name at me, and turned to climb his trellis.

I walked only as far as the taxi stand a quarter of a mile from home. Taking the carriage would have resulted in more questions, and our drivers—notorious gossips who supplied the household staff with the majority of their information— would know exactly where I'd been.

The streets were a bedlam of shopkeepers and merchants opening stalls and setting out wares. The gas lamps had long since been doused, and I recognized the man who I sometimes saw lighting them in the evenings leaning against the flower stall, chatting up a pretty girl within. Our neighborhood had been the first to be lit some five or six years ago, and Father was considering having lighting installed at home.

I approached the taxis—a line of small open carriages strung up near the gate. I walked down the line of horses, as if picking my mount for a carousel ride. I came to the last one in the queue and found its driver snoring loudly in the seat.

"Sir?" I said.

He did not stir.

"Sir?" I repeated, this time leaning in and speaking a bit louder. At this he jumped, feet slipping from the rail.

"That's right, Joe," he seemed to say to the horse, "I'm awake, I am."

He still hadn't noticed me. I half wondered if he thought the horse had spoken. "Sir!" I said again, this time a bit exasperated.

He rose to his feet and climbed onto the bench mounted between the horse and the carriage. "Morning, miss. May I be of service?" he asked, as he wiped the corners of his mouth with an open hand.

"Are you available for the morning?"

"Always available if a fare is legit, ma'am."

I reached into my bag and found a coin. I held the half crown up to him. He raised his eyes in appreciation.

"That'll do, miss," he said, as he donned his hat and nodded toward the carriage.

I climbed in. "The British Museum, please," I said, settling in for the ride.

Chapter Eight

❧

The driver steered the hack into the wide gravel half circle leading to the building's entrance. It was quieter than the busy lane we'd just left—a gardener here and there, and a few souls carrying bundles to a small door to the left and below the main entrance. I hadn't visited the British Museum in ages. The last time I'd been here was when the first of the mummies went on public display, but it looked the same as I remembered.

"You meeting someone, miss?" the coachman asked.

I ignored his question, simply stepped from the carriage and called to him as I made for the entrance. "Wait here. I do not know how long I will be, but if we are later returning to the Park than eleven, I shall be inclined to pay you more generously."

I didn't wait for a response, not wanting to give him a chance to argue about advancing him half his fee now.

I hurried up the staircase, breathless by the time I reached the broad, columned patio sweeping out from the front doors. I passed through the one open door, realizing I must be among the day's first visitors.

Inside, a marble statue bloomed at the center of the foyer, the liveliest thing in the room. Arched hallways to the exhibits branched in three directions from the statue.

A porter appeared. "Morning, miss."

"Good morning, sir," I began. "I was wondering if you could direct me to—"

"Egypt rooms. Townley Gallery, second floor. Those stairs there at the back hall."

I froze. "How did you know?"

"Steady stream of curiosity seekers since that mayhem over at the Park two nights ago."

I thanked him, declined his offer to show me the way, and hurried through the archway toward the exhibits. I felt his eyes follow me as I paced the long hall, lined with more marble statuary. I took the indicated stair as quickly as I could and found a sign pointing out the direction of the Egypt rooms. I traveled another corridor, this one lined with tapestries, before reaching my destination. As it was early, I found the room still and quiet. The light was dim despite the morning sunshine I'd left behind. The windows were small and set high near the ceiling. On my last visit, our guide had told us that this curious feature was a caution to protect the artifacts displayed from direct sunlight. But the placement and infrequency of the windows, and the resulting perpetual shadow, only made the setting feel all the more like the tombs and caves the objects had been taken from.

Sarcophagi flanked the perimeter, like soldiers standing vigil over the contents of the room. Their eyes, some painted on stone, a few on gold or silver, seemed to follow me, daring me to disturb the collection of pots and jars arranged in glass cabinets. Near the extreme end of the room, a living shape hunched over the open case of a mummy, carefully brushing dust from its surface with the tip of a feather. A candle blazed from behind a glassed lantern on a cart beside him.

"Pardon me?" I said.

The figure unbent itself from the work. He was tall and surprisingly young. And familiar. When his eyes met mine, I realized where I'd seen him before and started.

"Yes?" he asked, eying me curiously.

It was the young man from the party. The one who'd so painstakingly cataloged the findings on the body that night. The one Showalter had embarrassed. He stared at me with those deep brown eyes, and the effect was even more unnerving than that produced by the painted ones on the sarcophagi, though for altogether different reasons.

"Nine o'clock already?" His voice echoed around the empty room.

No recognition in his eyes or his voice. He viewed me solely as an interruption.

I swallowed. "Yes. I was hoping you could help me."

"I'd meant to finish this before opening," he said, annoyed, returning to his work.

"But this is an urgent matter . . ."

He applied the feather's tip to the sunken eye sockets on the wrapped corpse. "What could be so urgent—," he began before turning to face me again. "Come to ask about that curse business, have you?"

"That's not why I'm here," I said.

"Then out with it, if you please." He gestured toward the body. "I've work to do."

I nodded appreciatively at the mummy he was dusting, wondering if he feared it might wander off before he finished. "I need help identifying something."

"And what is this something?" he asked, placing the feather on a cart laden with the lantern and an assortment of other tools.

"Are you an expert?" I asked.

He hesitated, then finally nodded, drawing himself up a little taller. "Enough."

He couldn't be more than a few years older than me. "Forgive me, sir, you seem so young, and you are, well . . . *dusting*, after all."

He bristled. "I've been a student of the artifacts of Egypt for some years, and I'll have you know that we cannot trust the care of these specimens"—he gestured toward the body he'd been dusting—"to any scab who might know how to wield a rag and mop."

Having thoroughly offended him and wasted time in doing so, I hesitated no further. "Very well," I said, reaching into my handbag and pulling from it the iron dog's head.

I held it out to him. He took it in his gloved hands and over to his cart, where he pulled a magnifying glass from the tray.

"Where did you get this?"

"At a party last season," I lied. "I know the glyphs cannot be read, but I was wondering if you could tell me something about the object itself."

The young Egyptologist examined it closely. "Demotic," he announced.

"Pardon me?"

"They're not glyphs. These are demotic letters—much more recent than glyphs. The Rosetta Stone bears both," he said. "You've heard of the Rosetta Stone, I reckon?"

"Of course," I answered, glancing round the room. "But where is it? Last time I visited—"

"Off display," he interrupted me. "Temporarily. For cleaning."

I nodded. "But it will not help us with the script on that, will it?" I asked, pointing at the linen trailing from the dog's head.

He shook his head. "Don't need it. I'm fluent enough in reading demotic text to tell you this is gibberish," he said proudly.

"What?"

"Random characters. Bit of hocus-pocus to look the real thing. Like the dog's head. Actually, it's a jackal—a common motif in Egyptian art, easy mark for forgers."

"But how can you be so certain after such a cursory examination?" I asked, pressing toward him.

He tapped the metal with his fingernail. "This is iron. Iron was dear in Egypt, almost as precious as silver and gold. Maybe even more so, since they couldn't mine for it. What iron they did have was what they recovered from meteorites. Early Egyptians called it the metal of heaven, and didn't spend it on pieces like this one." He tossed the object roughly on the cart while keeping his focus on me. It landed dangerously close to the lantern, the metal clinking against the lantern's base, the scrap of linen resting across the glass.

He crossed his arms and stared at me. I knew that look from quarrels with my brothers. He was *taunting* me.

"If I may be so bold, could you tell me again your position with the museum?" I asked. If this object was not important, then it meant that I'd been wrong about someone searching for it.

"My position?" he repeated, suddenly defensive. "I'm an Egyptologist with special interest in the Rosetta Stone."

I eyed him again. Something was amiss. He was too young to keep company with true academics. Plus, he'd been relegated to menial clerical work a few nights before at the party.

"And your name, sir?"

He sighed. "Stowe, for what it's worth. Truth is, there are dozens of shavers out there more than willing to capitalize on the public's current fascination with Egypt rather than—" He turned to look again at where he'd tossed my dog's head on his tray. He stopped speaking abruptly.

"Rather than what?" I asked him, my patience wearing thin.

He said nothing, merely reached for his magnifying glass and bent over the jackal's head. He leaned in close enough that the glass caught the lantern light and refracted on the cases behind him.

"The devil . . . ," he said quietly. "There's something here."

"Of course there's something there—you simply cannot read it. Perhaps you could be so kind as to point me toward someone who can?" I said, reaching for the piece.

Stowe ignored me, picking up the metal shape and stretching the scrap of linen taut between his two hands. He then proceeded to hold it closer to the lantern, pressing it flat against the glass.

"I cannot make it out," he said, sounding painfully confused.

"I believe you established that several moments ago—," I began.

"No," he interrupted. "I can't 'cause it's in French."

I was now thoroughly convinced that this Egyptologist was little more than a dustman. "Mr. Stowe, if that were French, I'd have no reason to trouble you—"

"Would you listen? Not the message you brought me," he said, handing me a magnifying glass and making room at the cart. "This one."

He repeated his motion with the scrap stretched across the warm glass of the lantern. The letters he had dismissed as meaningless remained, but incredibly a new message appeared in faint white script. It slanted at an angle, the words seeming to have been written hastily.

And recently.

I stood and whispered before I could catch myself, "Bloody hell, it does look like French!"

"Miss Wilkins, you—"

I froze. "How do you know my name?"

"You pretended not to know me," he accused.

"And you me!" I shot back.

He relented quickly. "I . . . recognize you from the party. I had to write your name in my ledger." He paused. "And you were rude to me."

I shook my head. "Not you," I said quickly. "I was objecting to Showalter's *treatment* of you. But how did you know if you do not speak French?"

"An insult in any language has the same ring of superiority about it," he said hotly.

I started to protest, but instead reached out and snatched the jackal's head from him. I leaned over to press it up against the lantern myself, then watched the words reappear.

This time I peered closer and actually read the line.

I read it a second time.

And then a third.

It can't be . . ., I thought.

"Well?" Mr. Stowe prodded.

I stood.

"Are you all right?" he asked me, offering his arm.

I shook my head. "The message . . ." I faltered, leaned against a display case. "The message reads '15 May 1815— Cairo. W's standard in the great London pyramid. This is the key. Emperor advised and awaiting delivery.'"

My head swam and my heart raced, though I still could barely credit the reason.

"The emperor?" Stowe said. "But if it's written in French and references the emperor, they can only be talking about—"

"Napoleon," I finished for him. "The message speaks of Napoleon."

Chapter Nine

"Napoleon?" Stowe said. "You're sure?"

"This is common French, there is but one emperor—"

"You having me on?" he asked.

I shook my head. "This is no joke."

I thought of all the events of the last two days. The party, the strange fates that had befallen those of us around the corpse. The nature of the message. And I began to feel something like the fear I'd felt that night the man had followed me in the garden.

Mr. Stowe swallowed hard. "You sure you're not having a laugh?" he asked again, this time sounding as if he wished I were.

I shook my head, fought to control the trembling of my hands.

"Swear it," he said, nerves fraying his voice, eyes wide.

"I promise," I said.

"Tell me again what it says," he demanded, grabbing pencil and tablet.

I held it back to the heat of the lantern light and read it again. "'*15 mai 1815—Le Caire. Standard de W dans la grande pyramide de Londres. C'est la clé. Empereur ausé et attend livraison.*'"

He looked up at me. "English, please?"

I nodded and repeated my translation slowly as Mr. Stowe recorded the words on the paper. As he wrote, I asked, "How is it you speak ancient Egyptian and not French? I thought any classically trained scholar would have had at least some French."

He wrote for a moment more, then looked up. "My learning is a bit of a gallimaufry."

I squinted. It was the third or fourth time he'd used a word I wasn't entirely familiar with. I knew it was slang of some sort, the thing Mother would call gutter talk. But it chapped me a bit to think that I might converse freely with an Indian, but couldn't keep up with a young man from a different neighborhood in London.

He noted my confusion. "A hodgepodge? A bit of this and that, made up of what I can manage?"

I still wasn't understanding. He rolled his eyes, sat up taller, and put on a voice a bit more posh. "My training has not been what one might consider classical."

I waited for him to elaborate.

"I'm something like an apprentice," he said.

"An apprentice," I repeated, wondering exactly whom I'd finally managed to trust my secret to.

Mr. Stowe read the message again, as I pressed the scrap against the light. The strokes that appeared were uneven and messy, as if they'd been written hurriedly. Perhaps it was the years of eavesdropping on Father's fireside conferences, but cryptic references to a standard and London pyramids sounded suspiciously like code. And coupled with the fact that it was written in some sort of invisible ink and tucked inside the wrappings of a mummy . . . it was more than even Father would believe.

I stood and found Mr. Stowe eyeing me with suspicion. "You didn't get this at a party last year, Miss Wilkins," he said, pointing at the transcription he'd recorded on the paper. "The date of the message gives you up." He paused, then stepped forward and closed a hand around the jackal's head as if to take it from me. I held fast.

"Where'd you get it?" he demanded.

"Mr. Stowe, what is your *exact* position with the museum?" I shot back.

There was a long pause where we both stared, each with a hand on the jackal's head, the iron closing the circuit passing between us. His gaze was bold, serious, but the smile tugging at the corner of his mouth surprised me.

"Birds of a feather, we are," he said finally, adding, "Of the bald-faced lying variety."

I failed to suppress my own smile.

"I *am* an apprentice here," he began. "In the main, I clean exhibits and assist senior researchers. I've no formal training, but I know a fair bit."

"And how did you acquire this knowledge?"

"Through my father, mainly," he said. "He was a surveyor in the British army when I was a boy. He was on the ground with the lobsters in Egypt when Nelson's fleet routed Napoleon at the Nile. He'd no learning either, but he was bright and curious. When he returned, he filled my head to bursting with stories, and I've been hungry for more since." He shrugged. "Been here at the museum in varying capacities for almost three years now."

"And your work with the Rosetta Stone?"

"A bit under the rose," he said, adding, "But just because they don't know about it doesn't mean I'm not on to something. I'm quite close to a breakthrough, I believe. And when I achieve it, my future will be assured."

At his confession, I decided I must make one of my own.

"I might have brought the jackal's head from Lord Showalter's party by mistake," I admitted.

"By mistake?"

"It might have found its way into my bodice when no one was looking."

"You *filched* it?"

I shook my head, then told him my reasons for keeping it—that Showalter had promised me we would be permitted to take the items home with us, that it seemed so insignificant, that by the time I realized what was happening it would have been impossible to return it without making a scene. I left out the part about being unwilling to invite Showalter's attentions once again.

"It came off the *mummy*?" Mr. Stowe's eyes widened even farther. Clearly, pilfering an artifact from an antiquity was a greater sin than merely nabbing a trinket off someone's mantel.

I nodded meekly. "When I took my turn at the unwrapping."

He slumped against a case of jars, each labeled with cards covered in precise script. LIVER, MASON, UPPER NILE DELTA, 1000 AD. HEART, PRINCESS, LOWER ASSYRIA, 1100 AD.

"And people looked at *me* as if they worried I might nick the silver candlesticks," he muttered.

I tried to tug the jackal's head away from him. "Do you intend to scold me or help me?"

"Help you what? Return it? Pawn it?"

"Of course not! I—," I began, but the truth was, I was even less certain what to do now than I had been when I walked in. If the message did indeed reference Napoleon, would that make it valuable enough to kill for? Was this responsible for the waiter's fate?

He looked puzzled. "You have no plan?"

I shook my head.

"Lord Showalter doesn't know you're here?"

"No one does," I said.

"The authorities?"

"No one," I repeated. "I thought it best to gather more

information before trusting someone else. It's what Father would advise."

"Your father?" he asked, pulling a face.

I explained Father's position and expertise, as well as how my plans to speak with him had been thwarted thus far. "But that was before I realized this could be so serious as to involve Napoleon and the war," I said, fighting the fear rising in me. I should have been more persistent with Father yesterday.

"When's he back?" Mr. Stowe asked.

"Tomorrow evening," I said quietly. "Though sometimes these trips turn into even longer affairs. . . ."

"One day is a long time," he said, nodding his head, "long enough for all manner of things—"

"Perhaps you're right," I said quickly. "Perhaps I should find someone else to tell, someone Father might approve of." One of his trusted associates might be still in London. But I didn't know where to begin, and suddenly, holding something potentially so important in my hands made me even more wary of trusting anyone.

"No!" he said, holding out his hand. "That's not what I meant. I meant that it's long enough for—"

I looked up sharply. "For what?"

He released his grip on the jackal's head and leaned against the edge of the open case. He stared at the floor for several moments before continuing. In the silence, I thought of turning and going, reasoning that I'd learned as much as I could hope to present to Father. But Mr. Stowe knew my secret, and that fact kept me rooted to the spot.

"What if this is an opportunity," he began, looking at me, "for us to help each other?"

I crossed my arms. "In what way?"

He stood, leaned closer. "You've committed an indiscretion—"

I flushed. "It was nothing so scandalous."

He waved a hand at me. "Never mind the scandal. But you find yourself needing to return a sensitive object and make sure no one finds out that you filched it."

"Go on," I said.

"And then you have me," he said, placing his hand on his chest. "A young man with nothing but his passion for his field to recommend him. No connections, no paper from Oxford—"

"The point, Mr. Stowe!" I said.

He smiled as he leaned even closer. "But if I brought to my superiors a mysterious artifact . . . an artifact of great interest to Bonaparte . . . and I had a chance to study it, work out its significance—"

"You would use this object to buy your future," I said quietly.

"Earn it," he corrected. "But whatever word you prefer, the solution is clear as clear can be, right?"

I took a step back. "Enlighten me."

"Give it to me," he said. "I will relieve you of the burden, discover its importance, and ensure that I don't spend the rest of my life dusting cases. When your father returns, you can tell him all and he can do as he wishes. But in the meantime, I have a day to try to figure what's what, and you can return to the very important business of fancy dresses and balls."

I hugged the jackal's head to my chest and felt my face grow warm. "You think that's all that matters to me?" I said, drawing myself up taller. "I wouldn't have come if that were all I cared about!" I spoke loudly enough now that my voice echoed off the vaulted ceiling, loudly enough that Mr. Stowe took a step backward.

He looked surprised, shocked even that I wasn't as eager to relieve myself of the mess as he expected. "I meant no offense—"

"How do I even know that I can trust you? How do I know that you were not the intended recipient of this object and its message all along?" It felt good to accuse him, though I didn't believe it even as I said it. It merely assuaged the sting of having been mistaken for a silly, empty-headed girl.

His mouth fell open. "*Me?* I had even less reason to be at that party than you. I was only standing in for Banehart. He took ill at the last and sent me."

"You could be lying," I pointed out.

"Wouldn't I have already taken it from you if it were meant for me?" he asked, shaking his head. "A simple offer of assistance to a lady in distress and this is what it gets me . . ." He turned and walked a few paces away from me.

I looked at his back. He was handsome enough to be the rakish sort of fellow who broke hearts and promises in an A Lady novel. Ambitious enough, certainly. And maybe I was as foolish as any of those girls who fell for a Willoughby or a Wickham.

But Mr. Stowe was right on one point at least. I could not do this alone. Already having stumbled into trusting him, I should wait now for Father before risking more. And when I did speak to Father, if I could bring with me some evidence that someone with Mr. Stowe's experience could supply, so much the better.

"I need no rescuer," I said evenly, "but I do need your help."

He turned and looked at me.

"We will work together," I said finally.

Stowe squared his shoulders, lifted an eyebrow. "Together?"

"Only until Father returns."

"Fair enough," he said. "So long as you promise to ask him to speak on my behalf."

"Agreed," I said, extending my free hand. "And if we are to work together, please call me Agnes, Mr. Stowe."

"If you like," he said. He eyed my hand, still hanging out in the air, but he didn't move to take it.

I pulled it partway back. "And I'll go on calling you Mr. Stowe, then?"

"Oh!" He closed the gap between us, tugged off his glove, and placed his palm against my own.

"Caedmon. My name is Caedmon."

His touch was warm and dry, slightly calloused at the fingertips. "This could be dangerous," he pointed out.

"Shaking hands?" I said.

He released his grip. "You know what I mean."

I nodded. It was already dangerous. I'd already taken the jackal's head. The man at the party had already been murdered. My neighbors had already been vandalized. I was already in too deeply now to abandon the cause. And if it was possible that Napoleon was after something that we could prevent him from getting, then I was obligated, wasn't I?

"You've pluck about you, Agnes," he said, releasing my hand. "I'll give you that."

I almost blushed. In truth, I surprised myself. As dangerous as all this might be, as inconveniently as it might have been timed, part of me was grateful. Grateful that I'd been given the gift of something important, something exciting, perhaps something that mattered more than cotillions and curtsies. In a part of me that I would never reveal to anyone, it felt like a last blessed grasp at living before I settled into the life everyone else was planning for me. That same part of me silently thanked heaven that Father had been as busy and unavailable as ever.

After too long a silence, I cleared my throat and spoke again. "Where should we begin?"

He looked at the jackal's head resting in my other palm. "It seems we have two challenges: divining the meaning of the message on that scrap, and sussing out who might have been meant to receive it."

"It could be anyone," I began, "anyone at the party—"

"A guest, or a member of Showalter's household," Caedmon mused. "Or even the rum ned himself."

"Don't be absurd," I said, wrinkling my nose. "It is far more likely to be someone working with the museum if the body was meant to come here in the first place!"

"Then we begin with the message itself. Shall we have another go?"

He did not wait for my reply as he turned and grabbed his tablet. "W's standard," he read aloud. "That seems to be the first order—" But he caught himself, looking over my head toward the entrance to the room. I turned to follow his gaze. A man in a black suit wandered in and began a circuitous path between the cases. The point of a finely carved cane tapped the wooden floorboards with a muffled thud.

"Perhaps," Caedmon whispered as I turned back, "perhaps we should continue this somewhere more private . . . at another time?" He quickly replaced the lid on the case he'd been cleaning and began to secure the items on his cart.

I knew he was right. We couldn't risk discussing the jackal's head in front of anyone, and if I didn't get back home soon, I'd face more questions than I could come up with answers for.

I stared at the jackal's head, reluctant. If someone truly was looking for this, they'd come looking for it at my door soon enough. I wasn't sure I could hide it properly at home.

"Will you keep it for me?" I whispered hastily.

He looked taken aback. "I—I—"

"It will be safer for all of us if you do. No one knows I've been here."

"Now you would trust me?"

"I already have," I said, folding the jackal's head into his hand.

He nodded gravely. "All right."

"I'll come tomorrow. I should be able to slip away in the afternoon," I said.

"Not here," he whispered. "Meet me at the south gate of the Tower," he said, referencing the old fortress on the Thames. "I know someone who can help."

"Can he be trusted?" I asked, rankling at how already he was taking charge.

"He served with my father," Caedmon said quietly, in a tone that made me realize I should ask no more.

Chapter Ten

❧

Mother hadn't even noticed my absence the morning before, and Clarisse was as discreet as I knew she would be. But keeping my appointment with Caedmon the next afternoon presented a greater challenge.

"But Aunt Rachel is out," Mother said when I begged her to allow me to go to the dressmakers to see about a bit of ribbon for my presentation gown. Aunt Rachel's absence was precisely what I'd counted on. She met with her missionary alliance from the church on our at-home day. I told Mother that the shopgirl had informed me that it would be the last shipment from the Continent for some time—so little was making it through the blockades of late—and that if I didn't go now, there'd be slim chance of anything being left by tomorrow.

Mother considered this.

"You *will* need something for the train."

"All four feet of it," I agreed, trying not to sound too eager. If I overplayed this, Mother might suspect I had other reasons for the errand. I rubbed the wing of my jade butterfly nervously.

"And maybe a little something at the waist—just on the fifth rib where we agreed it would hit."

"Yes, Mother."

I didn't care if it hit the fifth rib or my second knuckle so long as she let me go.

"But why such interest now?" she said, setting aside her embroidery.

"It *is* my presentation dress. And I am making more of an effort, Mother. After I saw what Caroline Hallishaw wore at the unwrapping . . ."

She rolled her eyes. "So inappropriate for a garden party . . . now what will they have her wear for her debut?"

"Exactly," I enthused.

Mother hesitated. "Very well, but don't be long, please. The Martins are to call later, and I can't be made to endure her comparisons of her own silly daughter to you if you are absent."

"Back before you even know I've gone," I promised.

Mother relented with a wave of her hand. I popped down and kissed her cheek, dashing out the door before she could change her mind.

The ribbon was the only believable errand that would put me in distance of my rendezvous with Caedmon. Woolsey, our carriage driver, deposited me at the curb in front of Boulton's dress shop. While most of my contemporaries would be crowding the shops in Bond Street, Mother swore by the dressmakers near the river and London Bridge—and conveniently, the Tower.

Inside, I hastily picked out ribbon as promised.

"It's lovely, miss," gushed the clerk as she handed over the ribbon. "I only saw the fabric once, but from what I recall, this color ought to be perfect."

Boulton's had imported the silk, but like the gown I'd worn for the unwrapping, Mother insisted that this dress be made away from prying eyes, and fitted at home when the time came. "All this secrecy is nonsense," I offered.

"We had a girl last week who insisted we bury her gown underneath piles of scrap muslin when we weren't working on it," the girl said, smiling. "Your mother's not the only one afraid of spies."

I couldn't help but smile to myself. "No," I said, turning, "I suppose she's not."

Outside, Woolsey leaned against the carriage, staring into the shop windows for a glimpse of a certain seamstress I knew him to be sweet on. I'd requested him—and not our other driver—for precisely this reason.

I told Woolsey I'd walk awhile and inquire about a volume of poetry at the booksellers up the lane. He made no attempt to conceal his delight at having the good fortune to stay behind and stare at the pretty golden-haired girl through the windows of the shop.

I made for the Tower. It was as lovely to be alone on a busy street today as it had been yesterday morning. But as I drew closer to the point at which I'd agreed to meet Caedmon, my thoughts occupied themselves with how best to proceed with this young man.

While I was brave enough to flout convention with my appetite for education and my penchant for shirking a chaperone, I confess that even in my most rebellious of moods I had not conceived of spending time alone with a young man. Even close conversations with Showalter made me more than a little nervous, despite the constant presence of Mother or Aunt Rachel. So going to meet Caedmon—though an indiscretion born of necessity—was all the more unsettling. An indiscretion complicated by how very attractive and very irritating he managed to be at the same time.

But there was nothing for it. Until I spoke with Father, there was little else I could do but follow where fate had led me.

I found Caedmon sitting cross-legged like a child at the corner of the lawn, the gray-brown stones of the Tower piling up behind him, oblivious to the pungent smell rising from the stale waters of the moat behind him. He was staring intently at the scrap of paper on which he'd recorded the translation of the secret message yesterday.

I thought of what it might mean if someone saw us together unescorted. Girls' reputations had been ruined for less. Mother would lock me away for the rest of the season, perhaps longer. Showalter might withdraw his interest. And the fact that this prospect bothered me gave me even more pause. Could it mean that I was developing feelings for Showalter? Or that I was already so conscious of my pride that even the possibility of his refusal was difficult to stomach?

But the fact that neither was enough to make me turn around and scurry back to the carriage meant something else entirely, I suspected.

"Good afternoon," I said. He looked up at me and scrambled to his feet.

"H'lo," Caedmon said. "Wasn't sure you'd turn up."

"I said I would, didn't I?"

He nodded. "Thought you might have second thoughts is all."

I'd had third and fourth thoughts, but didn't bother telling him that. He held the paper bearing his translation of the message out to me.

"Honestly, I think if it were a proper code or cipher or hieroglyph it would almost be easier to make out." He shook his head.

"You've had no luck, then?" I said.

"Maybe one bit. I think 'standard,' because it apparently belongs to somebody"—here he pointed to the possessive *W*— "can only be one thing."

I waited for him to finish. He waited for me to ask him to do so. I won.

"I think it's a standard like a king's standard," he said finally.

"Like colors?" I asked, thinking of the ceremonial banners the guards carried at the front of a royal procession.

"Spot on. Given the other possible meanings of the word, it's the only one that really squares. Each pharaoh and even some of the generals had their own standards smithed. What Napoleon, if he is indeed the emperor referenced, might be seeking would be some carved or wrought-metal job they could affix to a wooden pole. Deacon can tell us for certain."

He steered me past the Tower grounds and into an alleyway with a hand lightly touching my elbow. I almost objected when his fingers landed there. Such a gesture by anyone other than my father or brothers was considered highly inappropriate, but Caedmon didn't live in my world.

And if pressed, I might have been forced to admit that I rather liked it. There was something familiar in the gesture, something comfortable.

"Who is Deacon?" I asked, to pull my mind back to the matter at hand. A pack of ravens scattered as we approached.

"My godfather. He was a military man, but his knowledge of Egypt and the artifacts outstrips even the most senior of men at the museum. My father served with him in Egypt. Pa thought he was tip-top, used to bring me along on visits to his place when I was younger, after they both returned to London. Of course that was before . . ." Caedmon trailed off.

"Before what?"

He hesitated. "Deacon was more than just a soldier, and

he distinguished himself when my father served under him in Egypt. Pa was never clear about what Deacon was up to or how he helped him, but I have my notions."

"Notions?"

He looked away. "You'll think me cork-brained," he said.

"I might, if we weren't having this conversation the day after finding a secret message attached to an ancient ornament."

Now he smiled. "I think Deacon was a bit of a spy," he said slowly.

I stopped. "A spy?" Suddenly I felt as if I were listening again at my fireplace.

"Something like. When we visited him in the Tower, Pa told me Deacon worked for the ordnance board, devising explosives for the army and navy."

It was true the Tower had since fallen to this purpose, a strange evolution from its years as a prison so long ago. It also held a zoo, the crown jewels, and half a dozen other odd things.

"He and Pa always talked about their time in Egypt or some new book or discovery. But other times, my father would send me from the office out to the grounds to chase the birds. Still, I heard enough. But short afore Pa died, something happened and Deacon was dished up. He shifted here."

He stopped and pointed to a nondescript door.

"Difficult times," I said.

He shrugged his shoulders and brushed back a lock of hair

that fell across his forehead. "He's all right. Still awake about a thing or two. Forgotten more about Egypt than any of those triflers at the museum ever even knew, and if he was a spy—"

"Then who better to help us with cryptic messages about Napoleon smuggled into Britain by way of a mummy," I finished for him. He nodded and looked at me again, something like curiosity in his expression, a look he might give to some oddity under glass in the museum.

He looked longer still, his expression perhaps sliding from curiosity to appreciation. Half-afraid of what might come next, I reached out and knocked hard and loud on the worn wood.

The action broke the spell, as my knock elicited a string of oaths from beyond the door.

"What?" growled a grizzled man as he pulled the door open a crack a moment later, bright blue eyes wincing in the light. First his gaze fell on me, annoyance morphing into confusion, then it found Caedmon, and his face relaxed. "Well done, lad," he said. "Finally found yourself a girl." The door fell open to admit us.

I balked. Caedmon sputtered, "We—we need your help."

Deacon turned his back to us and hobbled toward a chair dwarfed by piles of books on either side. "Looks like you're doing quite well—"

"Uncle," Caedmon groaned.

I stepped across the threshold and spoke. "We've come to consult your expertise on another matter."

"Who is she?" the man asked.

Caedmon found his voice again. "Er, sorry. Miles Deacon, meet Miss Agnes Wilkins."

Miles Deacon eyed me carefully. "Your father Lord Wilkins?"

I swallowed the panic rising in me. If he somehow knew Father, he might even tell him before I had the chance to do so. "Yes, sir."

He nodded. "Good man. Always a friend to the service."

"I wasn't aware Father had ties to the ordnance board."

He shot me a look, then said to Caedmon, "What kind of nonsense have you been telling her about me?"

"Only that you might be able to help us with this," Caedmon said hurriedly, reaching into his pocket and handing a small bundle of cloth to Deacon. The old man unfolded it.

"Humph," he said, examining the jackal's head. Then he squinted at the characters on the attached piece of linen. "Gibberish. You must know that, Caedmon."

"He does," I said, and quickly explained the object's sordid history and our discovery of the hidden message. As I did so, Deacon's face grew grave.

"Let me see the translation," he ordered after I finished. Caedmon passed him the slip of paper. He read it, first to himself, then in a hushed voice aloud. We were quiet a full minute as we waited for him to say something.

"Bring the candle," he commanded me, gesturing toward the tallow puddling on the mantel.

Deacon held the scrap to the flame and the message once again came into view. He read it, then leaned in and sniffed the linen.

"Written with lemon juice," he said, sniffing again. "Or milk gone sour. Hard to tell the difference after a while."

He sniffed a third time, his eyes closed. After a moment, he looked up. "Well," he said, sighing, "you've found yourself in the middle of more trouble than you could ever hope to imagine."

Chapter Eleven

Deacon was transformed. Gone was the scowl. Gone was the hunch in his shoulders. And he'd shed that prickly attitude like an overcoat in August.

"Tell me again how you came to possess this," he commanded.

I repeated my story; this time he interrupted me with more questions, trying to place the date of the mummy's arrival in England, the condition of the wrappings around the object, the behavior of the man who followed me through the gardens.

"And this was quite buried within?" he asked, tapping the iron of the jackal's head with his fingernail.

I nodded and related my observation regarding the variation in color of the wrappings at the feet.

His face grew grave. "I warned them this would happen."

I looked to Caedmon. Them? What would happen?

"Uncle?" he said, begging an explanation.

Deacon sprang to his feet. "I told the ministry years ago

that French sympathizers would find new ways to smuggle their information across our blockades. Nobody fancied they'd be so bold as to conceal it within a body, but I knew it wasn't beyond them. And Bonaparte has had spies in Egypt since we ousted him. Any one of them might have had access to a shipment bound for the museum, none of which are searched properly for contraband. . . ."

"Because anyone paying the expense of bringing them here would have a fit if the artifacts were disturbed before they'd made it to London. And if you've pockets deep enough to get the items, you can afford to bribe a port officer," Caedmon finished.

"But why bother with Egypt? Wouldn't Napoleon's intelligence resources be better used within England, collecting information on our deployments and strategy?" I asked.

Deacon stopped and stared at me. "Got more of your father in you than just those eyes, haven't you?" I blushed for the second time, and didn't answer. He went on. "Boney's got plenty of spies here in London working those angles, a few we know about, and too many we don't. But to answer your question, it's obvious he's still looking for it."

"Looking for *what*?" Caedmon asked.

"Come, boy. We've discussed this." Deacon's tone grew impatient.

Caedmon looked confused. "The standard from the message?"

"Of course the standard! It's written right here, isn't it?" he said, waving our transcription in the air.

"But *W*?" I said. "What is *W*?"

"Not what . . . *who*," Deacon said ominously, letting the word echo in the silent room.

Caedmon clapped his hands abruptly, making me jump in my seat.

"Wepwawet!" he shouted, springing to his feet. He pounded one fist into his other hand and bolted for a stack of books in the corner.

I played the name over in my mind and, coming up with nothing, looked to Deacon.

"Wepwawet," he began, reaching for the book Caedmon had extricated from the pile, "was an Egyptian deity. Very mighty. His cult"—he paused here to check the index in the giant volume, red leather creaking as the spine bent open—"was among the most powerful in all of Egypt, spreading the entire length of the Nile."

"Cult?" I asked.

Caedmon took over as Deacon began thumbing through the moldy pages. "Religion in Egypt at the time wasn't at all like it is today. There were thousands of recognized deities. A person had a great many more choices than, say, your average Londoner whose only real choice is which Church of England congregation to join."

Deacon resumed the thread. "They simply ascribed greater

devotion to one in particular. Sometimes their choice was based on geography. Sometimes on their vocation, or family tradition . . . or an appetite for influence," he finished as he handed me the open book.

"Wepwawet's cult was powerful?" I asked.

Caedmon nodded. "Wepwawet was the god of war, oversaw the funerary cult—"

"How many cults could one person fall in with?" I asked, staring at the drawing of a regal-looking man, heavily armored. In his hands, he held a pole. Atop this pole sat a figure on a stool. The figure had the body of a man, but the head of a jackal, long-snouted, with pointy ears.

I swung around to look at Caedmon. He nodded. "Wepwawet had the head and strength of a jackal. Cock of the walk, he was. And he could open the way between the living and the dead."

Deacon broke in. "Hence his position of importance in the funerary cult. Anyone mummifying a loved one would have prayed to Wepwawet to speed the body and soul along to the afterlife, and the waiting judgment of Osiris or the keeping of Anubis. And with the vast number of mummified remains throughout Egypt—"

"His cult would have been enormous," I finished.

"And," Caedmon said, "because of the war bits, the pharaohs were devotees."

"Then the cult *itself* was powerful as well."

Deacon hesitated, gave a slight nod. "Somewhat. We can only

rely on what little of the surviving historical record we've been able to translate. We can never know if it was the cult's high-level membership that made it influential, or if the magic itself merely attracted those souls. The Ptolemys were particularly devout."

"Ptolemy from the Rosetta Stone inscription," Caedmon supplied.

"But the message," I said, shaking my head. "Unless Napoleon intends to have himself mummified, what does Wepwawet have to do with—"

"He's after the standard," Caedmon said.

"Why *now*?" Bonaparte commanded some half a million men at present, a force larger than any he'd ever assembled. The papers indicated that they were marching on Brussels, with the Prussians and English poised to converge on him.

Deacon leaned toward me. "He took forty thousand troops into Egypt, where he knew he'd find no opposition, and proceeded to occupy the entire Nile Delta, sending out archaeological teams. He'd dug up half the country by the time England decided we couldn't allow him a strong base from which to threaten our empire in India."

"And some say he still hadn't found what he'd come for in the first place," Caedmon interjected.

"This standard?" I guessed. Both men nodded solemnly. "But how did he even know to look for it?"

"Boney's an odd one," Deacon said, "which is what's made him so difficult to outflank all these years. He's as taken with

Egypt and the Old Kingdom as he is with overthrowing royals and chasing women. And he's been after that standard for ages."

"But it's just a hunk of metal!" I protested.

Deacon took too long to reply. "I saw things in Egypt that I cannot explain. Things that haunt me still." He shifted in his seat, stared out the dingy window, and shook his head softly, remembering.

"But you can't believe that this standard actually has some sort of supernatural power?"

He looked at me. "I don't *disbelieve* it," he said carefully, his caution eerily reminiscent of Showalter's two mornings ago at breakfast.

Caedmon went on, "If what we reckon from the history is right, the standard could only be wielded by true kings."

"And Napoleon certainly fancies himself that," Deacon agreed.

"But what can it possibly do besides fetch a premium from a collector? Why would he bother looking for it now?"

Deacon shifted in his seat. "All the available sources indicated three things about the standard's mystical properties. First, it meant that the bearer could not be defeated in battle. Second, it assured that the bearer—when he did die—would ascend immediately to the skies and bypass the potential unpleasantness of judgment and the underworld."

"But that's just superstition, isn't it?" I asked, looking uncertainly to Caedmon.

Deacon and Caedmon were quiet long enough to exchange a glance, long enough to indicate that neither was ready to discount any rumor regarding the standard's power. "There is still more," Deacon said quietly. "It is also said that whoever bears the standard can summon Wepwawet's power to bridge the kingdoms of the living and the dead."

"I don't understand." The room seemed to grow colder.

"It means," Caedmon said gently, "that the pharaoh who carried it could resurrect an army of the dead to fight alongside his living soldiers."

"Now you're trying to scare me!" I forced a laugh.

Neither Deacon nor Caedmon cracked a smile.

Finally I found my voice. "But that's preposterous! There can be no more power in this thing"—I pointed toward the drawing in the book—"than there is in a cup of twice-steeped tea leaves."

"If I learned anything in my time in Egypt," Deacon said, "it's that the foolish man disrespects legend. And foolish men did not survive. There are powers and things beyond our understanding. And if history is correct, this standard is one of the most powerful weapons ever forged."

I realized I desperately wanted a rational explanation. "All of London is now mad with notions of the mummy's curse, but we know it's someone searching for this!" I waved the jackal's head before them.

"Fair point," Deacon said. "So let's suppose that the standard really is nothing but a plate of bronze with a harmless figurine atop it. Consider the example you just shared with me. You said yourself that all of London is under the spell of this mummy curse. They have almost *no* evidence to support it, but the idea has taken hold nonetheless."

"Museum attendance has increased tenfold since Showalter's party," Caedmon offered.

Deacon nodded. "Compare that fervor with what might result from an actual object once carried by the rulers of the world's first empire. An empire ruled by kings revered as gods."

"Men like Napoleon," I whispered.

He nodded. "Think on it, Miss Wilkins. Bonaparte has already cheated death countless times, and politically resurrected himself from death twice. He's done the impossible again and again. He stands poised to overrun the Continent, leaving little hope that England will be able to outlast him. He enjoys almost fanatical adoration from his people. So give that man an object that supposedly gives him complete invulnerability . . . and the power to raise an army of ghost soldiers from the millions of Frenchmen who've died for his cause—"

"And people will believe in the legend whether there's evidence to the contrary or not," I said quietly.

"Precisely," Deacon said. "Alexander the Great went to the Oracle at Delphi to receive his prophecy, ordering the seer to tell his generals who'd accompanied him that he could not be defeated in battle. The Oracle inhaled the vapors at the altar and foretold the exact place and time of Alexander's death. But when he dragged her by the hair outside the temple and held a knife to her throat in front of his men, she said exactly what he wanted them to hear. And he went on to win countless battles that according to all historians should have been utterly unwinnable. He understood something fundamental about leadership. Far more important than your actual ability is what those who follow you believe you can do. Napoleon knows this better than any man alive."

"To say nothing of what it might mean if it actually works . . ." Caedmon trailed off.

"And I wouldn't be so quick to dismiss a mummy's curse in the end," Deacon said carefully.

I waited for him to go on. "I was present at excavations in Egypt a time or two," he began, "and things never seemed to go well for the people involved. I once observed the removal of some items from a tomb near Alexandria—"

"Father told me about this," Caedmon said, leaning forward.

Deacon nodded. "He was there with me. Within a fortnight six of the crew—including the senior archaeologist—had died."

I gulped. "Six?"

"All in different ways—one from a fall, another seemed to have some sort of stroke, still another was bitten by a snake. There was nothing to connect the deaths. The men were from different villages, of different ages, all in fair health. . . ."

"Then you mean . . ." My voice failed with the knowledge of what they were telling me.

"If there are curses," Deacon said carefully, "sometimes the means by which they are visited on the offenders are more subtle than we might imagine."

"You're saying the person responsible for the break-ins might actually be the instrument of the curse?"

"Stranger things," Deacon said quietly.

My heart seemed to have slowed. The room was eerily still, but my thoughts roiled. An object of possible mystical power, a curse that might be real, a curse that still might find its way to my door eventually.

I tried to forget my own possible peril and focus on the greater problem at hand. "Then what you're saying," I said evenly, "is that if Napoleon recovers the standard, whether it functions according to legend or not—"

"Then God help us all."

I thought of my brother aboard his ship, somewhere at sea. Of all those soldiers marching on the Continent.

"But he doesn't have it yet," I said, with more conviction than I felt. "We have the message—perhaps its location. What is the great London pyramid?"

"Well," Deacon hedged. He shook his head, turned to Caedmon. "I'd heard a few years ago that French archaeologists and historians had taken to calling your museum something like that."

Caedmon sat up straighter. "The museum?"

"Frogs still resent having their hard work stripped of them all those years ago. And since we've occupied Egypt, their access to artifacts and dig sites has been carefully controlled," Deacon explained.

It taxed even my imagination to see the pillars and square profile of the former mansion as anything so exotic as a pyramid. I fell quiet as I considered this, tracing the seams between the stones of the uneven floor with my eyes. Outside, a brief chorus of cawing erupted from the ravens at the Tower.

"There's logic there," Caedmon said as he began to pace the small room, the space of which he covered in three strides before he had to turn back around. "If a pyramid was for piling up all the treasures and riches and history of a life so that it could live forever with the owner . . ."

"Then a museum becomes the modern equivalent," I said, rising to my feet.

"Which means that the standard is somewhere in the museum," Caedmon said, sounding less enthusiastic than I'd thought he might.

"Then all we have to do is find it!" I cried. Perhaps we'd succeed after all, perhaps our efforts to keep the standard from the hands of Napoleon would cancel out whatever evil I'd managed to rouse when I took the jackal's head.

"Easier said," Caedmon replied, lifting the paper up. "If this message came from Egypt with the mummy, it means it was planted by a French agent there. According to the date, a month has passed."

"So?"

"So . . . artifacts flow in and out of the museum all the time, some on loan to high-water patrons, some simply stored elsewhere because we haven't the space to study or exhibit them. On top of that, there are thousands of items currently on display or in the back rooms," Caedmon said, leaning against a door frame.

"We could ask for help," I offered, though as I said it I knew it was a bad idea.

"What would your father say to that, Miss Wilkins?" Deacon asked.

"My father?"

He nodded. "What might he have to say about involving a larger group of people in the search for this item?"

"He'd say that the more individuals with intelligence of this kind, the greater the chance of the message making it to the ears of its intended recipient."

Deacon nodded. "And that's the most pressing question for the moment, at any rate," he said. "You can assume, at least until a second message might make its way from the Nile, that no one of consequence knows the truth."

"So you suggest that we figure out who this message was meant for instead of recovering the standard?" I asked.

"Short list of suspects," Caedmon said.

I turned to him. "Meaning?"

"Meaning it had to be someone who was meant to receive the mummy in the first place. Not many a man in London with the coin to traffic in 'em."

I shook my head. "Not your Showalter suspicions again." I stifled a laugh at the thought of my neighbor engaged in high treason. When Caedmon didn't break a smile, I sobered. "Come now—it's far more likely the person awaiting the message works within the museum. They're the ones who commandeered the mummy away from Lord Showalter. Isn't it at the museum now?"

Caedmon nodded. "And far worse for the wear. By the time I saw it the morning after, it looked to have been properly gutted. And no one's in a hurry to really do anything with it."

"Odd, given how urgently they required it of Lord Showalter," I said. "Makes whomever demanded its surrender fairly suspect."

Deacon nodded. "She's right, Caedmon. There are a few sharks over there I'd keep an eye on, if I were you."

"Not many beside Banehart who could have given such an order," Caedmon offered.

"He's as likely as anyone to be mixed up in this," Deacon said.

"True. But we can't dismiss the possibility that if it's not Showalter—"

"You only suspect him because he was rude to you that evening," I put in.

"You refuse to entertain the possibility because he's caught your eye!" Caedmon said.

I gaped at him. "He's done nothing of the sort, and if you think for a moment—"

Deacon rose to his feet and raised his hands. "You two can bicker when we've sorted other more pressing matters. For now, perhaps we can all agree that it could just as easily have been someone within Showalter's household, or someone the sender knew would be at the party."

"Someone like me?" I said hotly, still smarting from Caedmon's accusation.

Caedmon sighed and rolled his eyes. "No, maybe that waiter, or—"

"Oh!" I yelped, another face coming to my mind. "Tanner— Showalter's valet. He's got a runny eye. Always lurking. I saw him follow when the waiter slipped away from the party that night."

"A runny eye and penchant for lurking are not the tells of a great spy," Deacon said with a kind smile, "but he's worth being wary of."

Outside I heard the bells above the Tower toll. Woolsey would have been waiting now for nearly an hour. I sprang to my feet. "I must go," I said, feeling a bit like Cinderella at her ball.

Caedmon started, "Already?"

I shook my head and explained my abandoned driver and the fact that Mother expected me at home to receive the Martins. I felt silly as the words passed my lips; I wished I had something legitimately urgent to carry me away.

I wished it even more when I noticed the withering look Caedmon sent my way. And at the same time, a fury tore through me. "Who are you to judge—," I began, my voice as hot as my temper.

"Enough!" Deacon roared. "We all do the best with what we can. And I must ask you both again to save your bickering for a time more convenient."

Deacon's outburst silenced us both.

"Now," he went on. "Caedmon, you will return to the museum and make a careful inventory of any object bearing any relation to Wepwawet's cult—however tenuous the connection might appear."

Caedmon nodded.

"And you, Miss Wilkins," he said, turning to me. "You will speak to your father about this at the earliest possible moment. You are right to be cautious in trusting others, but your father most certainly must know what is afoot."

"Yes, Mr. Deacon," I replied.

"Have your father send for me as soon as you have spoken with him," he ordered, wrapping up the jackal's head and handing it back to me. I held it a moment before returning it to Caedmon. It was still safer with him than at my home.

"Right, then?" Deacon asked us both.

Caedmon and I looked at each other. I looked to Deacon. "Fine."

Deacon studied us as if he didn't quite believe us. "You've

fallen into something here," he said carefully. "But soon enough we'll make sure the matter is in safer hands."

He crossed between us and opened the door. "Now walk her to the end of the lane," Deacon ordered Caedmon. "And no arguing on the way. You'll draw far more attention if you're picking at each other in the street than you will if folks think you're simply a couple out for a stroll."

My cheeks burned as I ducked out the door and hurried up the alley.

I heard Caedmon exchange good-byes with his mentor before he ran to catch me.

He fell into step beside me. "I'm sorry if I gave offense," he offered.

I kept walking, eyes ahead, but slowed my pace. "Thank you," I said. When I spoke next it was to ask him if he agreed with Deacon's plan.

He hesitated. "Deacon knows his business."

"I will still recommend you to Father, if that is your concern," I said.

"It's not," he said, "but I'm obliged."

We sidestepped a hansom cab barreling up the lane. "I had no right to sing small of your duties," he said, "when mine amount to little more than cleaning up displays and carrying post for my employers."

"You like your work, though," I said. "And toil in hopes of greater fulfillment to come."

"Don't you?" he asked quickly. "Have hope?"

I thought about Showalter. About the life a marriage with him would promise. A life free of worry, conflict, want, and complication.

And then I thought about my life at this moment. A life so terrifying and thrilling and challenging . . .

"It is hardly a fair comparison," I said, sounding sadder than I meant to.

He smiled. "You're welcome to come paw through moldy papers and crammed storage rooms with me."

"Oh, that I could," I said, smiling sadly. "I don't know how I might slip away, though. I'm running out of excuses for Mother."

He grinned. "Should you change your mind, you'll know where to find me. I'll be at the museum all day. Might even rough it there tonight."

"Won't you be missed at home?"

"No one at home," he said simply.

"You live alone?"

He nodded. "Mum passed five years before Pa. My sister had enough education to secure a position as a governess in the Lake District. I haven't seen her in three years, though we write now and again."

"You must be lonesome," I said, stealing a glance at him. And as many times as I'd wished to be able to do what I wanted, to have no one directing me, I wondered now, looking at Caedmon, if I ought not be more careful what I wished for. I began to pity rather than envy him, began to think how hollow life might be without Mother or Father, or even Rupert to spar with.

"I'm rather lucky, I think," he said, though he didn't sound entirely convinced. "No distractions, free to focus on my work . . . to pursue my ambition."

I wanted to press more, to ask more, to find out if there was anyone—a landlady or a flatmate or a sweetheart—who might wonder where he'd gone. It shouldn't have concerned me, but for some reason it did. For some reason I didn't like to think of Caedmon working away in anonymity only to be just as unnoticed or unmissed at whatever place he might call home.

We reached the end of the dressmakers' street, where I'd left Woolsey and the coach. "This is far enough," I said.

"You're sure I can't walk you the whole way?" he asked.

We were far enough from my neighborhood and it was early enough that it was unlikely I'd be seen or recognized by anyone of consequence. Still, I'd probably tempted fate far enough walking with him as long as I had.

"Thank you, but our coach driver is as loose-lipped as any girl I've ever known. I'll send you word when I've spoken to Father. He'll want to see you and the jackal, I believe."

"I'll be waiting," he said.

I looked up at him. Smiled. "Good-bye."

"Good-bye, Miss Wilkins," he said, nodding. I turned and made for the corner.

As I strode away, I felt that touch again at my elbow. I stopped and looked back at him. "Take care, Agnes," he said, using my Christian name for the first time since our meeting at the museum.

I smiled at his kindness. "Thank you, Caedmon."

I hurried across the bridge. Upon passing the bookshop I recalled my fib to Woolsey and ducked inside.

"Have you Goethe's *Faust*?" I asked the clerk quickly. "In the original German?"

He held up a finger, then disappeared into a tower of shelves and emerged a moment later with the volume.

I took the book and handed over the required coins, "*Danke,*" I said, sailing out the door.

I found Woolsey dozing in the seat, the pretty young seamstress no doubt having tired of being stared at and retreated to another location within the shop.

"Look sharp," I ordered. "Mother will be waiting."

Woolsey smiled, stretched, and snapped the reins, stirring the carriage to life. My mind raced as I sat inside the box, reflecting on what I'd discovered this morning, how the time spent in Deacon's hovel was like the best sort of dream—the kind that I could remember clearly, replaying again and again in my thoughts. And I realized as we neared the Park that despite the dangers, despite the gravity of the situation itself, I was already mourning that my moment in this story was drawing to a close. I would tell all to Father, I would give up my place in the events to others more suited to the task. I would surrender the excitement and the intrigue that could not be matched, no matter how scandalous the rest of the season proved to be.

There was something else, though, that troubled me more. Something I couldn't quite define. Something I suspected I would miss only after I realized it was gone.

I supposed it had to do with Caedmon.

He was exasperating and accusatory, yes. But he was also earnest and intelligent and brave. And it bothered me more than it should that this might have been my last opportunity to see him. Once I'd told Father, he'd take over, ending my chances to speak again with Caedmon.

But then perhaps it was merely my worrying about him being so lonely, having no one to look after him.

But was it more than that?

Had I grown *fond* of him?

At our initial meeting in the museum, I'd found him annoying and less than forthcoming. But then, so was I.

And of course he could stir up a quarrel faster than I could blink.

But all the same, I *did* like him.

Realizing it almost made me laugh. And then I did laugh to think that no matter how charming I found him, no matter how handsome he was (and this, too, I was forced to admit, was the case), it couldn't possibly matter. I could no more choose him than he would even want me. There were lines between our classes, between our stations and families (or his lack of one).

No, despite his many finer qualities—character and otherwise—they would never be enough to convince Mother to allow him at table, much less earn him a place in our society.

My amusement at my own silly heart was beginning to give way to something like regret at the injustice of it all—for I told myself it was the outmoded social mores I was bemoaning and not something more personal—as Woolsey dropped me inside our front gate. I took the stairs to the entry hall slowly, less than eager to meet with Mother and the Martins.

But further thoughts on Caedmon were interrupted by what I saw sitting on the table in the foyer: an officer's hat, brushed clean and bedecked with two gold bars and a simple white feather. Within I heard delighted laughter, one warm voice ringing out above the rest.

My brother David was home.

Chapter Twelve

❧

I flung my hat onto the table next to my brother's and sprinted for the drawing room, nearly knocking Mrs. Brewster flat as I barreled in. "David!" I shouted.

"Aggie!" He bounced to his feet from his seat beside Mother on the sofa, gathering me into a hug.

"But what are you doing here? I thought you wouldn't be home again for months!" I buried my face in his wool jacket.

"You are happy with your surprise after all, then?" my father asked from the armchair nearest the sofa.

I released David and flew to Father. "You knew?"

He laughed. "He was half the reason for my errand to Tilbury," he explained.

"And you kept it from us!" I said, eyes wide.

"Father thought it might be a nice surprise. And with Mother so worked up over your debut, he thought it best to not give her any more reason to throw the household into a state," David explained.

I turned back to my brother and looked him over. There were faint lines around his eyes that hadn't been there when we'd seen each other last almost two years ago. And the uniform that once seemed to hang from his shoulders now fit him perfectly. He looked more man than the boy I'd grown up chasing down the back stairs, but he was still my brother.

"You're taller again," he said, somewhat sadly.

"I haven't grown since my fourteenth birthday."

"But you're always taller than I remember you," he said. "It's just that my baby sister is not supposed to be so . . . *adult*."

I jabbed him in the ribs. "And you are supposed to write more often."

"You sound like Mother," he said, laughing and gathering me into his arms again.

"Why *are* you home?" I asked again, grateful that he was safe with us rather than preparing for battle at sea.

"I just finished telling Mother, but . . . ," he said, sitting down.

"But I'm sure you won't mind telling it again," Rupert interrupted from his chair in the corner, where he managed to look bored already with my brother's return.

"It seems your brother has distinguished himself as quite the hero," said a voice I was not expecting to hear. Showalter! I was stunned to find him leaning against the mantel, eyeing me curiously.

"What are you doing here?" I asked.

"Agnes, *really*," Mother hissed.

"I'm only surprised to see you, Lord Showalter. Please take no offense," I said, curtsying. I wasn't unhappy to see him. In fact, it gave me great pride to show David off to him.

"Of course not. I simply came to call on you and your mother. I'd thought to arrange that visit to the museum we spoke of, but was pleased to find David here to meet instead."

"I'm glad that you were able to meet him," I said politely, then turned back to my brother. "David! Tell me what you've done."

David ducked his head. "Only my duty."

"David," my father said, "hobble your modesty and tell her before I botch the story myself."

My brother smiled and settled back beside Mother on the sofa. I perched on the ottoman at his feet to hear his tale. His ship had caught up with a French corvette south of Spain. They'd received dispatches that this very ship had made a sly approach up the Welsh coast after some local fisherman spotted her in waters she had no real reason to be in and alerted the navy. David's ship was lucky to stumble across and corral her in a shallow inlet. "I led the boarding party," David concluded.

"You never!" I said, my eyes widening at the thought of my brother, sword drawn, jumping to the deck of a French ship.

"Calm yourself," he said with a laugh, "there was no blood spilled. In fact, the crew offered no resistance. There were no marines aboard, only some very light artillery, and the captain himself surrendered, willingly offering that the ship had been sailing reconnaissance missions up and down the coast."

"Thank heaven you caught up to them!" I whispered.

"So we took the captain prisoner, locked up a few of her crew for good measure, supplemented with our own, and I was given command to bring her back as a prize to England."

"Your first command!" I shouted.

"His first command!" Mother echoed.

"His first command," Rupert chorused with mock enthusiasm, adding in a mutter, "And all he had to do was climb onboard and turn the boat around."

"Not quite," David said coolly. "Captain Hoyle wisely ordered us to take the corvette due west into the open sea for several hundred miles before tracking back east for England."

"To avoid any possible encounters with French naval forces that might wish to reclaim her," Father supplied.

"Precisely. And as soon as we set sail, it was a wonder no one pursued us to the ends of the earth. I've never been aboard a trimmer vessel. She fairly flew over the water, hardly any draft at all, and laden with sails that seem to make their own winds rather than wait around for it to start up a blow. . . ."

David looked wistful. He looked enamored. He looked like Caedmon when he talked about the Rosetta Stone. I wondered if I'd ever find anything in my own life that made me look that way.

"David?" My mother's voice nudged my brother back to his story.

"Right. As I told you, the crew when we took her was small,

really less than half strength of what one might expect of a ship of her class. But if, as they said, they were meant to provide reconnaissance, it was logical that they'd run her skeleton. But as we sailed, I began to notice that one of the topsail men didn't know his business at all."

"How odd," I offered.

"For heaven's sake, Agnes, the more you interrupt, the longer it takes him to tell the bloody story again," Rupert groused. I waved him off, and David went on.

"The man couldn't tie a knot to save his own life. And then my lieutenant, he said that when we'd first boarded and he'd secured all the prisoners while we took inventory of the ship, that man's hands had been as smooth as a virgin's throat and that he was no more a sailor than the king himself."

"David, your language," Mother warned. We both ignored her.

"Then what was he doing aboard a corvette running at half-strength?" I asked.

"Hiding, as it turns out. I left the man on his sails, though I detailed another hand from our ranks on the *Hyperion* to quietly double-check his work. And then I instructed my men to pump the other sailors for what information they could. They were a tight-lipped lot—and so few of my men spoke French as to make it even more difficult—but we did learn from one with a fondness for drink that the ship was engaged in transport, and supposedly returning a very important person to France."

"A spy!"

David and Mother looked taken aback; only Father did not flinch. Rupert crowed, "A debutante figures out in half a minute what it took you weeks to learn, *Captain*."

I glared at Rupert, but David only laughed and said gamely, "Yes! How did you—," he started to ask me, but I couldn't divulge the fact that this unique brand of intrigue had been dominating my thoughts for the last few days.

"What happened when you brought him into port?" I cut short his question.

My brother smiled. "He tried to slip away—and the other French crewmen even made a halfhearted effort at helping him, and had we not been watching him secretly, he might have succeeded. But we rounded him up and carried him into the war department, him refusing to speak a word. We thought we were going to have a time figuring out who he was and why he'd have been so important to Napoleon as to risk bringing him back to France now."

"But it turned out that when we handed him over to the army, he was recognized. He'd been serving as a desk officer for nearly four years. He disappeared two weeks after Napoleon returned from Elba, having somehow received word from France to head home."

I shuddered. "To think what Napoleon might have done with what the man knew . . ." I trailed off. "You *are* a hero, David."

"And your father kept us *all* in the dark," Mother said, though she couldn't bear to be unhappy.

"The army summoned me to Tilbury to await the arrival of the ship and its prisoner. I only learned of the affair a few days ago, and thought it best to keep it quiet in the event David was not granted leave to come back with me."

"So tonight we celebrate." Mother beamed. "We dine together, as a family."

She quickly looked to Showalter. "You will join us, of course, won't you, Lord Showalter?"

I sucked in my breath. The entire room was quiet. I knew Mother was being polite. But I also knew that her invitation was another step in signaling to Showalter how accepted his attentions were toward me. Including him in a family dinner— one featuring the rare joy of David's presence—was an unmistakable encouragement of his advances.

Showalter smiled, bowed slightly to Mother, and accepted her invitation. "But please excuse me now, for I've business to attend to before we meet again."

Father rose, clapped a hand on David's shoulder, and escorted Showalter from the room.

After they had gone, my mother gave me a look. "Agnes, you must encourage him a bit more," she chided.

"You encourage him enough for the lot of us, Mother," I teased.

"He really does seem a good sort," David agreed.

"And he's rich as a sultan," Rupert said, rolling to his feet. "I've also got business to attend to," he announced, though I suspected he was only slinking off to take a nap or round up a drink at the club.

"And I've got to consult with Cook—we've a special meal to prepare in honor of David's return," Mother said, leaning over to David and offering him her cheek before she rose and disappeared into the hall.

My brother and I sat quietly for a moment before I managed to ask the question that we'd all been too afraid of uttering.

"When do you go back?"

He sighed. "Tomorrow morning—early. I'm to rejoin the *Hyperion* by way of a supply ship this weekend. The corvette will take some weeks to refit to our naval standards before she's in service, and it's unlikely her command will fall to me. Besides, we've all got this business with Napoleon to get through before anything is decided."

"Where to this time?" I asked, bracing myself.

"Just into the Channel, off the Belgian coast," he said. I cast my eyes to my lap, afraid of showing my disappointment that he was in fact heading straight for the coming storm.

"I see."

He nodded. "The next few days could well spell the future for us all."

My thoughts drifted back to my conversation with Deacon and Caedmon. I thought to tell David the whole story; I knew he'd scold me less than Father and possibly gain as much joy from hearing of my adventure as I had in learning of his.

But the time wasn't right. And with David only home for such a brief visit, I began to doubt that the time was right to tell Father, either. I knew that as soon as Father learned what I'd discovered, he'd be bound to work as quickly as he could. And if David had to go in the morning, a few hours more couldn't hurt. We could have one evening without the distractions and obligations of war to simply enjoy having David home.

I must have mused too long. David leaned forward to catch my eye. "I wish you wouldn't worry," he said. "You should be happy. That's why we're out there. To keep the likes of you safe from harm, so all you need to do is worry about not falling into the prince's lap at your debut."

I groaned. "Don't remind me."

He smiled. "Though I confess it is a fate more fraught with peril than the life of a navy man."

"I just don't suppose I'm terribly excited about all of it. I often feel as though I'm performing my duty, nothing more. Like you joining the navy."

"I suppose a choice between the clergy and the navy really is no choice at all." He laughed. "Duty calls one way or another."

"I just imagined I might be happier about it when the time came."

David considered this. "I don't see my life that way. It's been hard, sure, but I get to sail, see the world, do something that matters, maybe even make a pile of prize money—"

"Pirate," I mumbled, smiling in spite of myself.

"No more pirate than a debutante who marries solely for position or wealth," he said.

"Quite," I said formally, a little stung. "But he hasn't even proposed or spoken to Father. Nothing is settled."

David took my hand. "I shouldn't tease you," he said. "I'm lucky that the things I like best are all part of my life at sea. I only hope you'll at least reach for the same satisfaction in the life you choose."

"But even second sons have more choices to make than daughters." Tears stung my eyes.

"True enough," he said, squeezing my hand. "But—Agnes, look at me." His voice softened as he leaned round to catch my eye. "I think there is a place for each of us where our duties and passions can coexist."

I said nothing as a tear slipped down my cheek.

"Just don't give up on finding both," he said. "Maybe even with Showalter. He seems a good sort."

I nodded. He was a good sort. "I'm just not sure I'm ready is all."

"Where's the fun in being ready? I wasn't *ready* for sea. And I had no idea how much I'd love the life until after I'd been aboard ship awhile. Maybe it will be the same with you and your choice. Maybe you'll grow to love your lot after you've set sail."

I prayed David was right, both for my sake and for Showalter's.

Chapter Thirteen

✤

After feting David with a dinner laden with roast potatoes, fresh vegetables, pastries, and other favorites deprived him at sea, we retired to the garden. In addition to Showalter, two of David's Eton friends living in London joined us. The three of them laughed raucously as they smoked near the lilacs. Mother and Father sat on the patio, content. Rupert nursed a glass of brandy (his fifth at my last count). I hoped he was stewing in the knowledge that he was a worm for having done so little with his life in comparison to his younger brother.

Though I'd have given anything just to sit next to David and take comfort in how near he was to us, it fell to me to entertain Showalter. We strolled the garden path, exchanging a comment with Mother or Father when we came near, sometimes pausing to listen to one of David's friends recount some mischief they stirred up at school.

"May I say again how lovely you look tonight, Agnes?" Showalter asked me.

I smiled as sincerely as I could. "You may," I said, but I was painfully aware that he was simply saying so because he had run out of conversation. Still, it never stopped him from nattering on. He truly did love the sound of his own voice, truly did appear to love an audience, even if it was only an audience of one. His chatter was diverting enough—his observations on the plants in the garden were astute, his musings on the stars we could see through the treetops overhead were entertaining, but they required nothing of me but an appreciative expression and perhaps a well-timed question here or there to keep him going.

I was doing as David asked, giving Showalter as much of the benefit of the doubt as I could. And I found him as agreeable as ever. But something was missing.

It was so very different talking with this man—a man who'd known my family for years—than it was talking to Caedmon, whom I'd known barely a week.

It was not the first unbidden comparison that sprang to mind wherein Lord Showalter fell short of his unknown rival.

"I do hope you'll allow me the pleasure of the first dance at the ball next Saturday?"

I looked down. "It's over a week away," I said. "I hardly think my card will be full. . . ."

He smiled. "Just so. You promise you'll save me at least one?"

I nodded, again a little pleased about how it felt to be pursued. Even if I sat out half the dances that night, someone had

already asked me for the first. But Showalter was not done with
his compliments.

"First balls, then the world!" he said grandly. "You'll steal
the heart of every man on the Continent when you finally make
the tour one day."

"I'd rather they simply understand me. I do so hope that my
Greek proves adequate. I've had no practice speaking," I told
him. While I was confident in my reading and writing abilities,
having taught myself after exhausting my language tutors in
German, Italian, French, and Spanish and that kindly old rabbi
Father unearthed to help me with Hebrew, there had been no
suitable tutors for Greek or Hindi, and my progress suffered
for it.

"I'll never understand the point of learning all those languages," Lord Showalter said. "You can easily pick up a trans-
lator anywhere we might go."

My toe caught on a corner of one of the flagstones. But the
word I'd just heard him utter was even more jarring. *We.* It was
the closest he'd come to declaring himself. My heart made an
odd flutter, but for all the wrong reasons—I felt as though the
garden was closing in on me, and something like panic rose in
my chest.

What was I doing? It had been fun to play the debutante,
to flirt a bit, to think that I had managed (with Mother's help,
of course) to win the affections of someone as perfect as
Showalter. But now that it appeared I'd succeeded, now that he

was signaling me so openly, it made me acutely aware of what I really was: a girl in a lady's dress, a girl who'd been pretending *too well*, a girl who would now suffer for it, and possibly cause a perfectly good man to suffer in the bargain.

I silently prayed that Mother hadn't overheard his slip.

Showalter offered me a steadying hand as he went on, "I hear that even in Egypt, most of the natives speak enough English or French to translate for outsiders."

"Translators muddy things," I said, unable to voice what I really meant. I resented that the life I lived—that the world women were allowed to live in—was often little more than a translated, simplified version of the world belonging to my brothers, my father, to Showalter.

"All this assumes anyone will even be able to make the tour as before," I added.

He sighed. "I'm sure your husband, whoever the lucky man might be"—he paused and smiled sideways at me—"will be unable to deny you such a trip, whether Napoleon is firing cannon shot over Vienna or not."

I flushed, then sought refuge in safer topics than possible marriages. "The war does seem interminable, does it not?"

"Yes, well, I have a feeling all that unpleasant business of war will sort itself out very soon somehow."

I almost laughed aloud. If only he knew just how unpleasant things threatened to become. Resurrected armies of the dead . . . domination by Napoleon.

"Then perhaps we can rest easier knowing that David won't be hurling himself aboard enemy ships."

He laughed. "And the trade routes will open back up properly. It will be better for all of us—on both sides of the Channel," he said. "And some even suggest that a peace—however it is achieved—would result in shared scholarship on Egypt and the artifacts."

"For now, I suppose we'll have to settle for our unwrappings and visits to the museum," I said, feeling compelled to respond in some way.

"And we'll make that trip very soon," he supplied. "Your mother and I settled on Thursday morning. You'll luncheon with me at my home afterward."

A whole morning? With just my mother and Lord Showalter? Then lunch? We'd be hours, hours I should have been using to sneak away and see to the search for the standard. Hours wherein I'd feel the same mixture of nerves and regret that I felt now. "How nice," I managed to say.

"There are a number of new acquisitions at the museum," he said genially. "When was the last time you visited?"

I hesitated before letting the lie slip past my lips. "Years ago. Even then I found myself torn—"

"Torn?"

I nodded. "As marvelous as the museum is, part of me can only wonder if the items belong in the places they originated, to the people whose ancestors created them."

"Agnes Wilkins!" he teased. "You harbor dangerous sentiments!"

I looked at him, alarmed. But he grinned, then leaned closer to whisper. "If it comes to light that the daughter of a prominent member of the House of Lords harbors such anti-imperialist views . . ."

"You are mocking me," I said, smirking. So he had a sense of humor after all. I realized that I couldn't stop myself from checking off his attributes, that I couldn't keep from cataloging what I liked and didn't like about the man, that despite my reservations, I couldn't think of him as anything other than a suitor.

He shrugged. "Think what you like, Miss Wilkins. But politics aside, I rather believe having the place brought to you rather than enduring the dust is infinitely better. Did you know that one of my associates just made a journey to a dig site outside Memphis and was forced to ride a camel? Really, I can't imagine perching atop one of those spitting beasts."

"Riding a camel? I think it sounds marvelous," I said, adding with another smirk, "provided I was clear of the spitting end."

"I'd like to see some of those curators at the museum on a camel."

"Have they been quite cross with you?" I asked as casually as I could manage, avoiding his eye, looking toward the tree line, where the first of the evening's fireflies had begun to flicker.

"Hmm?"

"About the mummy we unwrapped by mistake?"

"Oh, that! Well, they worked themselves up, as if I'd inten-tionally taken the wrong specimen. But I paid for them both, so they can't be too indignant. Unless they start charging admis-sion in that place, they need men like me to keep them going."

I watched one light blink on and off, tracing its slow path across the shadow of an elm. It felt dangerous, this questioning, even if there was no way Showalter could know the real reason for my curiosity. I took a steadying breath and asked my next question.

"And were they quite satisfied that all the items from the wrappings had been restored?"

I felt the arm he'd extended to me at the outset of our stroll stiffen ever so slightly. "I believe so," he said. "Why do you ask?"

The firefly I'd been following with my eye seemed to hover in place, flashing more rapidly now, not moving across the trees, as if it were stuck fast in a spiderweb. I hesitated, wishing I had Deacon or even my father to advise me on how to proceed. I chose my words carefully.

"I only ask because I wonder if your guests were the only ones with access to the body."

"What are you suggesting?" he asked, leaning around to try and catch my eye. I looked quickly to his face and then back to the firefly stuck in the web.

"Simply that even in the finest households, servants are tempted by the attractions of wealth."

He stopped to stare at me. "You really are a *curious* girl," he said.

I realized that I might have pushed too far. That the limb I'd decided to venture out on was growing less sturdy the farther I climbed. Over my shoulder, I heard Rupert snort at something David said and found my excuse. Widening my eyes to look as innocent as possible, I turned my face to Showalter. "At breakfast this morning, Rupert and I were talking. And he's always accusing our servants of misconduct. I suppose his suspicion is catching. Particularly with things as they've been lately."

"Doesn't hurt to be careful, I suppose." His tone was once again cheerful.

"Thank you, sir. But I must confess something. Your valet, Tanner—"

"Don't let that buggy eye put you off. He's as loyal as they come."

"It's just that . . . ," I began, faltering in order to appear distraught at conveying such bad tidings, "I've been wanting to tell you . . . I think I saw him follow that murdered man from the party."

Showalter's expression was unreadable, distorted by the shadows cast from the lamps and the rising moon. Past his shoulder I could see that same poor firefly winking in the distance.

Finally he laughed. A sure, satisfied laugh that rang around the garden like music. "You're a jewel, Agnes Wilkins," he said, taking a breath and sighing, "such an imagination . . ."

I started to protest, to assure him that it was not my imagination. But a flurry at the patio caught my eye.

Clarisse burst onto the terrace and hastened to my mother's side, panting and near tears. I watched her whisper furiously to my parents. My father stood, spilling half his drink in his haste. Mother sat frozen in her chair.

"Assemble the servants in the hall," Father ordered.

The rest of us sped to him from our various positions within the garden.

"What's happened, Father?" David asked, grasping his arm.

"Lord Showalter, would you be so kind as to escort Mrs. Wilkins and my daughter to the drawing room? You boys come with me," he said to my brothers and our other guests.

Showalter helped my mother to her feet and guided her into the house and toward the sofa in the drawing room. I lingered behind, peeling away when we reached the hall.

"Father ordered you to the drawing room," Rupert hissed as I followed the men thundering up the carpeted stairs. I ignored him and trailed the party to my brother's open door.

"What the devil?" Rupert cried out as he shot past my father and into his room. I stopped short of the doorway. It looked as if David's ship had opened up its cannons and fired in. Rupert's clothes were pulled from the wardrobe; desk drawers had been emptied, their contents spilled into drifts of paper. The linens had been stripped from the bed, the washbasin, overturned, left water puddling on the rug.

"Capital," Rupert cried, kicking at the chamber pot.

"Is this what happened to the other party guests?" David asked quietly as he crossed the room to the open window. Despite Mother's insistence that we confine our conversation to lighter matters for the hours we had David with us, Rupert must have at some point told him of the events in our neighborhood of late.

My father nodded. "Clarisse discovered the mess and the man who made it when she came in to light the lamps."

"She saw him?" I exclaimed.

My father started at hearing my voice. "Agnes, I asked you to wait in the drawing room."

"Clarisse saw him?" I demanded again.

"Only for a moment. She was carrying a candle to light the wicks. He leaped from the window when she entered," he said.

"He could have used the trellis here to climb in," David said, crossing to the window.

I surveyed the disorder, and the thought struck me that if Rupert's room had been burglarized, then—

I turned abruptly and fled up the hall to my own chamber. Clarisse always lit the lamps on Rupert's side of the hall first. My door was shut fast, no light creeping from beneath it. I scooped up a lantern from the table in the hall and pushed open my door.

Inside, dresses and hats and hair ribbons littered the floor like scattered leaves. My books, too, had been disturbed, the spines uneven as they lined the shelves.

I took a few cautious steps in, picking my way through the debris. A glint from the floor beside my dressing table caught my eye, and then broke my heart.

My jade butterfly lay shattered. I'd tried to wear it tonight, but Mother had forbidden it, had said the green was garish next to my dress, had complained that I wore it too often as it was.

It was the only thing in the room that I could see that had been damaged in some way. It made me wonder if whoever had done this might have somehow known how precious the item was to me. Had the burglar sought and found the most readily available means to injure me?

A fury I'd never known threatened to choke me, but out of the cloud of anger emerged another thought.

My heart hammered, and I grasped the door frame to steady myself. The burglar, perhaps the very one who'd been meant to intercept the message, had been *here* moments ago. Now he'd made complete his inventory of the people at the mummy—

But he still hadn't found the jackal's head.

Caedmon had it and the message safe. My instincts had proven out!

And if the burglar was the agent of some evil curse, had it passed us by as well? I hoped so.

I hurried back up the hall to rejoin Father and the others to tell them that my room had also been ransacked. I now realized there would likely be no better moment to tell Father what I knew, what I'd done.

I expected he'd be proud of me, after all. And there was little lovelier than Father's praise.

The men still gathered at the window.

"Father, I—," I began.

"Not now, Agnes," he said.

"I really must tell you something—"

"Agnes, you have already disobeyed me by following us upstairs. Do not incense me further by ignoring—"

"But Father—"

"Not now, Agnes!" he said without turning.

Well.

I stared at the back of Father's head as he conferenced with the men by the window. If he did not wish to hear from me, I could oblige him. I fumed, thinking of all the trouble I'd gone to, all the very useful things I'd already learned, but even Father was ready to dismiss me out of hand. So, if he wanted my silence, he could jolly well have it.

On all points.

I'd had more than I could stomach of people assuming I was incapable of handling life's challenges because of my sex. Even Father, the most open-minded man I knew, thought I belonged downstairs, protected from the unpleasantness in my own home.

Perhaps it was time to demonstrate how capable I was.

Perhaps I would ignore Deacon's order to tell Father.

Perhaps Caedmon and I would continue our own search. Perhaps the best time for Father to hear of it would be when all was settled, when Caedmon and I had secured the standard. After all, the burglar had come and gone empty-handed; the greatest of any danger had passed.

It would serve them all right.

So resolved, I stooped to collect up a handful of Rupert's books that had been knocked to the floor. I placed the volumes back on the shelf, but hesitated as I discovered among them a small notebook bound in soft leather. It bore no title on cover or spine, and when I flipped it open I found the pages covered with Rupert's handwriting, arrayed in careful columns and stanzas. Poems, I realized as I glanced at the title of the one I'd landed on. "To Emmaline." Emmaline? The only Emmaline I knew was Julia's chaperone, Mrs. Perkins.

Rupert was on me in a moment. "What are you doing?" he yelped, snatching the book from my hand.

"Nothing," I managed, "I was merely—"

"Isn't it enough my room has been vandalized by a stranger? Must I endure your invasion of my privacy as well?" he fumed, placing the book in the drawer of his writing desk and turning to find us all staring at him.

Father broke the silence at last. "Rupert is right," he said. "We should avoid disturbing the room further until it has been thoroughly examined." He motioned us all toward the door, dispatching David's friends to fetch a constable.

"Let's speak no more of this tonight," he said, clapping a hand on David's shoulder. "We've precious few hours left with our young captain. We'll go down to the drawing room and collect Mother and Lord Showalter and salvage what we can of this evening."

"You'll want to have a look at my room before that, I think," I said coolly.

Father turned to me. "Your room?"

"Rupert's wasn't the only one disturbed," I said, leading them up the hall.

Father hurried past me.

"I tried to tell you," I said as I pointed toward my open door. Father and the others looked in.

After a long moment, Father reached for me. "Agnes, come here," he ordered. I let him fold me into his arms.

"Forgive me for being so curt with you before," he said. "I didn't realize—"

"It's all right, Father," I said evenly.

"You are an unusual girl, Agnes," he said, holding me at arm's length. "Sometimes even I manage to forget that."

"Thank you, Father," I said, sure he'd never forget when Caedmon and I succeeded.

Chapter Fourteen

Both Father and David were gone the next morning when I came down to breakfast. Father had ridden back to Tilbury to escort David to his ship, observe questioning of the prisoner, and meet with various commanders encamped there before they shipped across the Channel to face Napoleon's forces. Now that he was gone, I wondered if I'd done right in waiting to tell him.

Mother put down her teacup. "Don't look so grim, Agnes," she said. "Father is due back Friday afternoon—"

"It's not that," I said quickly, realizing as I said it that I couldn't tell her exactly what it was that had me so distracted, so I added even more quickly, "I miss David."

She lowered her eyes, nodded once, and lifted her napkin to her lips. "We all do," she said. "But we must soldier on, mustn't we?"

She was, as was often the case, more right than she realized. Caedmon would need my help now more than ever.

I spent the morning concocting a careful lie about visiting friends who were up from the country. Later that morning, I presented Mother with my story, convincing her that a fellow debutante, Fiona Delacroix, had hired a small skiff, with the intent of taking some of us cruising in the harbor. There would be no room for Aunt Rachel, who was prone to seasickness anyway. I assured Mother that Fiona's chaperone would be in attendance, that I would keep my hat on the entire morning, and that I would be home in time to make our appointed visit to Julia's at three.

Once outside, I did not take one of our drivers, instead sneaking off to hire a cab. I had him ferry me on a circuitous, lengthy journey covering half of London before I consented to tell him my real destination.

At the museum, I found Caedmon in one of the small side rooms flanking the main display gallery, and greeted him with a smile that was hardly proper or ladylike. I could not help it. I was so pleased to see him.

"I have the most interesting news," I gushed as I tugged off my gloves. He was positioning an information card in front of a display of embalming tools. He grunted something and tossed me a dismissive look.

I ignored his sullen expression as I related the adventures of last night, trying not to boast of my unforeseen genius at having deposited the jackal's head with him.

"So for a time at least we are in the clear," I finished up.

"Whoever is looking for the object must think by now that I do not have it and will be forced to look elsewhere."

Caedmon nodded. "Grand," he managed, picking up a sharp, hooked object and polishing it with a square of cotton.

"But this is wonderful! The burglar will be searching between here and Egypt for the message. An impossible task!"

"D'you know what this is?" Caedmon asked quietly.

I stopped, hearing and noticing for the first time how utterly exhausted he looked. "No."

"This is the device the Egyptians used in the earliest stages of mummification, to draw the brains from the skull. They had no regard for the brain, didn't even trouble with preserving it with the other organs for the afterlife."

"Caedmon?"

He pointed toward the hooked end. "This got shimmied up the nose, and then they tugged the brain out bit by bit."

My smile faded. "Revolting," I murmured.

"I reckon I know how it feels now," he said. "I've spent every moment since we parted searching the museum's stores for someplace the standard might be hiding. And when I wasn't doing that, I was hunched over the Stone, wondering if there aren't answers still for us there."

I hung my head. "My brother—"

"All the while I expected word to arrive from you or Deacon."

"Caedmon, I'm sorry."

"So if it's an impossible task that puts the color in your

cheeks, you've come to the right place." He turned and walked slowly away.

My heart sank. I spoke in a torrent, flinging out my tale of David's visit, the break-in, my decision not to tell Father, and now his renewed absence, before Caedmon could argue or object.

"Away?" Caedmon repeated when I finally finished.

"At Tilbury," I said quietly. "We expect him home Friday evening."

"Then he knows nothing of the standard?"

I shook my head. Caedmon swore. "Deacon will be furious! I'm going to him straight after work. He needs to know what you've done."

"Fine," I returned. "If he wants us to send for Father, I'll do it."

"He will!" His eyes burned brightly, making the deep hollows beneath seem all the darker.

"I don't understand!" I cried. "I thought you'd be pleased to have more time to work. You were the one who wanted to capitalize on this opportunity!"

"That was before we knew how important this is!" he shot back. "You're acting like it's all some ruddy game!"

"I'm not!" But was I? No. I knew how grave things were. The affair had occupied my every thought for the last two days, and Caedmon with it.

I wished I could tell him how many times I'd thought of him since we'd last met. How he'd never left my mind as I rode home yesterday, as I spoke with David and saw so much of the passion and dignity that I admired in my brother reflected in him. If only he could know how often I'd remembered him last night as I walked with Showalter.

But putting it into words was the trick. How could I say all this without making it sound as if I had feelings for him?

Which I didn't.

Or more to the point, which I shouldn't.

"I'm sorry," I said finally, reasoning a general apology was the only safe course.

He said nothing. I watched as the anger seemed to melt, giving way to only exhaustion.

"And I'm here now. Willingly . . . *dutifully*," I said.

His shoulders relaxed a bit more. "What can I do?" I asked.

He sighed and started walking again, gesturing for me to follow. "I don't know," he said. "Until I started looking, I hadn't truly reckoned how much we actually had."

"How many items in the collection?"

He threw up his hands. "The catalogs are such a kettle of fish that it's like trying to number the drunks along the Thames. They don't lend themselves to lining up and being counted."

We entered the great room with its sarcophagi.

"But if the object is meant to contain the standard some-how," I ventured, "surely that rules out the smaller pieces."

He nodded. "I suppose. But we don't know its size, or how it could fit inside something else."

I thought for a moment. "Couldn't we focus on the displayed items only? Wouldn't it be reasonable to assume that the spies are familiar only with the limited items in these rooms?"

He shook his head. "Doesn't hold up. Especially if one of the conspirators is associated with the museum itself somehow." He glanced toward the archway, then added, "Someone like Banehart."

"I met him at a lecture once. Quite ghastly."

Caedmon suppressed a smile. "Try working for him. He's made no bones about his longings for peace with France and partnership to share the collections. Mind you, his only motivation is scientific. He's got it in his head that if our collections are combined and our experts collaborate, we'll work faster on translating the glyphs and finding new sites to excavate."

I nodded, remembering that Showalter had said something like that last night. "You believe he'd sooner see England fly the flag of France than lose out on some trivia about a dead civilization?"

"Barmy, I know," Caedmon said. "But if we're to believe even a word about Wepwawet's standard, Egyptology can hardly be considered trivial."

"I only meant—"

"I know what you meant," he said. "I'm sorry. I'm tired, that's all. And I've been shirking my other work since all this started."

I felt horrid again for having abandoned him. "My brother

would commend such sacrifice as honorable in a time of war," I told him with a smile.

He almost laughed, then crossed his arms over his chest. "Pity we're the only ones who know I'm sacrificing. My employers will only think I'm trigging it," he said.

"When this is over and you're discovered for the hero that you are, you can quit the lot of them and have your pick of positions at any Egyptological collection in all of England," I tried to assure him.

He laughed. "The British Museum is the only one in the world with a collection like this."

"Then you'll start your own. You'll make expeditions to Egypt, unlock the Rosetta Stone's secrets; I'm sure Lord Showalter would happily throw piles of money your way."

His smile faded. There was an awkward silence as we crossed the room and approached a door in the back bearing the words STAFF ONLY. I gave it a glance and followed him within.

"Where are we going?" I asked as we left behind the gleaming cases for a narrow hallway, crammed floor to ceiling with long drawers, a few spilling dusty corners of paper.

"Workroom," he said. "You really shouldn't be back here, but the bigwigs are in conference. Have to be quick, though. The bosses are meant to return by noon."

I glanced at the clock. Twenty to twelve.

Caedmon led me through the passage, pointing toward a door indicating the offices. The hall spilled out into a great jumbled storage room of sorts. Urns of varying shapes and sizes grew like a dwarf forest across the floor. Canopic jars containing the pickled remains of the vital organs of Lord knew how many princes and kings, nobles and artisans lined bays of shallow shelves. Gold headpieces and masks littered a long table in the center of the room. A collection of long wooden staffs, many crooked at one end, stood like cut flowers in an old umbrella stand.

It was dim and quiet, the air cool and slightly damp, somehow stale and musty. And given the exotica of all the items that surrounded us, it was even easier to imagine what the interiors of one of the pyramids in Egypt might feel like than it was in the gallery.

A disembodied arm at least as tall as me and thicker at the wrist than I was at the waist sat like a fallen tree trunk beside the table. I reached down to stroke the gleaming granite shot through with pink glints.

"That's Ramses II. His arm, anyway."

I snatched my hand away, awed. "Ramses from the scriptures Ramses?"

Caedmon nodded and smiled. "Very good. The rest of him is fragmented outside his temple. This arm was the smallest of the pieces . . . only thing they could manage onto a boat. Weighs nearly a ton."

"Fascinating," I said, imagining how grand the complete statue might have been. And yet . . . I couldn't help but think it seemed a pity to dismantle something so magnificent.

"Moving the big'uns has always been the puzzle," Caedmon told me, walking toward a row of sarcophagi neatly lined up like runners about to begin a footrace.

I joined Caedmon, reaching out to stroke the painted and gilt interior of one elaborate coffin leaning against the shelf. Its surface warm and rough to the touch, unlike the smooth chill of the stone. I hadn't expected that.

"That one's wooden. Cedar, actually," Caedmon explained. "Queer for its time. Over three thousand years old. Lumber of any quality greater than palm had to be imported from Lebanon, so masonry and marble work were the order of the day. But the craftsmanship here is tip-top."

I nodded. "It's very beautiful."

"Should be," he said. "According to the markings, it once bore the body of one of the pharaoh's favorite concubines. Upon his death, she consented to have herself killed and mummified to make the journey to the afterlife at his side."

"How awful," I said. "I can't imagine having to make such a decision."

Caedmon shrugged. "If she'd refused, they'd probably have had her killed anyway. This way at least she was guaranteed an afterlife. Women didn't have a lot to say about anything."

"Still don't." I knew women whose husbands died and left them with daughters and no sons. Their homes and property were taken and entailed away to some nephew, the poor women given meager allowances and forced to shove off. As if even the law decided you might as well be dead if your husband went first.

"But look at this. The wood wrights were apparently ordered to protect her body from grave robbers, so they did something I'd not seen before," Caedmon said as he closed the lid, the casket wobbling slightly. It gave a soft click as he pushed it home, the seam between the door and the box almost completely disappearing. On the surface, I could plainly see the outline of a woman, dark kohl eyes staring demurely to the left.

"Why isn't she looking straight on like the others?" I asked.

"They would have placed her next to her king so she could gaze at him for all eternity."

I found the notion curiously nauseating and romantic at the same time.

"But see here," he said, taking my hand and placing it on the edge of the door. A warm sensation spread out over my arm.

He didn't seem to notice. "Go on, open it," he urged.

I tried to wedge my fingertips into the spot where I thought the edge of the door should be. I pulled. It didn't budge. Then I applied both hands and pulled even harder.

"It's stuck."

He grinned, enjoying this game. "They were about to take a pry bar to it when I convinced them to give me a go. I reckoned the fact that it was made of wood had to mean something. And the only other bits of wood we see through here are curio boxes."

"You mean like a puzzle box?"

"Spot on. We don't have many examples, owing to the fact that the wood rots a sight quicker than stone. But knowing the Egyptians were keen on them made me wonder if this"—he ran a hand along the box's edge—"might be built along the same lines."

"And you were correct?"

He lifted a shoulder modestly. "After a bit of trial and error, I managed to lick it."

He crouched down, slid the feet over, pushed the entire piece down half an inch, and then stood.

"Mind you, this was done strictly in the name of science," he said, blushing, as he reached out and pushed the left breast sideways. It slid open to reveal a small recessed panel with a wooden tab. Caedmon pushed this tab, producing the same click I'd heard earlier when the lid shut tight. He then lifted it open, revealing the inside once again.

"Bravo!" I applauded quietly.

He laughed and stepped back, admiring the casket.

"Can it be opened from the inside?" I asked.

He shook his head. "They didn't figure she'd be letting herself out."

"Do you have the king's sarcophagus?"

"Here," he said. At the end of the row an enormous stone box lay on the floor. Its lid sat a few feet away, leaning against the wall.

"Are you sure he didn't take another of his concubines in there with him?" I asked, marveling at the size.

Caedmon laughed. "He was gone before we got the sarco-phagus. But his sweetheart is on the display floor now."

"I wonder if she was as beautiful as the markings indicated," I mused, looking back at the puzzle box.

"She wasn't to my tastes," he said dryly.

Could the way he avoided my eyes as he said this indicate what I thought it might? Was he actually paying me a compliment?

He stepped away quickly and looked around the room. "I've hunted back here and on the floor, but nothing's turned up. A thorough search would take months, maybe even longer since I have to sneak about to do it."

"I'll help," I offered again.

He shook his head. "I only have the run of this place when the senior staff has meetings."

"But they're not here at night, are they?"

He shrugged. "Not as late as I am, usually. After hours is the only time I can devote myself to that," he said, pointing toward a display table on which lay what looked like a giant rock, broken jagged at the edges, but polished to gleaming on a sur-face etched with tiny characters.

"The Rosetta Stone!" I cried, rushing forward. In size, the Stone looked like it could have been a grave marker from Westminster Abbey. Nearly a foot thick, and probably at least up to my shoulder if it were standing on its end. The Stone was so dark that it seemed to pull the light toward itself, like water slipping toward a drain.

"A damned puzzle," he said, though with greater affection than the oath indicated.

It wasn't beautiful, yet it was attractive—magnetic, even. I couldn't resist touching it. "Imagine what it must have been like when it was actually in use," I mused. "Don't you wish you could go there? See things like this where they were made? See the people? Hear the language? The music? Eat the dates and figs and . . ."

I stopped and looked up to find him staring at me, smiling. "Pardon," I said. "I find myself carried away."

"No!" he said quickly. "So do I. Sometimes when I'm working on the beast I think about what she might have looked like whole and proud, and I think that maybe some man like me might have leaned up against her side to take a rest. And I can almost feel the heat from the sun rising off the surface, like the kissing crust when a loaf is drawn from an oven. . . ."

I gaped at him, realized that there was someone as wistful as I was, someone as desperate to see someplace else.

"Someday I'll go," he said, without taking his eyes from the Stone.

I spoke without thinking. "I believe you will."

He smiled, a bit sadly, as if he thought he had less chance of realizing this hope than I did. Perhaps he did. I cleared my throat and leaned over the Stone.

"Here's the demotic, and these must be the hieroglyphs," I said, letting my fingers float above the upper portion bearing the pictographs. I peered closer at the middle section and squinted in the low light. "I'd forgotten it had Greek inscribed on it!" I said, delighted.

Caedmon smiled. "Most people are surprised to find it there."

I began to read the text aloud. "'In the fourteenth year of Ptolemy . . .'"

"You can read Greek?"

"Read, yes. Speak, I'm not so sure."

Now Caedmon was impressed.

"But I presume I'm not the only one who can read the Greek. And if the demotic and the Greek say the same thing, doesn't it stand to reason that the glyphs are a direct translation?" I asked.

"Picture writing is far more nuanced than written script. More than half the population couldn't read. Hieroglyphs were like pub signs or signal flags, almost. And adding them up together is the difficult part. On top of that, there appear to be slight but significant variations between the Greek and demotic texts," he explained.

"Didn't you say that the Ptolemy referenced on the Stone is the very one who last bore the standard before it disappeared?"

He nodded.

"Then the Stone might contain some clue to finding it?"

He shrugged. "That's what I've been trying to work out, but . . ."

"Is Wepwawet mentioned in the demotic or Greek texts?"

He shook his head. "I don't think I would have missed that."

"But couldn't this be him here?" I asked, pointing to the top edge of the Stone, where the piece had broken away in a jagged hunk. Below the edge, a curved line, leading into the bottom of what appeared to be an open mouth, was plainly visible. Caedmon leaned closer, inspecting the incomplete hieroglyph.

"No . . . ," he began, fumbling in his pocket for the jackal's head. I snatched it from his grip and held it to the bottom outline. The contours matched exactly. It was my jackal's head in miniature. I gave a short, explosive giggle and turned to see Caedmon's cheeks burning.

"Of all the chuckleheaded things," he said sheepishly. "I only focused on the complete characters."

"Sometimes a puzzle requires a pair of fresh eyes," I consoled him.

"And my eyes are anything but that at this point," he said, still embarrassed.

I wanted to take his hand. I wanted to reassure him that anyone could have made the same mistake. I wanted to promise him that we would prevail. Instead I made a promise that I could keep.

"I'm coming tonight to help you."

I was pleased more than I could express that he did not argue.

He did say we needed to leave now—the supervisors would be back in moments—and led me from the chambers and back toward the hall. As we rounded the corner, a living, breathing person far more frightening than any of the mummies blocked our path.

"What is this?" spat the figure, clad in a severe black suit, a polished leather briefcase tucked under his arm.

Caedmon's face went ashen. "Mr. Banehart, I—"

The man looked even ghastlier than I recalled from having met him last spring at a lecture I attended with Father.

"You *know* these areas are restricted!" Banehart seethed, edging closer, his pale skin aglow in the dusky light. "And to bring a *woman* back here," he added angrily, looking to my face for the first time. A hint of recognition seemed to spark in his eyes. I fanned it into flame.

"Mr. Banehart, please don't be angry with"—I turned to Caedmon and looked at him as if I didn't know him—"with Mr. . . . Mr. . . . ?"

"Stowe," Caedmon squeaked finally.

"Our dear friend Lord Showalter often encourages me to see the collection, and since his party I confess I've been even more curious. I wandered back here by mistake, and Mr. Stowe was good enough to help me find my way back to the exhibits."

"Forgive me, miss, but I have a difficult time believing that someone like yourself—that is, someone who can *read*—could have failed to notice the posting on the only door leading into this facility," he said with carefully controlled menace.

"Very true, sir. But I found the door ajar, and I confess was so taken with the mystery and beauty of the artifacts that a long hallway and tumbled storeroom seemed to fit right in with the stories I was concocting in my head."

"Of all the nonsense—," he began.

"I'm sure that were I with Lord Showalter I'd be granted access to these rooms?" I asked after he continued staring at me.

Banehart forced a polite smile. "Of course. Please give him my regards, Miss Wilkins. You are both welcome to return *together*."

"I am very grateful, sir," I said as evenly as I could.

Banehart glared at Caedmon. "Escort her out, and then report to my office."

As he stalked away, I breathed, letting the adrenaline ebb as Caedmon took my elbow and pushed me down the hall.

"Stowe!" Mr. Banehart snapped. I froze.

"Yes, sir?" Caedmon said quietly.

"This came for you by messenger. I don't know how I let the brat persuade me to ferry it to you, but here it is." He held out a scrap of paper, forcing Caedmon to walk back to him to get it. Once he had, we continued toward the main door and out of earshot.

Banehart was as awful as I remembered, and I found myself thinking how lovely it might be if he did indeed turn out to be the culprit. How convenient it would be to have Banehart proven a traitor and Caedmon revealed as a hero simultaneously.

It might even elevate Caedmon far enough to make him admissible to society.

I was theorizing just how respected he might have to be in order to merit no objection from Mother and Father when Caedmon stopped abruptly beside me.

He held the note out. "It's from the public hospital."

My heartbeat quickened.

"Deacon's there. He's . . . been attacked . . . and is asking for me."

"Oh, no!"

"I have to go," Caedmon said, hurtling toward the door.

"No!" I said. "Banehart won't stand for it. You're already going to have to answer for my being in the restricted area!"

"But—"

"No. We'll go tonight . . . together."

"But he has no one else," Caedmon argued.

"And he of all people knows how important it is that we continue the search for the standard. And if you lose your position here—which is sure to happen if you disappear now—we'll have no access."

He started to protest.

"You *know* what he would say," I said.

Caedmon nodded weakly.

"I'll meet you at ten," I said firmly, "at his rooms near the Tower."

Chapter Fifteen

❧

"Honestly, Agnes, you eat like your brother," Mother complained.

"If we weren't in such an infernal hurry," I said around a mouthful of bread, "I could slow down and be a bit more lady-like. I think Julia and her mother will understand if we're late."

"A lady is never late," Mother replied.

"A lady doesn't bolt down food, either, but that's what you're forcing me to do!"

"Whatever you are in private matters less than what you are in public, though to have mastery over both arenas is preferable. But *you* cut this fine, so you've no one to blame but yourself."

I nodded, swallowed, wiped my mouth, and followed her out the door.

"You're so completely distracted, Agnes," Mother said as we rounded the gate at the front walk.

"It's a busy time," I said simply.

"Don't tell me about it," she said. "I had my season as well.

And I know how busy it is. And believe you me, shepherding you through your first season is almost as trying as my own debut."

"I'm sorry, Mother."

"But it isn't that only"—she paused to tug the cap sleeve of my dress into place—"you seem so disconnected. Even when David was here, your mind always seemed elsewhere."

It was. It was in the museum with Caedmon.

"I can imagine how Showalter's attentions have your head spinning," she said, now pulling at my other shoulder's sleeve. "Which reminds me: I sent him a note inviting him to take Father's place with us at the opera this evening. He wrote saying he'd be delighted to escort us."

Oh, not the opera now. I'd have to figure a way out of *that* in order to meet Caedmon this evening. "But we're already engaged to spend the morning with him tomorrow—"

"The man knows how to seize an opportunity, Agnes. Something I hope you'll take a lesson in," she said, looking sideways at me. "He's indicated that he's very eager to speak with your father upon his return."

I stopped walking altogether. "What do you mean?"

She quit fussing with my sleeves. "Well, he can't very well ask you for your hand until securing your father's permission. I suspect if your father had not been called away so unexpectedly, and had David not come home, maybe we'd already be planning an announcement," she said, almost cooing with triumph.

Planning an announcement? To marry? I found I suddenly had to remind myself to breathe.

I didn't want to accept a proposal, much less marry. Not yet at least. But it was more than that.

A snippet of *Sense and Sensibility* winged its way into my mind. *"I want no proof of their affection, but of their engagement I do."* The words slipped out in Spanish before I realized what I was doing. *"Quiero ninguna prueba de su afecto, sino de su compromiso lo hago,"* I whispered.

My mother took my chin in her hand and gently turned my face to meet her eyes. "Are you sure you're all right, Agnes? You look a trifle peaked."

"Just a little tired," I said, wishing my anxiety would manifest itself in a way less obvious than nervous eruptions of A Lady passages. But I had plenty to be anxious about. I was flattered by Showalter's attentions, even if it was a little surprising how easy making a match had turned out to be. But perhaps that was part of the problem. And what of that sinking feeling that I felt when I saw him, or was about to see him? I thought of how excited I'd been to meet Caedmon at the museum . . . how excited I was to meet him again tonight.

It was comfortable with Showalter. Easy knowing how much he professed to like me. He was an excellent match. But he did not excite me. He did not vex me. He did not draw my thoughts back to him when I was away from him, despite the magnetism others claimed he possessed.

He was not Caedmon. The realization struck me with such force that the line popped out again, this time in Dutch. *"Ik wil geen bewijs van hun genegenheid, maar ook van hun betrokkenheid ik doe."*

"You *are* agitated," Mother said, new concern lacing her voice. "That translating habit always worsens when you're working yourself up about something."

I swallowed hard. "I suppose it is all a bit overwhelming."

Her eyes softened. "I think a nap is in order after we return home. I'm sure Mrs. Overton will understand that we must cut short our visit."

She pulled me by the hand through the Overtons' gate and up the front step as the bread and butter I'd gulped down threatened to make a reappearance on the Park's most fashionable street.

"I know you'll feel better after all is settled with Showalter," she said, pulling the rope for the bell, the sound muted by the leaded glass.

"Do you think he loves me?" I asked Mother abruptly, surprised as she was that I'd posed such a question.

Mother hesitated. "Agnes—"

"Could he?" I asked again.

She took my hand. "Love grows, dear. And I've no doubt he'll find even more to love in you than any man could hope to."

She wasn't any surer than I was. But it didn't bother her.

And for the first time I began to feel a bit annoyed that she'd never once asked what *I* thought, what *I* felt.

"But I've scarcely even met any other suitable men . . . the season is just starting. What if there's someone . . . someone more—"

"Don't be absurd, Agnes! Lord Showalter is by far the most desirable match—all of London knows it. What more could you want? And what more could *he* want? You are witty, talented, and beautiful. Any man would clamor to make an early engagement with you."

It was hard to think on what Mother was telling me. That love was secondary—both in order and importance when making the choice that I would live with for the rest of my life. The line crept up again, this time in Greek. *"Θέλω δεν απαιτείται καμία απόδειξι της αγάπη τους, αλλά και της δέσμευσής τους να κάνω."*

Mother closed her eyes and took a deep breath, exhaling slowly through her nose before opening her eyes and looking at me kindly. "Enough of that, my love. And don't speak of it to Julia. Boasting of a match before it's announced just isn't done," she said, smiling in a way that made me know she ached to gloat to Mrs. Overton.

"Yes, Mother," I whispered as the door opened and the Overtons' downstairs maid admitted us inside.

"Agnes!" Julia rose from the settee as we entered the drawing room, and took my arm.

"Hello, Julia," I said, kissing her cheek. I turned to her
mother and curtsied quickly. "Ma'am."

"Oh, there's the girl who's stolen the heart of London's most
eligible fellow," Mrs. Overton squealed.

I shot a look at Mother, who managed to look satisfied and
surprised all at once.

"I'm sure I don't know what you mean," I said.

Mrs. Overton repositioned her wide hips in the wing chair.
"Rightly said, dear girl. Rightly said." She leaned forward and
winked. "Don't want to jinx it now, do we?"

The Overtons were new money, having made a fortune in
trade and essentially purchased their way into the world that had
once been the exclusive domain of men like my father. They'd
spent years trying to make everyone forget that they'd come
from nameless families in the north, but now and again Mrs.
Overton would pop off a remark that undid all her pretending.

Not that I cared. I adored Julia.

Mother took her place in the chair next to our hostess. I
joined Julia on the settee. We spoke of the weather and the next
ball until the tea arrived, and then Julia began whispering to me
behind her cup while Mother entertained Mrs. Overton with
news of David's visit.

"He really has set his cap for you," Julia said.

"It's utterly ridiculous," I said. "I've hardly spoken ten words
together to the man."

"Perhaps he's less interested in your conversation than he is in your other attributes." Julia giggled. "Whatever has captured his interest, I should think it only fitting that the most eligible man in London should be caught with such unprecedented speed. I'd expect nothing less in a season as eventful as ours has already proven."

"You heard about what happened at our house, then?"

"No thanks to you," she teased. "Truly, the fact that I have to learn of the break-in from the servants and not from you is almost unforgivable."

I was glad to have sidestepped the subject of Lord Showalter for the moment. And even more glad to let my mind spin through the rest of the adventure. And I didn't think I could keep myself from smiling. Julia knew me well enough that she'd suspect more. "Speaking of hired help, what news of your chaperone's attempts to make you a Wilkins?"

Julia shifted in her seat and glanced at her mother. "I believe she and Mother have abandoned that scheme. Emmaline is convinced his heart belongs to another," she whispered.

"Who?" I asked, though the pieces were beginning to come together in my mind.

Julia shrugged as she bit into a triangle of shortbread. "Didn't say. I'm not sure I'm entirely disappointed. Honestly, I was more excited about the prospect of being your sister than I was about being Rupert's wife. And that is no reason to marry the man, even if he wanted me." Her voice sounded braver than her eyes looked.

I wished I could reassure her of my brother's affection, wished I could somehow salve the pain of the rejection. But more than that, I itched to ask her if she'd any evidence of some attachment between my brother and her chaperone. Because if Lady Perkins was indeed the Emmaline referenced in Rupert's little book, the scandal that might erupt would be sensational. Perhaps even so great as to dwarf all this business with the mummy.

But Julia didn't need public insult added to the sting of losing my brother, no matter how lucky she was to be rid of him. So I simply took her hand and said, "You've always been the nearest I've known to a sister. And always will be, marriage or no."

Julia nodded, eyes shining. We said nothing for a moment, my mind wandering to Caedmon and the museum and the jackal's head.

"Agnes, have you been angry with me?"

I turned to her, spilling tea on my skirts in alarm. "Of course not!"

"It's just that you've been so silent since the party. I rather hoped we'd spend some more time together before you are whisked away to marriage."

"I'm sorry, Julia. I've just been busy is all," I offered lamely. "With the fittings and David's surprise visit home, the days simply aren't long enough. I've not even been reading lately."

"Oh!" Julia said, my neglect forgotten. "I've finished your *Sense and Sensibility*." She popped up from the settee and fetched

the book from the mantelpiece. Her mother noted her movement.

"Ooh, I rather liked that one too," she admitted. "Have you
read it, Lady Wilkins?"

Mother shook her head and grimaced. "No. But Agnes has
quoted it with such frequency, and in so many languages,"—she
threw a teasing look my way—"to make me believe I have."

"I'm quite taken with that A Lady," Mrs. Overton continued.

"As is Agnes," Mother said. "When she was thirteen, do you
know that she tried to convince her father to exploit his connections to discover the author's true identity?"

It was true. Father had laughed at my obsession. That
was the summer that Julia and I had concocted scheme after
scheme to try and suss out exactly who A Lady was.

"Well, do you know what I heard?" Mrs. Overton leaned
forward in her chair, lips pulled to one side of her face, eyes
begging me to ask the question.

"Mother," Julia said, rolling her eyes, "that's idle gossip."

"The best kind," her mother rejoined. "I heard from my
cousin over in Bath that A Lady is really a Miss Austen. Spinster
daughter of a parson!"

I laughed. "Preposterous! A spinster could not invent the
passion of *Pride and Prejudice* or the heartache of the Misses
Dashwood!"

Mrs. Overton shrugged. "Perhaps not. But wouldn't it be
lovely if she could? Wouldn't it be lovely if a lady really could

invent whole new lives for herself on the page, ones she'd never hoped of living? Just by scrawling them down?"

The room fell silent, four women wondering just what it might be like to make decisions entirely their own, even if they were only in fiction.

"Lovely," I murmured, and reached for the teapot, filling up the cups and trying to shake the cloud that had settled over the parlor.

❧   ❧   ❧

"I am only bothered by a bit of cramping," I said to Mother. We'd left the Overtons' at half past two, and I'd been dozing in my room since. I was supposed to be dressing for dinner and the opera now.

She felt my forehead, placed her hand across my belly. "Is it your time?"

I shrugged. "Nearly. But just because I am unwell doesn't mean you should miss it. Rossini is your favorite. And I hear that *L'inganno felice* is wonderful."

"Lord Showalter will be so disappointed," she worried.

"But even more so if I am unfit to visit the museum with him tomorrow," I said.

Mother considered this. "You are right," she said at last. "He might take it poorly if you cannot step out with him tomorrow, as he's made special arrangements—"

"I'll be fine by morning," I said, clutching my abdomen for good measure.

"I suppose you're right," Mother said, patting my hand.

"But do take Aunt Rachel along in my place, won't you?"

Mother looked confused. "She's quite hard of hearing, Agnes."

"But she so loves the spectacle," I said, hoping it was true.

Mother hesitated. "Very well, I suppose she's due for some entertainment, as you leave her behind at *every* opportunity."

I forced a smile. Mother leaned in to kiss my forehead. "I'll have Mrs. Brewster send up some broth," she said, gliding from the room in a rustle of silk and crinoline.

Now all that was left was to evade the servants. A few minutes later Clarisse brought a tray laden with the broth and a bit of bread—Mother's preferred remedy for female trouble. But when I found my time coming, I wanted little more than to be left alone with half a rack of bacon.

"Thank you," I said.

She placed the tray on the table near the fireplace. "Will that be all, miss?"

I nodded, trying to look pathetic as I sat up in bed.

Clarisse rolled her eyes. "You may have fooled Madame," she said, "but I know you better."

I froze. "Pardon?"

"You are not unwell," she said.

"Clarisse, I—"

"I thought you were slinking off to meet Lord Showalter

when you left so early the other morning," she said. There was mischief in her voice and eyes.

"I—"

"But tonight, *ma cherie*, you hide away from an opportunity to be with him," she went on.

"My stomach—"

She waved me off and barreled on. "And still you have that same look about you," she said, wagging a finger at me.

I opened my mouth to protest but found the words would not come.

"If you force me to guess, I would say you are waiting now for me to leave so you can sneak away again."

"This is—," I began, rising to my feet.

She wouldn't let me finish. "You *are* meeting someone, Miss Agnes," she said triumphantly, adding in a whisper, "but not Lord Showalter."

I looked at her. At the smile she fought to suppress. And suddenly I found myself smiling back.

"It's not quite what you think," I said finally.

She clapped her hands to her chest and rushed to my side. "You have a secret *amour!*"

I let her lead me to the settee and sat down beside her. Perhaps this was a blessing after all. I did have a secret, though perhaps not a love to go with it. All the same, I *was* going to go and meet a handsome young man, even if it was not for the reasons Clarisse had guessed. I could take her into my confidence without having to tell her the whole truth, particularly since she'd already been so good as to deliver a suitable alternative, ready-made for the purpose.

"You cannot tell Mother," I said finally. "Or anyone. You must promise."

"*Mon Dieu, non!*" she whispered. "What good is a secret lover if your mother knows?" she teased in a way that made me wonder exactly how many secret lovers Clarisse had entertained over the years.

"We are to meet tonight," I whispered, aware that I was barely able to keep myself from wishing Clarisse's notions were correct.

Clarisse squealed. "Where?"

"That matters not. But I could use your help," I begged.

She sat forward eagerly, making me wonder why I hadn't thought of relying on Clarisse even earlier. I knew I could count on her to be discreet. She was as romantic in her notions as the most starry-eyed of A Lady's creations. Worse by half than a Marianne Dashwood or a Lydia Bennet.

"At least tell me who he is!" she demanded.

"Truly, the less you know the less you'll have to own to should I be discovered," I reasoned.

She considered this. My parents might dismiss her if I was caught and they realized she'd assisted me. "Very well," she said finally, "but his name at least!"

I started to protest. Started to try and convince her that even that information was too much.

But I realized I didn't want to. I wanted to say his name to someone.

"Caedmon," I whispered, unable to keep from smiling.

Clarisse gave a little sigh, shoulders softening, eyes growing dreamy. *"C'est parfait,"* she moaned, repeating his name. "Caedmon."

I felt giddy at saying his name out loud and hearing it echoed back in Clarisse's wonderful accented speech.

"He is poor?" Clarisse asked.

I nodded.

"And handsome?"

I nodded again.

"And kind?"

I nodded a third time.

She sat up straighter, as if he had met some set of qualifications. "What can I do to help?"

I relaxed for the first time in days. "I have a plan. I need you only to make sure that none of the other servants see me go. And if you can keep Mother from checking on me when she returns from the opera . . ."

Her eyebrows shot toward the ceiling. "How long will you be gone?" she asked.

I shook my head. "I cannot say. But I will be back by morning. Can you give me that much time?"

She nodded. *"Oui.* But are you sure you cannot tell me more? Are you sure there is not more I can do?"

I shook my head. "It would be best if you went downstairs and told the other servants to leave me be for the night." I reached for the tray. "And take this—they'll be even more convinced when they see I haven't eaten any of it."

She collected the tray, then looked at me. "You will tell me all someday soon, will you not, miss?"

I squeezed her arm. "I'd like nothing better." And suddenly I realized I had two stories now in need of sharing. The one I had to tell Father, and the one I *wanted* to tell Clarisse.

Satisfied, she went to the door. Balancing the tray on one hand, she grasped the knob with the other, then paused. "Be careful, mademoiselle."

I bounded across the room, kissed her cheek lightly, and promised her I would. She laughed, muttered something about love, and disappeared into the hall.

I waited until nine before dousing my reading lamp, drawing the window shutters, and creeping to my door. A pair of my softest boots in hand, I peeked into the hallway. Clarisse was nowhere to be seen, and the only other upstairs maid was likely taking her dinner with the other servants below at this hour.

I took a deep breath and slipped from my room, gently pulling the door shut, taking care to avoid allowing the latch to sound. I hurried across the eight feet or so of carpet to David's door. As quietly and calmly as I could with my heart threatening to thump its way from beneath my nightgown, I opened his door and shut myself in silently.

David's room looked as abandoned as ever despite his recent surprise visit. The lamps were unlit and the windows shut, so I scrounged for a nub of candle in the bedside drawer and a tinderbox to light it with. I had to risk it, hoping that no one would even think to look in his room. Carrying the small candle, I opened his wardrobe, jumping when the door squeaked on its hinge. I froze a moment before breathing and moving again, this time working with haste. I reached into the wardrobe and withdrew what I suspected was the oldest suit of clothing yet remaining in the house. Mother had left David's room almost exactly as it had been when he'd entered the navy four years ago. This suit wouldn't have fit him now by any stretch, and the fabric was not only the wrong season, but also favored a style— the collar too high and the cut of the coat too long—that was now terribly out of fashion.

But for once dressing fashionably was not my duty.

Dressing as someone else *was*.

A young woman unescorted on the streets of London at night would prove a target for both the sinister and the noble. Either I'd be harassed by someone who'd had too much drink and too little sense, or some well-meaning soul would show concern and make sure I was safely escorted to whatever destination I was bound for.

But a young man in a secondhand suit could blend in easily. Tonight I'd be just another fellow looking for cheap ale or a long, lonely walk.

I rolled the waistband of my brother's trousers twice to make them sit at approximately the right height. They were meant to fit snugly, and I merely hoped in the darkness no one would pay attention. Just in case, I closed the jacket over them, buttoning down as far as it would go. It gapped at the shoulder and strained across the chest, but I found that if I slouched forward just so, I could persuade myself that no one would notice. The sleeves were just about right, and all in all the effect was not altogether unconvincing. There were no shoes in the wardrobe to complete the ensemble, but the ones I'd brought were the least feminine of the several pairs I owned. Going about barefoot seemed neither comfortable nor inconspicuous, even in the London heat.

I studied my reflection in the glass. It jarred me to see two legs in place of the long skirt, to see the waist of the trousers so near where my actual waist was. But I told myself that no one would see female where they expected male.

I reached for the only hat in the wardrobe, snapping the dust from it before lowering it onto my hair, and was shocked to find it snug.

Blast.

I removed it quickly and set about the task of tucking the length of my hair up into the cavity between my scalp and the top of the hat. When gravity seemed to get the better of my efforts—each time I tugged the band loose to slide a handful more hair up, another curl cascaded down—I bent over, removed the hat, and tried to coil my hair into the bowl before seating it on my head. After several attempts, I stood and saw that I was successful save for one small lock trailing over my left shoulder. Too afraid that I would never get this close again and worried that I was already running late to meet Caedmon, I retrieved a dull, forgotten shaving razor from the drawer.

"For England," I muttered, sawing through the stubborn tendril.

David's room opened onto the back garden. A tangle of ivy climbed the trellis. I stepped onto the wide ledge and pulled the sash almost shut behind me, careful to leave enough room to assure that my entry point remained upon my return. My hands grasped the weathered wooden slats as if they belonged to someone else. I swung one leg out, reaching as far as it would go, surprised by the freedom the pants allowed. Then I took a deep breath and shifted my weight to the toe now lodged in among the vines, placing the other on the trellis as I left the ledge.

Now it was a simple matter of descending the latticework like a ladder. Despite the fact that this was something I'd done only a handful of times as a child (young ladies of a certain age do not climb ladders), I told myself that it was nothing more than a very steep stile over an exceptionally tall country fence. Lizzie Bennet, I was sure, would have been proud.

I picked my way carefully down, and in a matter of moments, I was close enough to drop safely to the ground, where I landed squarely in a bed of day lilies. I whispered an apology to the broken stems, then gathered what I could and tossed them behind the shrubbery for fear that they'd be noticed and questions raised.

"Gardener's the only one who'll see," slurred a voice.

I shrieked—a scream completely incongruous with my apparel—and flattened myself against the wall. The sound of a glass bottle thudding gently to the earth preceded my brother's emergence from the shadow of a magnolia.

"For heaven's sake, Rupert," I muttered, scarcely able to believe I'd run into him again—me going out and him coming in.

He looked me up and down drunkenly. "Wot you s'posed to be?"

"Lower your voice," I hissed at him, adjusting my coat.

"You're up to no good, Aggie," he said, adding, "Naughty, naughty, naughty."

"Rupert, I think you'd better be in bed," I said. "And perhaps use the front door?" I worried about him climbing up his own trellis in this condition. And then worried a little at what might have caused him to be so far gone at so early an hour.

He collapsed into a squat and finally sat, without saying anything.

"Rupert?"

"She won't have me," he said.

I was confused. "Julia?"

"Not Julia. Julia's keen for it," he said, his voice again too loud.

"Rupert—"

"And the thing of it is, I know she loves me," he said.

"Julia will be all right—"

"Not Julia! Didn't I say that before?"

I took a cautious step toward him, "Rupert, you really—"

"She says just because she's so much older and a widow and all that, she can't give me what I need. That people won't stand for it. That Julia will be much better for me."

"Perhaps Lady Perkins is right," I said gently.

Apparently Rupert wasn't as drunk as he looked. "Who said anything about Lady Perkins?"

I hesitated. "You did, just now," I lied.

He started to argue, but gave it up, sighing. "Julia's a nice enough girl, but Emmaline is . . ."

I knelt beside him and pulled one of his arms over my shoulder, then slipped my other arm around his waist.

"I'm sorry, Rupert," I said, trying to heave him up.

"You don't love him, either, do you?" he asked.

I stopped pulling. "What?"

"Showalter. You don't love him. No more than I love Julia," he said, lying back on the ground.

"Rupert, you really cannot—"

"But we'll do our duties, won't we? Marry the right people, go to the right parties, have the right children."

I felt a stab of pain, knowing it wasn't what I wanted. Wasn't what my brother wanted either. Despite all his talk of who was worth what, my brother was far more complicated than I'd ever imagined . . . than I'd ever given him credit for.

Half a second later, Rupert was snoring softly.

I stared at him. Perhaps wearing a boy's clothing was going to my head, but I began to think that perhaps my brother's choices—or lack of them—were nearly as vexing as my own. He was a boy who wrote secret poems to a woman fifteen years his senior, who would one day settle for something as unsatisfying to him as my lot in life was becoming for me.

And there was nothing either of us could do about it.

I leaned over and kissed his cheek, reasoning that he was as safe in the garden for now as he would be in his own bed, and hurried away.

Chapter Sixteen

❧

Rupert, I decided, hadn't counted as a test of my disguise. Drunk or otherwise, he knew me well enough to spot me anywhere. I stepped from the darkness onto the sidewalk and headed toward the carriage stand.

My route took me past the darkened windows of Showalter's house, but I kept my head down and listened for familiar voices, ready to slip from the path rather than chance recognition. The walk seemed longer, though my steps were determined, trying to outpace the urgency that seemed to pulse in my veins.

I waited to cross the street until I'd come to the last in the row of carriages. I had my hand on the door and my body halfway inside the coach before the driver stirred. I held a half crown out to him, felt his hand close around the money while I hoped he didn't think my hand soft for a boy, and forced my voice low as I directed him toward the Tower. I didn't wait for comment, bundling myself the rest of the way into the hack and slamming the door as the driver pulled us away from the curb and bore north.

When the shadowed profile of the Tower appeared in the carriage window, I stepped down before it had even stopped moving fully and didn't slow at my driver's inquiry about awaiting my return. I walked quickly, emboldened by my success thus far. I was no idle young lady of London's elite. I was a man with a purpose.

Still, I wasn't brave enough to hazard a safer, more circular route around the perimeter of the Tower. Instead I approached Deacon's lodgings from the same alley Caedmon had escorted me down. I saw his silhouette pacing the street just ahead of where I knew the door lay.

I got within a few yards of him before he paid me any notice. And even that was a quick glance, a mumbled "Evening," and he withdrew toward the door.

I looked up and smiled. "Good evening to you, Mr. Stowe."

He froze, peering through the dim light at my face as I lifted my chin. He squinted. "Do I—"

He stopped, his eyes wide.

"Agnes?" he whispered.

"Mr. *August* Wilkins, if you please," I said, curtsying.

He gaped at me, finally managing to speak. "Y'ought to bow next time."

"Quite so," I said. "I forgot myself."

He still looked stunned. "Stampers are a giveaway," he said, pointing to my shoes, "but in the main you made a bang-up job of it."

I didn't know whether to be flattered or offended that I passed so easily for my brother.

"Shall we?" I asked.

He nodded and offered his arm to me. I looked at it, wanted so much to take it, to let my hand rest there . . . but it would only confuse matters. No point in starting something that had no hope of ending well. And there was my disguise to consider. I shook my head and tugged the brim of my hat lightly.

"Right," he said, setting off as I fell into step beside him.

We walked quickly, dodging clots of revelers spilling outside pub doors, and questionable women making even more questionable offers of service.

"I should have known you'd come dressed so," Caedmon said as we neared our destination. "But how did you give everyone the slip?"

"Well," I began, "there was one servant I took into my confidence."

"Who?" he asked, alarmed.

"My lady's maid. I didn't tell her about the standard," I clarified.

"And she just let you go?"

I hesitated. "She thinks I've come to meet a lover."

He seemed to stumble. "A what?"

"It was the quickest way to secure her cooperation," I said quickly. "Clarisse is a bit of a romantic."

He was quiet a beat too long. "I see."

Because I was too nervous to let it lie between us, I began to prattle on in painful detail about how I'd climbed out the window, found my brother, and then made my way to meet him.

Caedmon shook his head in wonder. "Pluck," he said, smiling.

And there it was again. That feeling that bubbled up when I saw him, when he said something that made some door inside me slide open, that made me believe his admiration was genuine, spontaneous, rather than rehearsed and performed the way Showalter's compliments sounded when he went on about how lovely I looked in a new gown. And it puzzled me that Caedmon seemed to see me more as I was, as I wished to be, even when I was dressed like this.

At the public invalid house, I allowed him to speak for us both, explaining to the porter that his godfather was within and had been asking after him earlier. After a bit of persuading, the old man admitted us and pointed toward a ward lined with beds on both sides.

I'd heard about hospitals like these, though they were still thankfully rare. My father worried that soon half of London would have no one at home to care for them—or no home at all in which to recover—and had been urging reforms to provide for the poor. He viewed these hospitals, funded largely at public expense, as a necessary evil.

I understood now what he meant.

The smell was like a wound itself, lingering and sticky. A poor soul moaned in his sleep from one corner, and another at the far end sat upright in his bed, rocking as if he were halfway to Bedlam already.

"Let's find him quickly," I whispered.

Caedmon nodded and moved slowly between the beds, scanning each occupant. We drew closer to the rocking man, whose eyes fixed on us vacantly as we approached.

"Here," Caedmon whispered as we reached the bed next to the odd man.

Deacon was sleeping, his head wrapped in fine white gauze, a dark stain seeping against the bandage.

"You're him," the man in the bed next to us hissed as he ceased his rocking.

I kept my eyes on Deacon's ashen face.

"Pardon?" Caedmon whispered.

"You're him . . . the one he was asking after," he said.

"I—I s'pose," Caedmon said.

"They hurt him bad," the man said, springing from his bed and causing me to edge backward. "Head all busted about. Hand twisted strange-like. But he wouldn't tell what happened. Just asked for you. Asked after you and after you and after you. Gave him laudanum to calm him down when you didn't come."

"Dear God," Caedmon said quietly.

I laid my hand lightly on Deacon's arm, hardly able to think about what he might have suffered on our behalf. What he might have suffered because of my foolishness in keeping the object in the first place.

"Has he been awake since?" Caedmon asked.

The strange inmate shook his head furiously. "Asleep with the sleep. They dosed him again for pain."

"He said nothing of his attackers?" Caedmon asked.

"Nothing. Just 'Fetch Stowe at the museum,' and then nighty-night." The man giggled.

We thanked him for his help, begged him to have the staff send for Caedmon again if Deacon woke, and made to depart before he stopped us.

"Who's she called?" he asked when we were halfway to the door.

I stiffened—he'd seen through my disguise.

Caedmon turned halfway round. "Say again?"

"Wot's her name?" he asked again. "So's I can tell him when he wakes up."

Caedmon looked at me. I shrugged. "Deacon will know who it was."

The man slumped against the wall and muttered, "Capital," as we hurried from the ward and back into the anonymity of the streets.

Outside, Caedmon stopped at the corner. "It's my fault," he said. "If I hadn't gone to Deacon, he wouldn't be lying there—"

I didn't allow him to finish. "If it's anyone's fault, it's mine," I argued. "I kept the jackal's head. I came to you for help, and Deacon is injured because of me."

"You had no way of knowing," he said, shaking his head and looking past me. He turned, gazing back at the hospital. "D'you think he's safe there?"

I swallowed hard. "I don't like that place," I said. "I don't like him in there with madmen and paupers." When Father returned and I begged his forgiveness after telling my tale, I would also beg to have Deacon moved to a place more comfortable, to have our physician sent to look after him. . . .

"It isn't right," he agreed, jaw twitching.

I reached out and took his arm. "It isn't. But there's nothing we can do about that now. And if we assume he was attacked because we went to him for help, then we have far more pressing problems than assigning blame."

He looked puzzled, but then his mouth slipped open, dark eyebrows lifted with alarm. "We were followed!"

I nodded. "Likely. At the very least, someone learned of my connection to you and yours to him. Whether they followed one or both of us is beside the point."

"It's very much the point," he said darkly. "Could mean that this person has been following us for days on the sly."

"You're right," I said uneasily, realizing that if we were being followed even now, we were making it awfully easy work by standing still in an empty street. "Shall we walk a bit?"

Caedmon seemed to understand, falling into step beside me. "The way I see things," I whispered as we hurried onward, "is that whoever is doing all these dreadful things and acting as Napoleon's agent—"

"Mr. Banehart," Caedmon said gravely.

"Whoever he is, he has not approached either of us directly to interrogate us. But the attack on poor Deacon proves that they know of our involvement, so—"

"So it means that they are waiting for us to find the standard for them?"

I shrugged. "Or they believe we won't surrender the message if we are openly approached." I thought of Deacon, of what he must have endured to protect us, to keep safe the secret of what I'd found. And it made me more resolved than ever to bring to light the people responsible.

Caedmon started to glance over his shoulder, but snapped his face back around to mine when I clicked my tongue at him. On the chance that someone was back there, it would be better if they didn't know we suspected.

"Is there a less public entrance to the museum we can use?" I asked him.

He fought to focus on my eyes. I fought to keep a clear head. Together we made a plan. Caedmon provided the location of a hidden entrance beneath an overgrown willow on the southeast corner. I suggested we'd stand a better chance at confounding a possible follower if we separated, both using as circuitous a route to the museum as possible, changing cabs and conveyance if the opportunity arose. Caedmon made a halfhearted attempt to protest my going unescorted, an argument he seemed to know he'd lose before he mounted it.

He slowed again as we reached the corner. "How do you know how to do all this?"

I wasn't entirely sure. It didn't exactly feel like something I'd learned. It felt a little like speaking French now did. I knew at some point I'd learned it, but now when I engaged in conversation or translation, it was as if part of my brain simply took over. It felt *innate*. This felt a bit like that.

But I didn't think I had sufficient time to explain this to Caedmon. "One can learn a great deal reading popular novels," I said, adding, "and listening at the grate of a well-placed parliament member's study."

I shook his hand abruptly before he had a chance to change his mind and marched past him, my shoulder brushing his chest as I did so.

"Good evening, sir," I said, and strode away without turning. I could feel his gaze on me, and hoped against all reason that my form looked reasonably well dressed in my brother's clothes.

Chapter Seventeen

❧

As I darted across a darkened park, clambered into a second carriage and gave the driver my fare and my destination, a thought struck me.

We'd been faced with the very likely possibility that someone had been following us. Yet my first reaction had not been to send word to Father or to rush to Scotland Yard or even find the nearest constable. Rather, I resolved to simply be more careful, to try and evade whoever might be following us. And Caedmon hadn't suggested otherwise. Something had shifted. We'd become a team of sorts. But were we being utterly foolhardy? Did we have a chance of finding the standard ourselves? And . . . was it possible that Caedmon was enjoying being with me as much as I was with him?

I found him pacing beneath the branches of the appointed willow.

"All right?" he asked me.

I nodded. "Perfectly. Were you followed?"

He shrugged. "No. Yes. Maybe. I'm half-mad thinking the whole world is after us now. And the other half is going mad thinking you're a sight better at playing the brave young man than I am."

"It's all show," I said, deciding to take that as a compliment. "How long have you been waiting?"

He sighed. "Bells sounded a bit ago. Not long."

"Good. And no sign of anyone?"

He shook his head.

"From the road, it's impossible to see you from beneath this tree, so if anyone has been following, they'll likely think we've already gone in. They would have approached by now to try and find our point of entry."

He looked at me, dumbfounded. "If you say so."

"Perhaps you're right. We should give it another quarter of an hour, just to be sure." I sank to the ground and tucked my legs under me as if I were still wearing a dress.

Caedmon sat and in spite of himself, smiled.

"What?" I asked.

"You don't look very convincing at the moment, that's all."

I reached for my hat and felt to be sure my hair had stayed hidden.

As alarming as it had been to be recognized by the hospital resident, I was just as relieved that Caedmon saw something that reminded him of who I really was, what I really looked like. We sat quietly for a few minutes more before the bells in the clock tower down the road chimed again.

"Time," he said, rising to his feet. He led me to a darkened doorway a few feet away. "I've used this entrance before to sneak in a few spare hours with the Stone when I couldn't sleep." A single pane of glass rattled in the door as Caedmon coaxed the lock free.

I followed him inside. "Mind your feet," he said, gesturing at the labyrinth created by piles of dusty papers and crates of books. "Acquisitions for the library," he explained. "First editions of the great masters."

"Will A Lady's works be represented?"

"Doubtful. These are heavyweights in here. The Gutenberg Bible, *Beowulf* in the original Old English. Romances and country stories don't quite make the mark."

"Clearly you've never read any of her work."

"I have—an older sister, you remember? A man will read anything if he's desperate enough. Not enough tragedy in them—that's the stuff that lasts."

"A Lady's endings do tend to be insufferably happy," I admitted, recalling all the virtuous young women who managed to marry for love and money simultaneously. Fantasy of the highest order.

"Walk soft," he whispered as we reached the top of the stairs. "I'm not the only one who works late now and again."

I nodded as Caedmon led me to the storage room we'd visited earlier today, though our approach was different. He motioned for me to wait, and I allowed my eyes to adjust to the blackness. A moment later I heard him rattling with a tinder-box, the flame sparking to life a few inches from the floor, where Caedmon held it to a nub of candle.

The room seemed to come alive as painted eyes stared, looking at me. I felt the odd sensation that they were annoyed by our disturbance of their quiet evening. A sculpted cat, ears far too long, loomed above me on a shelf. I stepped involuntarily to Caedmon's side. "Come," he whispered, leading me to the corner where the Stone sat on its pedestal. He left me there with the candle, crept toward the offices and the hall to the exhibit room, and disappeared.

Caedmon's absence was enough to resurrect the possible fear of the mummy's curse, if only for a moment. And his return was so silent and sudden that I jumped, spilling a drop of wax onto my wrist.

"All clear," he whispered, taking the light from my hand. He took another candle and a sheaf of papers from a wooden box shoved against the wall, placing the papers on top of the Stone, kissing the cold wick to the flame I held. Then he took both candles and positioned them near the top of the inscription.

"Cozy."

"Passable," he replied. "Cozy doesn't give you back strain and a squint."

I joined him in front of the Stone. "So, what now?"

He pulled a handful of papers from the pile he'd earlier produced. "I have a theory," he said, shuffling for a document.

"Something I pray the others researching the Stone have not reckoned on."

"Other researchers?" I asked.

He nodded. "Dozens around here. And even more on the Continent. Mostly in France, but a few Spaniards, and there is one persistent Austrian who—"

"But isn't this the only stone?"

"Yes, but loads of copies of the text are floating round," he explained. "Like this one." He dove back into the pile and produced a folded piece of fine, flexible paper. He handed it to me, its edges brittle in my clumsy fingers.

It was a rubbing, the kind of thing Julia and I used to do as children in the Lakes. We'd find leaves, feathers, butterflies, flowers, or anything we thought lovely and press them beneath a piece of onionskin paper, then scribble evenly across the surface to reproduce the image. We even went through a phase wherein we tried to make rubbings of the headstones in the local churchyard before her mother realized what we were up to and thought it an unsuitable pursuit for little girls.

"I cribbed this one when I first started working with the Stone. You can be sure the French made as many rubbings as they could before they surrendered her to the British army."

We stood close in the candlelight, him leaning over me as I studied the images on the onionskin. And it struck me that for the first time, we were *truly* alone. Before, we'd been on the street or in the museum, or at the hospital. Even in desolate places there was always the possibility of someone turning up.

But now? While the rest of London slept, we shared the feeble light of a pair of candles in the darkened back room of a museum that had been closed for hours.

Suddenly I felt nervous next to him. I leaned back and spoke too quickly. "How does it work? Understanding the glyphs?"

He sighed. "That's the trouble. General opinion holds that the Greek and demotic are literal translations, and the hieroglyphs will follow."

"*Где мнению носит общий характер, оно обычно правильно,*" I murmured, the words trickling out before I could clamp my mouth shut.

"What?" Caedmon asked.

"Nothing," I said. "Bad habit. It's a bit of A Lady: 'Where an opinion is general, it is usually correct.'"

"What tongue was that?"

"Russian," I said. "But it doesn't matter. Please go on. You were about to tell me how you think otherwise?"

He nodded, eyes still narrowed at me. He shook his head slightly. "They don't always square with each other. First I just figured I'd slipslopped it with my translating. But I did it over and over and they still don't match."

I considered this, thought of the way a word in Hebrew

often had no real counterpart in another language. "Translation is always an act of negotiation rather than a science, is it not?"

"But it's more than that," he said, holding the candle closer. "The words and structure of language—even Greek—at the time the Stone was inscribed were different than they are now. But *these* differences are a bit more havy cavy."

I thought of all the trouble and effort it would take to etch the words into a stone of this size. "For a civilization as advanced as the Egyptians, carelessness is suspect," he said, seemingly reading my mind.

I ran my fingers lightly across the Stone's surface. "Then understanding the glyphs relies on understanding how they took advantage of the differences between the other two texts on the Stone?"

He nodded eagerly. "Right as rain."

I lifted my hand and stared at the lines of symbols. "But that would mean they anticipated someone needing to translate the text at some later date. That would mean that they would have foreseen the fact that their civilization—despite the pyramids and other evidence to the contrary—would disappear."

He nodded solemnly, scratching the back of his neck. "A snarl, I admit. But only if you accept the supposition that all three texts were engraved at the same time."

The thought had never occurred to me. I looked at

Caedmon in admiration. "I suppose you have a reason for supposing otherwise?" I asked excitedly.

He rummaged on the table next to him and produced a magnifying glass, which he handed to me. "I wouldn't have noticed it had I been working only with the rubbed copies, but the hieroglyphs are a bit shallower than the other markings. Look."

He grabbed the candle and tilted it toward the demarcation between the pictures and the curves of the demotic script. I leaned in, acutely aware of his eyes on me, willing me to see what he had. As my eyes adjusted, I noticed that the rock behind the glyphs was not completely black, instead reflecting tiny pink glints back in the candlelight.

They did look a bit fresher, but it was hard to apply such a word to something as ancient as any of the markings I was looking at.

Caedmon replaced the candle in its stand. "If the hieroglyphs were added later, it's especially curious, considering the fact that hieroglyph usage was supplanted by the rise in popularity of the other two languages."

It was odd listening to him talk about the Stone. As if it demanded a whole new vocabulary of him. It seemed the slang that colored his speech dropped away as he slipped further into his description of his theory, as he delved into the science of his work. It gave me a new appreciation for him, for the way he could be as at home in the street as I imagined he might be with the most vaunted scientists. I looked again at the contour of the jackal glyph. "Then perhaps they added the carvings in order to hide something?"

He nodded and leaned on the Stone. "We've unearthed so many relics associated with the line of Ptolemy, it's queer one of the most important could be missing."

"Maybe grave robbers took the standard?"

He shook his head. "A bit of iron or bronze would likely have been shucked aside in favor of something that might fetch a higher premium from a collector. And if someone did know of its power, they would have used it or sold it to someone who would have used it."

He was right. An item that could potentially render its bearer invincible and allow him to raise an army of ghost warriors would certainly have merited historical mention.

"But why would Ptolemy hide it and deprive subsequent pharaohs of this power?"

Caedmon shrugged. "These folk sealed countless treasures into tombs. He could have planned to take it with him to the next world. Or decided that it was far too dangerous to leave lying around. Might have waited until he was certain the empire faced no threat, and then tucked it away until it was needed again by him or one of his descendents."

I nodded. "Very clever."

"Any pharaoh who spent more than a few years on the throne had to be a bit cagey."

"I wasn't speaking of the pharaoh," I said. Even in the faint light of the candle's glow, I could see that he was not immune to my praise of his work.

"Only a theory," he said, rubbing a spot on the Stone's glossy black surface.

"But if you're right, then all we have to do is compare the Greek and demotic, make an inventory of these intentional mistakes you've observed, and then use those and the text themselves to unlock the hieroglyphs."

"All of which may take a mite longer than a random search of the entire holdings of the museum," he said, his forehead sinking to the Stone.

"True. But we must try," I said. "Show me."

He propped himself up on his elbows, the candlelight catching the smile on only one half of his face. "You bear the bell, Agnes Wilkins," he said. "I mean, I knew you were clever, but you absorbed all this so easily."

I suppressed my own smile. "You explain it very well, Caedmon."

"But you're willing to credit it. Outside of Deacon, I've been too afraid to tell anyone what I've been working on. It's not just that I was scared of ridicule, but that I could be right and might have my hard work stolen away." He paused again, staring at me. "It's nice to have a partner."

I let the word settle between us. A partner. An equal. I knew others used it to describe marriage. To describe the relationship between husband and wife. Mother and Father certainly fit the definition. But I wondered, would I dream of applying it to Showalter and myself? Would it ever feel as natural as it did when Caedmon spoke it of us?

Finally I spoke, "Well," I said, surprised at the catch in my voice, "what kind of partner would I be if I delayed us any longer? Shall we?"

His gaze lingered on me a moment longer before he cleared the papers from the Stone, folding and tucking the lot of them into his waistband at his back. "I started with the dates and numbers. I noticed that the Greek and demotic reference the fifth Ptolemy—the Stone itself is a decree by the priests of his royal cult. He was only thirteen at the time of the inscription. This date," he said, pointing at a squiggle near the top of the demotic inscription, "is 332 AD. But this one . . ." He moved his finger to the Greek characters below.

"323 AD," I said.

"Nine years off. It seems to me that if one were going to all the trouble of inscribing something on a stone, you'd take care to get the numbers straight."

I nodded.

"And if you reckon that the name Ptolemy occurs as frequently in the glyphs as it does in the other two scripts, this cartouche must represent the king."

He pointed to a squarish oval set on its side in the middle of a line of hieroglyphic characters. The oval contained a series of carvings—a couple of shapes that might have been feathers, a snake, an ankh like Rupert had found on the mummy, and other shapes and squiggles.

"This is a name?" I asked.

He nodded. "More or less."

"The oval acts like some sort of punctuation, or calling someone Mr.?"

"Near enough," he agreed. "But note the differences between this one"—he scanned his finger across the Stone toward the corner where I'd found the outline of the dog's head last night— "and this one."

"There is an extra marking here," I said, falling under the spell that had so captivated Caedmon. I knew the joy of puzzling out a new language, but never before on a scale as grand as this.

"I reckon it's a number," he said.

"Nine?" I whispered.

He nodded. "And note its position?"

"Beneath the broken glyph of my jackal's head," I said.

"And the ninth Ptolemy is the last one reported to have used the standard in battle."

I stood. "Then that must narrow the search somewhat, mustn't it?"

"I—," Caedmon began.

Footsteps approached from the south hall. Silently Caedmon snuffed the candles and licked a thumb and fore-finger to quench the ember. I was helpless now in the dark, but Caedmon grabbed my hand and led me back the way we'd come. "Quickly," he called, his whisper calm but barely audible. I realized this wasn't the first time he'd nearly been caught.

When we reached the corner containing the sarcophagi, the footsteps abruptly changed direction. Now they were coming at us from the hallway we'd used to enter the rooms.

I realized I was holding my breath. Realized that I was hoping desperately it was merely another late nighter like Caedmon. Because if it wasn't, if we had been followed . . .

We had no clear line of escape. Without a word, Caedmon pulled me to the darkest corner bearing the largest of the coffins. "Inside," he whispered.

I obeyed, stepping over the edge and into the granite box. Caedmon followed, and I vaguely thought it funny that we were now testing my earlier observation that the sarcophagus seemed built for two.

Fear and joy proved a potent combination as Caedmon settled in next to me, and we lay on our sides facing each other. Now the walls of the stone box seemed even higher, a blessing since we would have been unable to lift the bulk of the lid even if we weren't trying to be utterly silent.

The footsteps drew nearer, and the glow of a light crept over the edge of the coffin like a slow sunrise, but did not trail down far enough to reveal us.

I forced myself to breath slowly, evenly though my nose, concentrating on the contour of Caedmon's chin, the smell of his washing soap, the feel of his body stretched out facing mine.

It was a moment before I realized that a second light had joined the first.

Two intruders. I longed to peek up over the edge, but doing so would have meant leaving our protected shadow. The voices were unrecognizable, their speech indiscernible. They spoke only a moment before the footsteps resumed, fading away in opposite directions.

All was dark and quiet once more.

We lay still for several minutes. Finally Caedmon whispered, "I think it's safe for us to get up now."

I was beginning to understand why Mother and Father and everyone else was so careful not to allow young men and women near each other. Beginning to understand how quickly feelings of excitement or longing could get the better of me. Because lying there next to Caedmon was the single most alarming and wonderful thing I'd ever experienced. It was strange to be so close to him, yet so oddly familiar, as if the space between his chin and chest were contoured exactly to provide a place for my head to nestle.

"Agnes?" he repeated. "I think we're safe."

Safe. We most certainly were not. I pushed myself up and over the edge before I lost my head.

He clambered from the coffin after me.

"I think I'd better see you home," he said, patently avoiding my eyes.

I consented to allow him to lead me from the room, back down our staircase, and outside.

At the street, he found a coach for me.

"Tomorrow?" I said, climbing in.

"It is tomorrow," he pointed out. "But given your—"

I cut him off. I didn't want to hear all the very good reasons he might have prepared. I didn't want to argue. I didn't have the strength.

"Good evening," I said, thumping the roof of the coach, ordering the driver to move before I could change my mind.

Chapter Eighteen

❧

Clarisse's entrance the next morning came painfully early.

"Busy day, mademoiselle," she said, crossing to my table.

By the time the coach had dropped me near home, and I'd climbed back up the trellis, returned David's clothes to his wardrobe, and deposited myself in bed, there were but few hours left until daylight. Most of those I'd squandered thinking about Caedmon, remembering what it felt like to have him look at me, what it felt like lying next to him.

I groaned, tossing the sheet from my legs and swinging my feet to the carpet.

"Though not nearly so busy as your evening?" she whispered slyly.

I could no more stop the smile that burst across my face than I could change the color of my hair.

Clarisse glanced toward the door to the hall, and then back to me. "You must tell me all," she ordered, "but not now. Your mother is already up and dressed. You are to be downstairs as soon as possible."

"Downstairs for what?" I asked, stretching, letting Clarisse slip the cotton dressing gown over my head. It was the most recent of my gifts from David, one he'd picked up when his ship resupplied in Morocco.

She shook her head. "You have forgotten him completely, have you? Your *other* suitor?"

I sprang from the bed. "Showalter!" I recalled, wondering how I'd spent the entire evening dreaming of Caedmon but hadn't managed to remember that Showalter was taking us to the museum this morning.

To the museum. "Oh, no," I said.

Clarisse laughed. "You have a problem, I do not doubt." She led me to the chair in front of the dressing table and began to work on my hair.

She couldn't imagine. Caedmon would be at the museum—he might not even have left last night. And Showalter would likely parade us through the Egyptian gallery, eager to show off how his largesse had made the collection possible.

"Love is always full of problems, *n'est-ce pas?*" she teased, reaching into her pocket. "But perhaps the morning's post will cheer you."

I took the letter from her outstretched hand.

"From David!" I said, tearing into the folds.

"Your mother had one for the family, but that one came special to you."

I nodded.

"Look up, please," she said. I obeyed, unfolded the letter in my lap, and lifted it to my eyes.

"What is this?" she asked, pulling back the tangles with the brush, revealing the sad little stump of hair I'd sawn off in my haste last night.

I glanced up from my letter and saw the ragged edge in her hand. "Oh, yes . . . *that*."

She shook her head. "Generally when a young lady wants to give her beau a lock of hair, she favors something a bit smaller," she muttered, "especially if she's bound to marry another."

I ended Clarisse's inquiry by burying myself in David's note.

> *My dear Aggie,*
>
> *Chin up.*
>
> *Yours ever,*
> *David*

I let my hands and the letter fall to my lap.

"He is well, miss?" Clarisse asked as she piled the braid she'd just woven onto the top of my head, securing it with pins.

"Better," I said. "He is brave."

"Of course, miss."

I prayed for my brother as the conversation we shared on the day he arrived echoed in my mind. I had work as important as David's to do.

"All right, Miss Wilkins?" Clarisse asked, working to tuck in the last bit of what I'd cut.

"Yes, thank you," I said quietly.

She squeezed my shoulders, hurried to the wardrobe, and withdrew a gown of fine pink linen.

"Shall I help you dress, miss?" Clarisse asked.

Finally I stood. "No, thank you. I'll manage today. Tell Mother I'll be down soon," I added, summoning my resolve.

"Very good," she said, inching from the room. "And I will be expecting a lovely tale this evening," she said, wagging a finger at me.

I stared at my reflection in the glass. What would I tell her? That what I'd pretended to secure her cooperation for was coming true? At least for me? That perhaps it had been true since I'd first laid eyes on Caedmon that evening at Showalter's?

I was grateful I had more pressing matters to offer some distraction. Because anything less than a threat to England's sovereignty seemed to pale in comparison to the questions troubling my heart.

⚘   ⚘   ⚘

I failed to persuade Showalter to take us somewhere else for our grand morning out, and we found ourselves at the museum just after the doors opened. Showalter led us inside as if it were his own home he welcomed us into.

"We haven't been here in ages," Mother said, looking round the entry hall. I caught the eye of the porter who admitted me the first morning I'd come, but looked away quickly, afraid he might give me away.

"Then I'm sure you'll be delighted by the wonders that await you. Despite the blockades, the museum has managed to keep a steady supply of acquisitions," Showalter offered. "There are plans in the offing for an expansion. I've agreed to underwrite some of the costs."

"Shall we have a look at some of those newer pieces?" I asked, desperate to avoid the Egyptian collection, as apprehensive about seeing Caedmon now as I'd been eager last night. "I understand there are some new marble friezes from Athens—"

Showalter waved a hand. "Nonsense," he said. "We've come to see proper mummies, and that's what we'll do. You were so keen at the party, and I had so little time to address your adorable curiosity. Now we must make the most of this opportunity, mustn't we?"

I forced a smile as he pulled me up the stairs. He was being so kind. So accommodating. So attentive. He was a good man . . . too good a man for me to be slinking about at night with no thought of how he might be wounded were I discovered.

I prayed silently that Caedmon might be occupied else-where, or even sleeping off the late night in a sarcophagus. But those hopes were dashed as we passed through the high door-way and into the now familiar room. Caedmon was occupied with his tray of tools, bent over another of the cases, cleaning and arranging as he had been that day I'd first encountered him here. In spite of the dread I'd been living in as I anticipated this moment, in spite of the circumstances of meeting him with my mother and my possible intended, my heart leaped like a fool pup yanking at a chain.

"Now we'll see if we can organize a proper tour," Showalter said. "Excuse me?" he shouted to Caedmon.

Caedmon rose and began to turn toward us. "Yes, sir."

He froze when he saw me, the smile starting at the corner of his mouth before he saw who accompanied me. His face blanched, the smile gave up, and he cut his eyes quickly to Showalter.

"Sir," he dropped his voice even lower, "how may I be of service?"

I looked down, fixing my eyes on the tips of Caedmon's boots.

"Mr. Banehart?" Showalter asked. "I was hoping he might be available to escort us through the collection?"

My head jolted up, panic arcing like lightning between Caedmon and me. If Banehart saw me again, he would surely—

"Mr. Banehart is otherwise engaged," Caedmon said, per-haps too quickly.

"Engaged?" Showalter said. "Surely if he knew who was asking for him—"

"He is in negotiations with a private collector," Caedmon said, a bit calmer this time, "in Sussex. He returns tomorrow."

Showalter shook his head and surveyed the open case where Caedmon had been working. "Rotten luck," he said. "Though I suppose you might be able to give us a bit of a show?"

Caedmon's eyes widened. "Me?"

Showalter nodded impatiently. "I presume you know *something* about the collection? Something that might make our journey here worthwhile?"

If he recognized Caedmon from the party, he didn't let on.

Caedmon put his tools down. "Glad to oblige."

Showalter snapped his fingers. "Right, then." He whirled round to me. "Where would you like to start?"

My shoulders fell. We were really going to do this. "I . . ." I cast my eyes about for something, anything. "I don't know where to begin."

"There are some absolutely enormous items in here, aren't there?" Mother said, surveying a granite spire that climbed halfway to the ceiling before breaking off in a jagged line.

"That's an obelisk." Showalter reached out and rubbed his palm against the carved side. "I've got some bits of these things back at home I can show you. They're not much to look at," he said dismissively, turning, eyes falling on the case behind us.

"But these little beauties," he went on, pushing past us, "these are stunning."

"And what are they?" Mother asked, pointing at the collection of polished stones in the case in front of her. They ranged in color from deepest black to a smoky green. But the basic shapes were all the same.

Caedmon stepped forward. "Heart scarabs, ma'am," he said.

"They look like giant beetles," Mother said dubiously.

"The scarab beetle was revered in ancient Egypt," Showalter offered, joining Mother and Caedmon at the case. "The natives associated it with the sun god."

"The scarab lays its eggs inside a ball it fashions from animal dung," Caedmon said carefully. "And it pushes the ball containing the eggs along the ground until it finds a safe place for them to hatch."

"How dreadful," Mother said, looking back and forth between Caedmon and Lord Showalter. I wondered what she saw when she looked at them. Wondered if she saw them as I did, if she ever could. If she could ever view Caedmon with the same hope and pride that I felt, or Showalter with the same kind of pity. Pity for pinning his hopes on a girl like me . . . a girl who felt too much for someone else.

And I wondered if she at least noticed that Caedmon was a bit taller, his hair a bit fuller, maybe even his eyes a bit kinder. . . .

I thought too how Caedmon must see Lord Showalter. Did he envy his luck at having been born into a fortune, a fortune that allowed him to indulge his passion for Egypt?

Did he envy him that that wealth also gave him access to me?

Was it awful that I hoped he did?

Caedmon was still trying to persuade Mother of the nobility of the scarab. "To the ancients, the sight of the young beetles emerging from the clod of dung was magical, a picture of life coming from a place it wasn't meant to be. And the sight of the beetle pushing the ball along the ground gave them an image for another myth. They thought the sun was pushed along in the sky by a giant beetle like the ones depicted here."

"The scarab was worshipped in Egypt, and the people there wore it as a talisman, like one might wear a crucifix today," Showalter said, horning in, perhaps afraid of being shown up by Caedmon.

"These all seem a bit big for wearing," Mother said, studying the pieces in the case below her.

"Heart scarabs were placed in the wrappings of a mummy, directly over the heart," Showalter supplied, falling easily into that role he loved so much, the role of expert, the role of lecturer. "Had we not been interrupted a few nights ago, we'd have likely found one in the wrappings."

"But I thought all the organs were removed from the bodies?" I said.

"All but the heart," Caedmon said, without looking up at me. "The Egyptians saw it as the most important part of the body. And on the journey to the afterlife, it had to be weighed and measured for purity by the gods. They put these scarab beetles over the heart in the remains to remind the dead to avoid confessing to any sins they'd committed in their lifetimes, lest they be denied their final rest."

"They used them to lie?" I asked.

I thought I saw Caedmon steal a glance at me before he went on. "More that they used them to hide. To shield their hearts, the things they'd really done"—he paused—"or perhaps had felt."

I felt sorry that these objects, which were so dear to the people who'd counted on them so long ago, were now under glass, dismissed by the likes of us who didn't know their real worth.

"How . . . *primitive*," Mother said after too long a pause. "Though it's a pity they couldn't have found a creature more noble for the purpose," she said. "Rather appalling to ornament oneself with an insect that cavorts around in excrement."

I wanted to apologize for my mother's comment, wanted to somehow make her see how lovely these things were. Wanted her to like them more, because in some odd way, it felt like if she liked them better, she'd like *Caedmon* better.

"It little matters what they were for," Showalter interjected. "These objects are highly prized by collectors. They fetch quite a price."

"We are very fortunate that we established such a collection," Caedmon said softly.

I surprised myself by speaking. "They don't belong here."

Showalter leaned in. "What's that?"

I looked quickly between him and Caedmon. "They don't belong here," I repeated. "They ought to be with the bodies, or at least back in Egypt where the scarab is understood."

Caedmon spoke without looking at me. In fact, he'd so far been able to avoid giving any indication of our association. And it bothered me more than I could say. Bothered me that he could see me with Showalter and carry on as if he didn't even know me. As if he hadn't been as rattled as I was by how close we'd found ourselves last night.

"Perhaps the work the museum does to help people understand outweighs—"

"No," I said firmly. "We don't want to understand them. We want to gawk at them and congratulate ourselves for having such precious things. Things we've rescued from ignorant savages around the world—"

Caedmon set his jaw, nostrils flaring, finally angry, finally showing something for me other than polite deference. "You presume too much," he said. "You're dead wrong to paint every person interested in antiquities or other lands with the same brush."

"But they belong in Egypt!" I said, pleased that some of his true speech was slipping out, that the mask of the academic was failing him.

"They belong where they can best be understood," Caedmon said evenly. "And perhaps the greatest gift we can give the people of Egypt in return is the benefit of our research. So that they might better understand their own history—"

"Now who presumes?" I said heatedly. "British citizens a thousand miles away know better what it meant to be a subject of the pharaoh?"

"You misunderstand me," Caedmon said, fuming, but I didn't let him finish.

"I think it is quite the reverse!" I said, feeling like a child for baiting him with an argument I knew he could not resist.

I realized Mother was squeezing my arm. "Perhaps we've had enough excitement for one morning," she said brightly. "Agnes has been feeling very tired by all the events of her debut, Lord Showalter," she said apologetically. "I'm afraid she's always veered toward petulance when she overexerts herself."

"I can speak for myself, Mother," I said bitterly.

Her nails dug into my skin. "You've left no room for doubt on that point, darling," she said. "But I think perhaps we might consider returning to the museum when you are a bit less excitable?"

Showalter eyed Caedmon carefully, looking for all the world as if he wanted to reprimand him for arguing with me. He started to speak to him, but I couldn't bear the thought of what he might say.

"Mother is right," I said quickly. "I am very tired and have

behaved very badly. I would be most grateful if we could luncheon earlier than planned and I might be excused to rest
this afternoon." I didn't wait for confirmation, didn't wait for
Showalter or Mother to say our good-byes to Caedmon. I threw
back my shoulders, lifted my chin, and stalked grandly from the
room. I knew that under different circumstances, my exit might
have drawn praise from Mother for its grandiosity, but I also
knew that when the time came for her to evaluate me, it would
draw something else entirely.

ᴕ   ᴕ   ᴕ

Mother and Showalter chatted politely in the carriage on the
way back to his home, both carefully avoiding any mention of
the scene I'd just made. I dreaded explaining myself later to
Mother, but not nearly so much as the conversation I'd have
with Caedmon eventually.

And I still had lunch to endure.

Upon our arrival, Lord Showalter's very annoyed housekeeper informed us that they hadn't expected us until twelve,
and the meal was far from ready. Mother and I followed
Showalter into the back gardens.

As we emerged, we were greeted by a terrific crack and
cloud of white smoke rising into the air.

"Capital!" Showalter cried out. "The morning may be
salvaged after all." He bounded down the steps to where his

gamesman stood next to a table bearing a small collection of revolvers.

"I was merely cleaning and testing the firearms, sir," the gamesman said. "I thought perhaps since you'd be away for the morning . . ."

"Your timing is impeccable," he said. "We find ourselves in need of some diversion. And I'm sure the ladies will not object?" He turned, his gaze seeking Mother's permission.

"Just the thing," Mother said genially, though I knew she loathed guns. It was expected for men to shoot pistols, and even common for women of the upper class to engage in the practice. But Mother forbade it at home and wouldn't allow it at our country house either if she was about. Rupert and Father always shot when she was away.

Showalter grinned, took up one of the pistols, and aimed at a target set up some thirty or forty yards away, near the entrance to the thicker part of the garden.

"Well shot, sir," said the gamesman to Lord Showalter after the echo of the gun's report faded with the cloud of smoke.

They set off for the target. I could see from here that the shot had found its way to the outer edges, leaving the cartoon of Napoleon's face untouched.

"You behaved abominably at the museum, Agnes," Mother said, without looking at me.

"I know," I said. I wished I could tell her why. Wished I could tell her what had come over me. Wished that she could understand what it felt like to have the two of them in the same room together, to have the two worlds crowding up against each other; what it felt like to see that it didn't bother Caedmon in the least to see me with Showalter.

"I'll thank you to acquit yourself more carefully this afternoon. If you can refrain from bickering with the servants, I'll take it as a personal favor," she said acidly.

"Yes, Mother."

I was saved further reprobation by the return of our host. He bounded back up the lawn to us, the gamesman following slowly as he retamped the barrel on the pistol.

"Nothing like a little target practice with old Boney," Showalter said, gesturing behind him.

"Very patriotic," I offered.

"Would you care to have a go, Lady Wilkins?" Showalter asked.

Mother shook her head. "Actually, I believe we'd be better off in your very comfortable drawing room. I'd hate to allow Agnes to become even more enervated by this sunshine."

"Go ahead, Mother," I said, knowing that if I went inside with her, I'd have more of her reprimands to endure. "I'll stay and watch. My bonnet should cover me quite well."

Mother started to protest, but Showalter interrupted. "In fact, Lady Wilkins, I'm happy to escort you myself. There's something in the library that I'd like to ask your opinion of," he said, smiling warmly at me. "I've purchased a gift for a certain young lady making her debut rather soon, and want a woman's refined perspective, you understand."

"I really don't think you should have—"

"Really, Agnes, I believe we've all had enough of your ill-formed opinions for one morning," Mother's barb landed with far more accuracy than Showalter's shot. She took our host's arm. "I'm happy to help."

They disappeared into the house, leaving me stunned in the yard with the gamesman.

"Want to have a go?" he asked, nodding toward the target.

Mother wouldn't like it. But she was already as angry as I'd ever seen her. "Perhaps just one shot," I said, looking over my shoulder to make sure Mother wasn't watching from the windows.

He extended the pistol to me. "She's already loaded."

I took a careful step closer and picked up the gun. Its weight felt unnatural in my hand. "It's remarkably heavy," I said, surprised as I stared at the pistol. The hammer atop the firing mechanism was carved to look like the head of an eagle, the powerful beak clamped tightly around the nub of flint.

"It's a new model," the gamesman said. "Don't know that we'll keep it round long, owing to some of the trouble we've heard about with it."

"Trouble?" I asked.

He nodded. "It's a little tricky. So long as you pay attention, and can aim true, it tends to find its mark. But if you leave it at full cock for any time at all, it's as likely to explode in your hand as it is to shoot where you aim."

"Oh, dear," I said, moving to return it to him.

"It's all right. Not even cocked yet." He moved closer and placed his hand over mine on the grip.

His thumb pulled back the ornate metal mechanism atop the pistol. It clicked once. "That's half-cock there," he said. "When I pull it all the way up to full, point at the target and pull the trigger with your finger. Problem comes when a body hesitates, and the powder has enough time to slip back in the chamber. Then the charge doesn't carry the ball forward."

"What happens when the ball doesn't go forward?"

He hesitated. "It has to go somewhere. Most often the pistol sort of explodes."

"Perhaps—"

Click. "There's full. Just don't wait too long, and don't shut your eyes."

I had no time to think. I pointed the barrel at Napoleon's face, straightened my arm, and squeezed gently on the curved metal trigger.

The noise was deafening, the flash of powder as it ignited blinding, the smoke suffocating. And the force of the shot threw me back several steps before I regained my balance.

"Nice and quick, miss," said the gamesman, his hand recovering the pistol from mine.

His voice sounded far away, accompanied by a ringing

in my ears. "Shall we go down and see if you've got him?"

I nodded weakly and followed him the length of the garden. What awaited shocked us both.

There was a new mark on the target. A mark through the French tyrant's left eye.

The gamesman whistled low. "We'd better not tell your mother about that, had we?"

I shook my head. "Perhaps not."

"Who's that wasting my ammunition?" Showalter shouted from the steps, smiling as he descended.

The gamesman and I exchanged a glance as my host jogged to our sides. I spoke before he could.

"This gentleman obliged me with a demonstration," I said. "So the fault is my own."

Showalter studied the target. "No fault in *that*," he said, fingering the sixpence-size hole in the paper. "Adams is the best shot in London. That's why I hired him."

The gamesman merely smiled, nodded, and looked at me. "You're too kind," he said, peeling away to head back up the hill to reload.

Chapter Nineteen

⤶

Mother's tirade that afternoon was legendary. She was so incensed that she ordered Clarisse to bring me supper in my room, requesting that I remain confined there for the rest of the evening in order that I might recover something of the sensible, respectable girl she believed me to be. I was barred even from attending Lady Kensington's card party with her for fear of what fool thing I might say next. She left me cowed in my room, framing excuses for my absence before she even reached the hallway.

She had no way of knowing how welcome her punishment was.

Mother's carriage pulled away that evening with Aunt Rachel beside her to take my place at cards. I watched them go, Caedmon's face drifting back into my mind, along with the expression of misery he'd worn when I stormed out of the exhibit hall. I'd wanted to provoke a reaction, wanted to believe he felt as anguished as I had at my being there with someone else. But as soon as I had, as soon as I realized I had injured him, I wanted to take it all back.

Still, despite my exhaustion, despite how badly I'd behaved at the museum, despite how difficult my reunion with Caedmon would prove this evening, I had to make the most of my opportunity.

Clarisse appeared at the door as Mother's carriage left the drive.

"She is quite upset with you, mademoiselle," she teased. "If she only knew . . ."

If *Clarisse* only knew.

"But at last I can hear your tale without fear of her interruption." She settled beside me and looked at me eagerly.

"I'm sorry, Clarisse," I said, "but I have to hurry."

She looked confused. "You go to him?" she asked. "Tonight?"

I nodded. "Though not for the reasons you might imagine."

She studied my expression, must have seen what looked like heartbreak there. "What has happened?" she begged.

I shook my head. What had happened? A pretend love affair already undone? It hardly seemed reasonable to feel so upset. But I was afraid if I let spill the story—or some sham version of it to pacify Clarisse—I would not be able to avoid very real tears.

"I cannot explain," I said simply, "not now. But I must go and see if I can make things right."

She hesitated, desperate for more details, but finally she

stood and kissed the top of my head. "I will do what I can to keep your mother from looking in upon her return," she said.

"Thank you," I said quietly.

She nodded. "Don't worry," she said. "Doesn't your A Lady say something about lovers' quarrels in *Pride and Prejudice*? 'Next to being married, a girl likes to be crossed in love a little now and then.'" She cocked her head. "Did I get it right?"

"Perfect," I said.

"It all makes it come out sweeter in the end," she said. "You'll see."

"Thank you, Clarisse," I said. She gave a quick curtsy and sailed out of the room.

I stared at the closed door for several minutes, still not eager to face Caedmon. I laid down on the bed sideways, hugged my knees to my chest and wondered if he could forgive me.

I hadn't meant to fall asleep, and woke in a panic a few hours later, the house quiet around me. Worried I'd given Caedmon even more reason to be upset with me (and aware that Mother and Aunt Rachel would be home soon from the card party), I hastened out of my room and into my brother's, dressing once again in his clothes.

By the time I'd hired a cab, I was feeling so rushed that I ordered him to take me directly to the museum, rather than the circuitous route I'd favored to avoid being followed. Along the way, I convinced myself that Caedmon and I had too much to do, faced risks too great to allow anything to distract us. He wouldn't let his irritation with me for my earlier behavior stand in our way. And I wouldn't let my silly hopes for his affections, or my futile wonderings about what lay ahead for us enter into our partnership. I knew he would agree, would allow us to once again find the proper balance in the partnership we'd established.

Because what lay ahead for us was of no consequence compared to what might lay ahead for the world if Napoleon were not defeated.

Caedmon was exactly where I expected to find him, hunched over the Stone, his chin in his hands.

"Miss Wilkins," he said, without looking to me.

"Good evening," I said, "or morning, I suppose."

Caedmon didn't even comment on my tardiness, and somehow this made it worse. I stood dumbly a few yards from where he worked at the Stone, his papers and a book I didn't recognize opened on its surface. He'd been here awhile.

"I am sorry for . . . this morning," I said.

He took a breath. "It was surprising," he said.

"That I came or who I came with?" I said, instantly forgetting my promise to myself to focus only on our task.

He shook his head. "That you provoked me," he said, "and that I let you."

"Please forgive me," I said. "I don't know what came over me."

"Showalter could have me sacked for less," he said.

"I'm sorry."

He hesitated. "He bluster like that all the time?"

I smiled. "Not all the time."

"Hmph," he said.

I started to explain, started to apologize, but found I really didn't want to.

"How is Deacon?" I asked instead.

"Same," he said quietly, explaining that he had looked in on his godfather before reporting to the museum this morning and that his neighbor had asked after me once again.

"I wish I could have gone with you. I hope my absence wasn't too keenly felt." I immediately regretted my choice of words. I hadn't been angling for him to declare that he missed me, but now that the phrase hung between us, I knew how it sounded.

"Always," he said simply, careful not to look at me. *Always?* I thought. Was there as much longing in the word for him as I wished I heard? Did he know it was hopeless, as I did? Or was it? If we could do what we'd done so far—evade Napoleon's spies, come close to finding an ancient hidden object—could we figure out some way to do the impossible again?

Caedmon's next words brought me back to reality. "I think I've found two more references to the ninth Ptolemy."

"Both in the hieroglyphs?"

He nodded. "Which supports the hypothesis that both the references and the glyphs were added at a much later date. If only the Stone were intact," he said, fingering the edge of the black rock above the broken jackal glyph.

"You really think it would have provided a clear location of the standard?"

Caedmon patted the Stone's surface the way Father did his favorite mare at our country estate. "I don't know. But I can't help feeling that it would have at least gotten us closer than it already has."

"What are these?" I pointed to the giant books he had stacked by his side, and what looked to be a leather-bound ledger beneath them.

"A hunch," he said. "I thought if I tried to focus on holdings related to Ptolemy the Ninth, then maybe something obvious would present itself. This book"—he tapped the open surface of the topmost volume—"is the most complete work we have on the Ptolemaic dynasties."

I examined the illustration on the page. "And this?" I asked, pointing to an engraving of a grand structure surrounded by pillars and pointed roofs.

"Ptolemy the Ninth's temple. A private expedition uncovered it several years ago. Most of his items we have came out of there."

I studied the architecture, surprised to find Greek again where it didn't seem to belong, this time as columns and porticos among the iconic pyramids. The artist had rendered it as it might have appeared thousands of years ago upon its completion, with its structures intact, altar swept clean, tiny figures scurrying about.

"Is this the entrance between these pillars?" I asked, pointing at a door between two massive columns.

He leaned in next to me and nodded. "Obelisks," he corrected, "like the one your mother asked after this morning. Like Showalter boasted of having."

I cringed at the mention of the morning fiasco.

"Tough things to move," Caedmon said. "We even tried to move these." He pointed at the illustration in the book. "There's a fellow in Egypt now named Bankes who's discovered a fine one weighing around six tons that he's managed to put on a ship. He's just waiting to sail home with it until after things calm down with Napoleon's return. I heard he's going to put it in his garden."

Garden. At the mention of the word, something clicked in my brain. I peered again at the picture. Beneath each obelisk was a massive base, twice as wide as the obelisk itself.

My heart began to race. "Did you say England tried to move these obelisks before?"

He nodded. "But we lost one of them at sea in a gale. The other broke off from its pedestal and into pieces when they tried to move it. They left the fragments behind, but did bring back a portion—"

"What part?"

"The base, I think."

"Where is it now?" I asked, my mind a tumble of thoughts.

He shook his head sadly. "I already checked. None of the pieces of those obelisks are in the museum."

"But what if it were one of the items on permanent loan to a patron? The message indicated that the standard was in the museum—"

He stopped, then snapped his fingers, his eyes now reflecting the fire I felt in my own. "And there's no reason an operative halfway round the world would know that several of the objects that are *supposed* to be in the museum are actually elsewhere!"

"But you can verify where it is now?" I had to be sure. . . .

He pushed back off the Stone and collected his candle. "There is another ledger for holdings outside the museum."

I followed him to the hallway, toward the patch of streetlight that fell through the office door window. I started to tell him what I thought I knew, that I might have seen that very obelisk, but halfway there, an unexpected sound stopped cold the blood that had begun to race in my veins.

An urn or some pot clattered to the floor in the darkness, perhaps twenty feet from where we stood. Caedmon and I froze. And though I could not see his face where we stood—on an island of darkness between the glow cast by his candles on the Stone and the light from the office window—I felt Caedmon's body tense next to mine.

Once again, we were not alone.

Chapter Twenty

Caedmon reached out and grabbed a long, crooked staff from the stand at the end of the shelf.

"Wait here," he whispered so silently it was almost like he forgot to give the words breath. A second later he was gone, and I stood, frozen in the darkness, the only light I could see glinting from the gilt eyes of a dozen Isis idols on the shelf. I knew his leaving me had less to do with chivalry and more to do with the fact that I'd surely stumble over something and give our position away. So I strained to listen for Caedmon's certain footfalls or any other sounds that might reveal the location of our intruder.

It seemed hours passed before I heard the scraping of a tinderbox and smelled the unmistakable scent of brimstone catching fire on the end of a match. When the flame flared, the scene it revealed terrified me.

Caedmon stood a few feet away from the point of a mean little dagger, poised in the hand of the man who held the match. I knew the profile instantly.

"Where's your *fella*?" Tanner asked, his sneer unmistakable.

"Who are you?" Caedmon asked, holding the crooked pole higher.

"Asked you first," he said. "Where is she?"

"I don't know what you're talking about. I'm here alone," Caedmon said.

"Bollocks. Followed her, straight here. She's getting careless," he said.

"She ran when we heard you," Caedmon said, though even as he spoke, I was edging closer.

"She'll be easy enough to round up. You're the one I don't know about," Tanner said. "Didn't figure she'd be so smart as to find all the help she has on this. And now I suppose you've a bit of information and a key I'm in need of."

A key? The note had mentioned the key. Caedmon and I had assumed the message was referring to the standard being the key to victory in the battle. We were to have found something else?

"I don't know anything," Caedmon said. "It's true we've been trying to figure out what that note means, but we haven't come up with anything."

"A body doesn't visit Miles Deacon without getting a few questions answered," Tanner said, grinning.

My mouth fell open. Caedmon's eyes grew wide. "What do you know about Deacon?"

"Miss Wilkins's carriage driver gave her up when I asked

him a few questions. Servants won't tell their masters what's what, but we learn a lot from each other. And anybody who knows anything about the craft knows Deacon's still lurking about the Tower."

"You're the bastard who banged him up," Caedmon seethed. I couldn't be sure, but I thought he could see me as I edged toward them. I stood next to the wooden puzzle box sarcophagus; Caedmon was opposite me, about eight feet away, and Tanner was between us.

Tanner nodded. "For all the good it did me," he said. "Deacon's seen my methods before. But I don't think you're made of as strong a stuff. I think you'll be telling me everything we need right quick." The match in his hand sputtered, and all was dark again. I realized at once that this might be our only chance.

"Caedmon! The box!" I shouted, hoping Tanner would turn at the sound of my voice, that Caedmon would have the presence of mind to know which box I spoke of. I reached for the wooden casket, grabbing the open lid in both hands.

Caedmon grunted as he lunged forward. I heard the sound of his staff swinging out and prayed it hit its mark. Something metal—the dagger, I hoped—clattered on the wooden floor. There was a crash of bodies tumbling toward me, and then I heard the weight of one of them fall into the coffin, followed by Caedmon shouting, "Close it!"

I slammed the lid home with as much force as I could

muster before the box's new occupant could realize what had happened. It clicked into place.

"Caedmon?" I said, my voice shrill with fear and hope.

"I'm here," he said, clearly in front of me.

From the inside of the box, Tanner began thumping wildly. "What the devil!" he shouted. The sarcophagus was still upright, but began to rock side to side with Tanner's flailing inside.

"Help me lower it afore it goes topsy-turvy and shatters," Caedmon ordered. I groped blindly at the edges and hugged the box. We gently lowered it to the floor as curses and oaths flew from within.

Caedmon seized my hand. "Stay close," he said, leading me expertly through the darkness toward the office.

He shoved open the door, fumbled with a tinderbox, and lit another candle. He looked at me.

"You realize what this means, don't you?" I asked him.

"That I'm likely to be sacked for using a priceless artifact to contain a dangerous criminal?"

"Apart from that," I said. "We know who the burglar is! Who was meant to receive the message originally. It means we're safe."

"Agnes, I have no idea how long that box will hold. And anyway, you reckoned we were safe when your room was tossed and the jackal's head was with me," Caedmon pointed out.

I paused, humbled. "Then Tanner knew from the beginning that I was up to something."

"Besides . . ." Caedmon hesitated a moment, thinking. "He said 'we'! He said 'you'll be telling me everything *we* need.'"

"He has an accomplice," I said, realizing he was right.

"Probably. And the only thing we can hope to do is move faster than whoever it is. And hope that he's not here with Tanner now." He pulled me into the office and shut the door behind us.

There were four desks, one pushed up against each corner of the room. Caedmon bolted for the one closest to the door and set his candle down. The surface was piled with papers. He looked sideways at me, seeming to note the mess all at once.

"I've not been back here all day," he said. "Banehart'll skin me for being late with his transcriptions, but—" He stopped abruptly and looked down at the desktop as he pulled down a large red leather-bound volume from a nearby shelf. He dropped the book when a plain brown envelope bearing his name scrawled in wild script caught his eye. He snatched it up. "That's Deacon's hand!"

He broke the seal, read quickly, and looked to me. "Deacon's awake," he said, eyes shining.

I glanced down at the note, saw that it bore today's date and read simply, *Come at once.*

"We have to go," Caedmon said, bolting for the door, both the note and the ledger in his hand.

I held the candle aloft so he could see, and struggled to keep pace as we hurried toward the back entrance.

He flipped through the ledger furiously, scanning down each carefully written column of lot numbers and descriptions.

"Here!" he said, pulling at my wrist to bring the light closer. "Lot 11987—obelisk pedestal from Ptolemy the Ninth temple. It's in London still!"

"Is there a name?" I asked, but I knew. I *knew.*

He shook his head. "No. But there is an address," he said as we barreled down the stairs and wove our way back through the crates of books.

"Park Garden Circle?" I asked.

"Number sixteen. How did you—," he began, pausing before we stepped outside. He lifted his eyes to meet mine. "No . . ."

I felt my skin chill and prickle at the confirmation of my suspicions. "Yes," I said, nodding. "The obelisk base is at Lord Showalter's house."

Chapter Twenty-one

❧

Despite the urgency, despite finally perhaps knowing where the standard was, we went to Deacon. I told myself that it was so he could advise us. But in truth I was as eager as Caedmon to see that he was well. Still, we had to hurry—if Tanner somehow managed to get free of that sarcophagus, he'd alert his accomplice. Worse yet, he might make straight for Showalter's, catching us again even if he didn't know to look for the standard there.

The front doors of the hospital were shut tight, the lamps all dark. There was no one to admit us as before. "Driver," I called up, "take us around back." We found a woman in a gray dress wrestling a sizable urn of milk over the threshold of the servants' entrance.

"Perfect," I whispered as we quickly disembarked.

"How do you figure?" Caedmon asked.

"Go and help her," I ordered.

He started to protest before he got my intent, and trotted over. I followed at his heel.

"Here, let me," he said, reaching for the urn. The woman looked up, revealing that she was in fact probably a year or two my senior, and despite her plain dress and calloused hands, she was unaccountably pretty. Wisps of blond escaped from beneath the wrap of muslin that kept her hair bound up on top of her head. Her blue eyes were as lovely as the tiny mouth that opened in a surprised O at the arrival of this strapping young man come to carry her burden for her. The delight in those eyes at seeing how handsome that young man was irked me more than I could say.

She stepped aside as Caedmon hefted the urn to his chest. He even managed to smile a little in return. He stood dumbly for a moment, looking at her, before she realized he was await-ing instruction.

"Oh! Through here!" She returned to life and ushered us into the kitchen. Caedmon deposited the urn on the floor in front of a table where she'd already laid out small stone pitchers for creaming tea.

"You're like angels, the pair of you," she said. "Dora took ill and I'm left to get the breakfast ready and up by myself."

I elbowed Caedmon, hoped he'd realize he needed to offer to help her. He did so, but with all the conviction of a bad actor in a melodrama.

"I couldn't dream of it," she said, not even thinking that we had appeared on her doorstep for any other reason than to help her with her chores.

"Do it," I whispered to Caedmon, this time perhaps too loudly, as the kitchen maid shot me a curious glance.

"I'm Molly," she said brightly.

I nudged Caedmon hard in the ribs a second time. "Caedmon," he said with a slight bow, "and this is my . . . brother, August."

"Right regal names those are," she said, eyes wide. Caedmon settled onto the stool next to hers and tugged the lid from the urn. She peppered him with questions, punctuated with furious bouts of batting her long eyelashes, as he told her we'd come early to visit our father in the ward before we headed off to our work at the docks. At some point I circled around behind her to fetch a towel when the milk she'd been ladling into one of the pitchers missed its mark because she refused to take her eyes from Caedmon. She noticed neither the spill nor my movement. I caught Caedmon's eye as I edged toward the door. He seemed to squint a bit at me—the only communication I received that he was annoyed at not having been consulted regarding the plan.

I touched my cap at him, slipped out the door, and fairly flew up the stairs.

I found the ward without trouble, most of its occupants still sleeping. I crossed quickly to Deacon's bed and noticed with relief that his neighbor who'd seen through my poor attempt at a disguise a few nights ago was sleeping with his face toward the wall.

I knelt beside the cot. "Deacon," I whispered, nudging his shoulder lightly through the sheet.

His eyes opened immediately, but he turned his head gingerly to meet mine.

"You," he said, smiling. "Jackson was right. You do make a poor boy."

I smiled. "Then we're lucky Molly had a far better specimen to serve as distraction."

He looked confused for a moment, but then relief washed over his expression. "Caedmon is with you? He's all right?"

I assured him Caedmon was fine, that we'd both escaped Tanner unscathed.

"But what of your father?"

"He's been away," I said, conveniently leaving out the part about how I'd elected not to tell him when I had the opportunity. "He returns this evening." I didn't want to rile Deacon, even if he was lying injured in bed. And there was nothing to gain by telling him now.

"Listen to me," he said, pushing up on one elbow, wincing, and looking round the ward to make sure no one was listening. "You must go to the authorities with this. If Napoleon's agents find the standard—"

"We've already found it, Deacon," I said, in as low a voice as I could manage.

"You—" He looked confused. "Caedmon?"

I nodded, then told him of our work thus far.

"Oh dear," he said. "Never did I think it would all come to this. I meant to secure some help for you both. Some protection."

"Protection? But how?"

He sighed and sank back on the pillow. "I hide things about myself a sight better than you."

"You know my father by more than his reputation, don't you?" I whispered.

He nodded. "He stood by me when that damned business about the assassination went awry. But the higher-ups were looking for someone to blame, and I wouldn't give up the names of my contacts, so . . ."

"You were dismissed."

"It was time anyway. I'd had enough. But then you two stumbled into my rooms and laid this on me," he said. "I was on my way to consult some men I knew I could trust when Tanner turned up."

I could hear cart and horse traffic increasing on the streets below as London roused itself from sleep. A few of the men around us began to shift.

"Will you be all right?" I asked him.

"Just a couple broken ribs and a nasty headache . . . nothing I've not dealt with before. But I'm safer in here than you are out there."

"We'll be careful," I said.

"Doesn't matter how careful you are," he replied sternly.

"There are very dangerous people about who clearly have had an eye on you two for a while. You must give me time to arrange for assistance."

"Any delay could give the French the time they need to get the standard. We must go now," I said gently.

"But you're not trained for any of this!" he said.

"We've managed," I assured him. "And the worst of it is over, surely."

He sank back on the pillow. "Tell me your plan."

I explained what we thought we'd learned, and about our planned errand to Showalter's estate. "We'll approach from the stream behind the house. The garden is dense there, and there are a series of paths leading to the pedestal—"

Deacon gripped my forearm, his face as grave as I'd ever seen it. "If you find it, what then?"

"Father returns this afternoon. Will he know what to do with it?"

"The things your father knows might surprise even you, Miss Wilkins," Deacon said. "Now go! Send word if you can. I'll try and rouse some support if I can get a message out."

I nodded, shifted my weight from my knees to my toes, and prepared to creep away. "I'm relieved to know you're well."

"I'm relieved to know you're on our side." He winked. "What those Frog spies would do with a prize like you . . ."

I squeezed his hand in gratitude for his praise and crouched to kiss his forehead. I gave him one last look before I turned to rejoin Caedmon, who I hoped hadn't fallen entirely for the milkmaid yet.

I burst into the kitchen and grabbed Caedmon by the sleeve as Molly was offering to let him stir the porridge burning on the stove.

"Good-bye!" Caedmon shouted as I dragged him back over the threshold and to the waiting carriage.

"Nice visit?" I asked.

"How is Deacon?"

I assured him that Deacon was fine, that he understood our situation, that he would get what help he could for us when he was able. We climbed back into the carriage, and Caedmon ordered the driver to ferry us to Hyde Park. The gray light of dawn gradually brightened as we drove across town, shop-keepers and servants already bustling about as we made our way toward the Park. It was nearly five when we left the carriage and disappeared into the tangled hedge, bearing toward the river and Showalter's gardens.

We hurried across a footbridge, coming out a hundred yards east of where I knew the path leading to the cultivated part of Showalter's garden ended at the river.

"Won't there be gardeners watering in the early hours?" Caedmon asked as we picked our way through a bramble toward the path.

I nodded. "But only closer to the main house. This part of the garden is mostly left to grow wild."

"And then?" he asked.

"We'll get the standard from there to my house and to Father," I said, adding, "somehow."

He hesitated. "And then?"

I tilted my head and looked at him. "If you're worried that I won't honor my agreement to recommend you to Father—"

"No," he said quickly. "I'm far more worried about what happens when we have no more reason to see each other."

My mouth fell open. Somehow I managed to speak. "Caedmon—"

He shook his head and seized my hand. "I . . . I could work in obscurity for the rest of my life if it meant I had some hope of seeing you now and then."

He did care for me. He really did. My relief at this news was so complete that I felt my shoulders relax, as if I'd let go a breath I'd been holding for a very long time. The old worries tried to crowd in, that he was an unsuitable match, that Mother wouldn't stand for it, that I would be breaking Showalter's heart . . . but they all withered in the glorious, searing knowledge that Caedmon cared for me. Perhaps even *loved* me as hopelessly as I did him.

But I would have to wait to find out.

"This really isn't the time," I said, mustering all the resolve I could.

"There is no other time! We're about to either save England or hasten its fall to France. Either way, I'll be dished up for cavorting about with the most marvelous girl I've ever known in the garden of the man who aims to marry her," he said.

Marvelous?

"No one's seen us," I insisted.

"But the story will come out. There's a man in a box back at the museum who'll be needing explanation. How willing do you think he'll be to keep mum about who put him there?"

"We'll think of something," I said, realizing I was talking about more than just Tanner in that box. I was talking about us. We would think of something, wouldn't we? But one thing I knew with certainty: I couldn't marry Showalter. Never.

He studied me, as if he wanted to say more, do more. He lifted my hand and kissed it delicately. "In the event that we don't," he said, almost sadly, "at least I'll have done that."

I felt the kiss linger there on the back of my hand, felt it travel up my arm and lodge itself in my heart like a promise.

Chapter Twenty-two

❧

I still clutched Caedmon's hand as we hurried on, the light of surprise intensifying with each step. I strained to listen for sounds of anyone deep in the garden at this early hour. All seemed quiet. The house was nearly invisible; only the three chimneys rose above the taller hedges, where the wilder part of the grounds gave over to the manicured paths and tidy rows of cowslips.

"There!" Caedmon whispered, pointing to the azure gazing ball in the small garden plaza. This time there was no red-coated waiter hiding in the brush.

I watched our distorted reflections in the surface of the ball as we approached; dew still clung like a veil to its surface.

In the daylight, I could see clearly that the gazing ball was a recent addition, affixed to a platform of some sort whose base had been anchored to the surface of the pedestal. I tried to imagine a forty-foot obelisk of granite rising past the treetops in its place.

"The hieroglyphs are oversize in proportion to the stone," Caedmon said, slipping into scholar mode as he traced the shape of one symbol. "I wonder if the companion base was marked similarly? Or if the obelisks themselves carried the same large characters."

As much as I loved the sound of his voice and the murmur of his thoughts coming unfiltered into the air, we had no time to waste. "Caedmon, suspend your rehearsal of your speech to the academy for a moment and tell me what to look for!"

He snapped back, "Some way to crack it, I reckon."

"Have you ever seen one open before?" I asked. He shook his head. "Perhaps it's like your puzzle box sarcophagus?"

"Then there should be some loose bit of stone," he said, as he leaned against its surface, both palms flat against the carved stone. I followed his example, pushing and leaning and shifting my way around the upper portions.

Nothing budged. I then ran my fingers along the edges, looking for a grip or handhold.

"There must be some way to open it," I said.

"Unless we're wrong," Caedmon pointed out.

"No. This fits too well. And it's our only possibility. It *must* be here," I insisted.

"If we're right," Caedmon began carefully, not meeting my eye, "then it's likely to mean Showalter is somehow involved."

I straightened. "What?"

Caedmon looked at me. "It's in *his* garden, Agnes," he said.

"You got the jackal's head at *his* party . . . you have to credit that it's a bit too neat to ignore."

I shook my head. "Impossible," I said. "We've known him for years."

He hesitated. "You don't want it to be him."

I stopped and let my gaze rest on the glyphs. I *didn't* want it to be him. But not for the reasons Caedmon thought. It was too difficult to think of how I'd deceived him already, how I would soon wound him with my rejection of his affection. I could not think him traitor and add insult to the injury.

But no matter what I thought, it simply wasn't possible.

"It won't matter what I want if we don't find it," I said. "But you're wrong. Showalter is many things, yet I know him well enough to say that he is no traitor."

Caedmon looked for a second as if he might argue. He set his jaw tightly. Sucked in on the inside of one of his cheeks. He breathed out sharply through his nose and sat forward, eyes once again on the pedestal base.

"What did the message say again?" Caedmon asked.

I'd mused on the message so many times it was becoming as familiar to me as an A Lady quote. "'W's standard in the Great London Pyramid. This is the key. Emperor advised and awaiting delivery.'"

"Damned puzzle," Caedmon muttered.

"Wait!" I said quietly, remembering my syntax and translation. "We've been assuming that the sender's hasty reference to the key meant that the standard itself and its location was essential to Napoleon. I supposed they meant it in the causal sense of the word. That 'key' meant necessary. But what if I misinterpreted . . ."

"Meaning 'This is the key' literally refers to—"

"The jackal's head!" I finished.

Caedmon couldn't speak fast enough. "That's what Tanner said back at the museum—that we had some key he was in want of!" He pulled a long leather cord from around his neck, tugging it out of his shirt. At the end, the jackal's head emerged with the scrap of linen still gamely hanging on.

"It must actually fit inside one of the glyphs." My voice had fallen to a whisper. The sun was warm on the back of my neck now. I was suddenly keenly aware that we were losing time.

"*That's* why they're sized this way," Caedmon said. "*Extraordinary.*"

We redoubled our efforts, now searching with eyes instead of hands. It didn't take long.

"Here!" I shouted as I rounded the back.

Caedmon scrambled over to where I crouched. At the corner of the pillar, half-hidden by a geranium planted at the base, sat a perfect carved version of the metalwork bauble that had started this whole affair.

We stared at it a moment longer, seeing now what we were sure must have been the twin of that broken glyph on the upper corner of the Rosetta Stone. Ptolemy, or whoever had hidden the standard, hadn't meant for it to be lost forever.

Caedmon fumbled with the knot he'd tied to the iron and freed the key from its tether, then hastily unbound it from the scrap containing the message. "Ladies first?"

"I think in the interest of science, you'd be the better choice," I said. "Besides, it's likely to try and bite your hand off or something dreadful, and I'd sooner that be you than me."

Caedmon took a deep breath and exhaled slowly. He repositioned his hold on the jackal's head so that the tips of his fingers barely grasped the edges. His shoulders straightened and his mouth set as he aligned the edges with the carved glyph. "For England," he said quietly.

"God save the king," I whispered, the last words drowned as the key disappeared inside the slot and a series of clicks and rumblings began to emanate from deep within the stone. The entire slab hummed like a beehive, the tone reverberating into the earth beneath us, tickling the soles of my feet through my shoes.

Caedmon gaped as a seam appeared in the surface of the rock. It had appeared to be an imperfection before, a faint, shimmering vein of mica like a ribbon of river on a map. But now the shape seemed to take the force of the vibration and tear. With a crack too loud for the quiet morning, the seam split wide, connecting itself to two other seams, forming a crude triangle perhaps a foot long on each side. As soon as the triangle appeared, it broke free from the surrounding granite and dropped inside the pedestal base. The shaking stopped as a cloud of dust rose—a cloud that impossibly carried the scent of sandalwood and earth and oil. The scent of an Egypt from two thousand years ago. I felt light-headed all of a sudden, to think that the last eyes to have seen what we looked at now belonged to those who'd hidden the standard here, knowing that some-day, someone would find it.

"This must be what it feels like to be at the opening of a tomb," I whispered.

Caedmon finally recovered his wits. "I should think this even better. There are many tombs, but that," he said, pointing through the settling cloud of dust into the pedestal, "is entirely unique."

The rising sun illuminated the interior of the base. Though the walls were easily three or four inches thick, the inside was hollow, like the trunk of a giant old tree, rotted out by time. The fallen triangle of stone that had been the hidden door now lay against a smaller stone pillar inside.

Atop this pillar sat the standard.

It looked remarkably like the illustration in Deacon's book. A human figure with a jackal's head sat on an austere throne. The jackal's feet and the legs of the throne melted into a narrow base about a foot long. Thin leather cords wrapped over the ends kept it upright on its stone perch.

"Remarkable," Caedmon whispered. "I really do wish I could write up some proper field notes."

I stared at him. "The scientific community will be forgiving in light of the circumstances." I reached out tentatively to retrieve the standard. When nothing roared or sank its fangs into my wrist, I reached a little farther until my fingers closed around it. "Help me with the lashing," I said.

Caedmon pulled the laces from the ends, and the standard came free in my hand.

Its weight was surprising. I drew it out, angling it through the triangular opening and into the sunshine, where the light glinted faintly off the bronze patina. Caedmon took it carefully from my hands, smiling at it as if it were a lovely toy.

"We did it," he whispered, looking up to meet my eyes.

"Almost," I said. "Let's celebrate after we've delivered it to more secure hands."

Caedmon stood, tucked the standard into the back of his waistband, and pulled me to my feet. I glanced quickly over my shoulder to make sure no one had heard the commotion. It seemed we'd make it after all.

But then the unthinkable happened.

Lord Showalter stepped from the undergrowth beside the path a few yards ahead of us.

"You there! What are you doing on my lands?"

Neither Caedmon nor I spoke. Showalter advanced on us. His boots were wet with the morning dew, his simple white shirt falling open at the collar. I'd never seen him so informally attired, and somehow it made me like him a bit more. I'd never even pictured him in anything but his buttoned-up shirt and vest, coat and hat brushed to perfection. But seeing him this way, as if he'd dressed quickly for a jaunt in the garden, made him more human. And made what I knew I must do later—put an end to his pursuit of me—even more difficult.

"Explain yourselves," he said, drawing within a few feet of where we stood and stopping abruptly. *"Miss Wilkins?"*

I sighed. Nodded. "Lord Showalter."

"Why are you dressed so?" he demanded of me, sounding almost stricken. Then he shook his head and turned to Caedmon. "Step away from this girl. I don't know what you are playing at, but I doubt any explanation could satisfy."

"Wait," I said. "He's a friend. And while you are quite correct in assuming that explaining these circumstances would require both a great portion of your morning and also a certain suspension of disbelief, we haven't the luxury of either at present."

"I demand to know what's going on!" he said, and turned to Caedmon again. "Move away from her!"

"Lord Showalter!" I took a step toward him. "We have no time to explain, but please believe me when I tell you that we've recovered an object of great importance and must deliver it to my father at once."

"Object?"

"Please, sir. I cannot tell you more. In truth, neither of us should know anything about this, and I'll speak to you at length about it sometime soon, but for now—"

"Perhaps you should give it to me," he said.

I felt Caedmon tense beside me.

"It's very important that we take it directly to my father."

"But your presence here must mean you found it in my garden? Surely I've a right to know what's being removed from my lands. And I've no reason to trust an apparent rogue who has been sneaking about with an impressionable young woman."

"I beg you, Lord Showalter. Only let us pass and I will explain all."

He studied me, face softening, shoulders relaxing slightly. "Agnes, you can trust me. I've all but made an offer for you. Are secrets like these any way to begin a courtship? Now be sensible and give me the standard to convey to—"

I staggered a step backward. "What did you say?"

"Agnes," Caedmon whispered, his hand on my arm.

Showalter didn't answer, but his eyes narrowed, and his mouth gave a twitch.

Could it be? "I—"

"He awake, Agnes," Caedmon said. "The only way he could know about the standard—"

"No," I said, taking another step back. It couldn't be. My father trusted him. Mother adored him. Rupert envied him, and the entire time he was pretending?

Showalter gave a tired shake of his head. His arm reached to his own waistband.

"Run!" Caedmon hissed, but he didn't move. Nor did I. It was hypnotic watching Showalter transform before me. The scales fell from my eyes as his expression altered, as if the very air around him had changed into something more malevolent and sinister.

He was not who I thought he was.

And all at once I understood what a fool I was. My head spun as I recalled how smug I'd been earlier at how easy it had been to fall into such a *fortunate* match. Pathetic for not having seen him for what he really was, for having defended him to Caedmon time and again. For having worried that I might hurt him in any way.

Because the man who stood before me now appeared incapable of being hurt. His stony expression was so foreign to me, so distant, that I might not have recognized the face that bore it in a crowd. He was someone else entirely, but he was suddenly entirely himself.

And the pistol in his left hand—every bit as alien on his person as the strange look in his cool gray eyes—was leveled squarely at my heart.

"No one runs," he said calmly, the hammer clicking open to half-cock.

Chapter Twenty-three

❧

"This is beyond all," I whispered, staring at Showalter as he closed in on us, pistol now trained on the space between Caedmon and me.

Showalter laughed, a knowing laugh I'd not heard before. "After all your deceptions the last few weeks, you stand there now attired in men's clothing and think that I'm as simple as you've always believed?"

It seemed the earth began to tremble beneath my feet as it had a few minutes ago when we'd opened the pedestal. I couldn't speak.

When Showalter saw my confusion, he laughed anew, edging a step closer. "*Wonderful*. So self-absorbed that you think you are the only one capable of some deception? I always thought you pretentious, but this is more than I even realized—"

"Speak plainly, sir," Caedmon said, an edge in his voice at Showalter's insult.

"Plainly?" Showalter repeated. "If I must. That bit of bronze

I saw you take from that pedestal is what I was sent here to await some five years ago."

"Sent here?" I asked. "Then that means you're in the employ of—"

"Good God, are you that dense? The emperor, Napoleon Bonaparte, yes. They thought of pulling me from the field during the last exile, but felt it in France's interests that I maintain my position."

"You're a spy!" I whispered, feeling suddenly as if I needed to sit down.

His gaze was cold. "Of course I'm a spy."

He had known the message would be in the body, had been expecting it. Deacon was right—the import of antiquities had been the perfect means for the French to smuggle information into London.

"You're—you're—a traitor!" I sputtered.

He laughed. "Again, you oversimplify me, Miss Wilkins. To be a traitor, one must have at one point held allegiance to the country in question. I was never such a man. Lord Showalter is a fiction, my past invented prior to my arrival here. Before taking up residence in your neighborhood, I served the Republic in Spain."

"But—but you're—" I found I couldn't settle on a word awful enough for what he really was.

"I'm what?" He edged closer. "I'm Showalter? The silly man with a taste for fine Egyptian antiquities? Your would-be fiancé?

I'm sorry to disappoint you, but I'm neither of those things. I'm simply very good at my job."

"A job that included pursuing me?" I asked, overcoming my shock to experience another emotion: indignation.

"Vile, isn't it? But it couldn't be helped. Even your precious A Lady was right about one thing. What's that first line of the one you like so much? Something about a man of good fortune needing a wife? Seems it wouldn't do for a man of my means and character to continue on as a bachelor."

The story began to take shape in my mind. Showalter had been ordered to court me. And he would have required as long an engagement as possible. During such a courtship, he'd have ready excuse to be in our home, ready means to keep track of Father's work, his sensitive conversations. If a girl with no formal training could glean as much as I had about Father's work, how much more could a trained spy make of such an opportunity?

"It was Father you were after," I said, simultaneously relieved and insulted. "You didn't feel anything for me at all."

He laughed, the sound cruel and sharp. "Irritation, mainly. You seemed so tolerant of my attentions, thought yourself so much better than me. It is the price I pay for performing my duty so well—I've never enjoyed appreciation from my audience for my work."

"That must be very hard for one whose ego is so prodigious," I said.

He smiled. "Oh, my dear girl. I was to be rewarded by my superiors if I did have to go through with the match." He arched an eyebrow. "They intended to make me a widower within the first few months of our marriage. I believe they planned your untimely end on the Continent during our honeymoon."

"You bastardly liar!" Caedmon roared, half lunging for him before Showalter straightened his arm and made ready to fire.

"*I'm* a liar? What of Agnes, then?" His eyes darted back to my face. "Pretending to be someone else for all these days. Pretending you didn't take that message and my key from the wrappings that night, manufacturing stories so you could slip off and consort with this." Here he gestured dismissively at Caedmon. "Truly, if I were who I pretended to be, this dalliance would be an insult I could not abide."

"You are not the only one who's suffered insult," I said.

"Of course not. I'm just the one for whom it doesn't matter. But nothing will matter in a few days' time. I'll deliver the standard to the emperor, his armies will enjoy certain and swift victory, and then perhaps one will finally be able to find a decent glass of wine in this swamp of a city. . . ."

I stared at him, but his words were just noise as a thought struck me. He was enjoying this. It was clear that finally unveiling himself to me, finally unmasking his intentions, was satisfying in some way. It infuriated me to think of him toying with me, with us, even to the last.

And if he was enjoying it, it meant that at least one small part of his personality hadn't been manufactured for the purposes of playing Lord Showalter.

The man—whatever he was really called—did love to hear himself natter on. Did love to bluster, as Caedmon had pointed out, and did love an audience, even if the audience was one he intended to shoot in due course.

Perhaps I could keep him prattling long enough to engineer an escape.

"But there are no instructions on how to use the standard," I heard Caedmon point out. "Boney just going to heave it up on a pole and hope for the best?"

"The emperor recovered a scroll covered with incantations and images of the standard years ago during his Egyptian campaign." Showalter's voice took on the tone of a lecturer delivering an address.

"But it can't work, can it?" I said. "Not as it is supposed to—ghost soldiers, an unbeatable king . . ."

He shook his head slowly. "Oh, it will work," he said. "I've seen things that defy description. It is real, this power that he seeks, and I am to be the man who delivers it to him."

If that was true, if Napoleon already had the means to awaken the standard . . . if it was all as real as it suddenly seemed it could be, then the standard really could decide the fate of England. We needed time, time to think, to figure out what to do next—

"But how did you know we'd be here?" I flung the words out as soon as they entered my mind.

He shrugged. "Serendipity, I suppose. Tanner was meant to have returned by now. I was about to dress to go out to look for him when I overheard one of the maids telling the housekeeper that she'd seen a pair of young men trespassing in the garden."

"You knew it was us?" I asked.

"I suspected. The servants were a bit surprised when I elected to see to the trouble myself, but they don't question me."

"Tanner's your man, then?" Caedmon asked.

"On the surface. It's far more a partnership. But for appearances' sake, it was imperative that he assume what in the eyes of the public was an appropriate role. Have you killed him, by the way?"

My mouth fell open. "Killed him?" The fact that he was so casual in asking about the death of Tanner was somehow more terrifying than the gun he held. He appeared to have no affection or concern for a man who'd apparently been his only confidant for five long years. And I realized that if that life meant so little to him, mine wasn't worth a farthing.

"Certainly not!" Caedmon said. "We trapped him."

He winced. "Pity for him. Our superiors will not be pleased to find he was bested by a pair of amateurs."

"How long have you known I had the key?" I asked.

"Almost since the night of the party."

"But who was the waiter? The dead man?"

He nodded. "Tanner recognized him as a British agent he'd tangled with in Prussia some years ago. Tanner couldn't let him report back, so he acted quickly."

"The waiter followed me when I took the key from the wrappings."

He gave an appreciative nod as if a final piece of the puzzle had just clicked into place. "I told Tanner we should have interrogated him, learned how he knew that I was receiving something in that mummy when I didn't. It would have saved us ever so much trouble if we'd been able to work out the location of the key sooner, but Tanner has a bit of bloodlust. And then he bunged it up even further when he loaded the body into a coach he thought was one of my spares."

"Then when you stopped the unwrapping," I asked, "that wasn't because the museum sent word?"

"Of course not. My contacts at the port have a signal—they have a particularly rare bottle of Scotch delivered a night or two in advance so that I know to be on the lookout for something extra in a shipment of goods. But the staff must have intercepted the bottle, mixed it in with the other provisions for the party that had been piling up all week. Tanner noticed it too late."

I was confused. Why hadn't he confronted me? Why had he let Deacon and Caedmon get involved? "You could have taken the key from me by force," I pointed out.

"A spy is nothing without his alias. If I revealed myself, or

Tanner himself, any further work in the positions we'd carved out would be jeopardized. No, it was far safer to follow and wait for you to find the standard for us. If we'd taken you and interrogated you, perhaps we could have found the key after a time, but this worked out far better in the long run. Mr. Stowe turned out to be unexpectedly helpful."

"You didn't know where the standard was?" Caedmon asked.

"Annoying, isn't it? If they knew it was in London, they certainly should have been able to tell me it was in my own bloody backyard," he said, "and then maybe your very promising career wouldn't have to be cut so short."

"How very careless of them," I muttered.

"Not really. They likely knew that as soon as I saw the key"—he nodded at the jackal's head in Caedmon's hand—"I'd immediately recognize what to do with it. We knew already that the standard had been hidden somewhere in Ptolemy the Ninth's temple, which is why we went to such trouble to get all those artifacts out of Egypt. We were sure we were on to something with those obelisks, but it never occurred to us that one might be hollow. But that's the way of these things," he said, shrugging. "Secrecy, codes, making do with what's at hand . . ."

"Don't you mean *who* is at hand?" I said. I couldn't tell if it was fear or rage that made my face grow hot and my blood boil under the surface of my skin. To have been used, exploited, and all the while he was looking forward to the way he might shed himself of the burden of me . . .

"You flatter yourself," he said. "But I must credit you for the find. So for that I—and the emperor—will be forever grateful. Of course forever for a pair in your position is a very, very short time." He aimed the gun at Caedmon's chest and pulled the hammer back to full cock. "Now, give me the standard."

Caedmon reached behind him and pulled the standard slowly into view. Showalter's eyes fixed on it.

But mine were on the pistol. For the first time, I saw the gun, saw the hollow eye of the carved eagle staring at me from down the length of the barrel.

It was the very one I'd shot that afternoon in his garden.

The very one with the nasty tendency to backfire.

"Caedmon, don't," I said, trying to remember exactly what the gamesman had said about how long it took for the powder and ball to slip back behind the flint. "He cannot shoot us. Even Lord Showalter won't be able to play stupid enough to explain away the corpses of his murdered neighbor and a stranger in his back garden."

"I won't have to. You're going to hand me the standard and walk down to the river. There, you'll tie each other's hands and jump in."

"Bollocks we will!" Caedmon shouted.

He sighed. "No. It's perfectly logical. And what a lovely, tragic, romantic story will emerge. Young Agnes Wilkins falls for her impoverished museum dustman, shuns her life of wealth and privilege as they seal their love in a suicide pact in the river.

You'll be the heroine of lovesick girls all over England," he said.

"And if we don't?" Caedmon asked.

"Then I'll kill you both where you stand. At a glance, it will look as if two thieves vandalized a priceless artifact on my property and then killed each other over it. Though I might have to stab you, Agnes, since I doubt you'll give me time to reload. At any rate, once investigators discover that one of the thieves is a parliamentarian's daughter in men's clothing, either the entire affair will be hushed away or explode into such a scandal that no one will know where truth begins and the stories end. Either way, I'll be free."

"Not free," Caedmon said. "Deacon, he knows—"

"Easy enough to remedy," Showalter said. "People die unexpectedly in those wretched public hospitals all the time. No one will even blink an eye at a washed-up old soldier."

He was a monster. I felt sick at the times he'd touched me, smiled at me, at how eager Mother had been to see me settled with him. Tears stung my eyes at the thought that this might be the end of things. That my life might end before it had even properly gotten its start.

But I was angry, too. Angry with myself for being taken in, for ever worrying that I might hurt Showalter, for dismissing Caedmon's suspicions. But something gave me even more reason to be furious: He presumed to write the end to my story . . . to manipulate the way the world remembered Agnes Wilkins.

But I had to keep a clear head. I had to keep him talking just a bit longer.

"Shall we, then?" He motioned toward the river, sounding as cordial as if he were inviting us to join him for a picnic at the water's edge.

"No," Caedmon said firmly.

I tore my eyes from Showalter and the gun and looked at Caedmon. "Step away from him, Agnes," he said evenly.

Showalter squared his shoulders and leveled the pistol at Caedmon's chest. "Stupid boy." He narrowed his eyes.

"He said himself he can't shoot us both," Caedmon reassured me. "One of us can run—maybe even keep him from getting his filthy hands on the standard."

Showalter smiled. "Clever, Mr. Stowe. You're right. This gun is handy for hiding in one's jacket pocket, but it has its limitations."

"Then neither of your plans will work," I whispered, backing a few steps away and toward the pedestal. I eyed the pistol. How long had it been?

He turned the gun toward me, and I froze. "But I do suspect Mr. Stowe has sufficient affection for you that any perceived peril to your life is motivation enough to do what I say," he said, moving toward me.

"Stop!" Caedmon called. Showalter kept the gun trained at my chest.

"Put the standard on the ground and take several steps back," he ordered.

"No," Caedmon said.

"Do it now or watch her die."

"Caedmon, don't. He'll kill us both anyway."

"You may be right," Showalter said evenly. "But there's always hope things will work out. Likely the same hope that let you"—here he turned to Caedmon—"believe a man of your status and prospects really might find the good fortune to fall in with a woman of Miss Wilkins's means. Hope that let you believe you might persuade her to forsake a suitable husband. I suspect you are the hoping kind, Mr. Stowe. All those lonely hours deciphering a stone that one of your superiors will likely steal the credit for. Hope is all you have. All you've ever had. Pity."

Caedmon seemed to deflate; I could see the venom of Showalter's words coursing through him.

"Just imagine how things might have played out if you two hadn't interfered. If only you'd remembered your place in the great scheme of things. A pauper and a girl and all their hopes? They don't belong in the real world."

Just a bit longer, I told myself. "We've managed to confound you so far." I flung the words at him, hoping the insult to his pride would be enough to stay his hand a moment more. Hoping he was petty enough to need the last word.

"But if you hadn't, you might have lived. And we wouldn't even be having this conversation."

"And Napoleon would have himself crowned in Westminster Abbey," I pointed out.

"But don't you see? He will be anyway. Despite all your efforts, you've only led us right to the point you were trying to avoid. You've simply made it more perilous for yourselves and tedious for me."

Surely it had been long enough now. It was time to force his hand.

I was seething, so angry that I'd nearly forgotten the gun he held pointed at my chest. "I suppose the way a stupid, self-involved girl and a museum lackey managed to get the better of you, France's most self-congratulatory espionage agent, *is* rather tedious," I spat.

He raised the pistol level with my brow. "I've so anticipated this moment." Anger frayed the edges of his words. "All those times you couldn't even be bothered to conceal that you'd rather be somewhere else than with me. I endured them all with the knowledge that someday, right before your death, you'd know who I was and what I've done. But you've managed to ruin this moment as well." He steadied his arm. "I suppose we can't always get what we wish for."

"No!" Caedmon shouted as I saw him shifting in my periphery.

"*Vive la France!*" Showalter whispered, narrowing his eyes as he pulled the trigger.

The pistol erupted in a flash of igniting powder. Smoke clouded the air between us. I wondered for a moment if I *had* been shot, if the lead ball had indeed hit me. But I knew it was the sound that caused me to stagger back, my own instinct to protect myself that forced me to the ground in the wake of the explosion.

My ears rang as I blinked away the flash spots swimming in front of my eyes. When I finally looked up, I was glad I couldn't see clearly.

Showalter's hand was a grisly mess.

The ball had indeed slipped back with the powder and backfired into his hand, just as the gamesman had warned. The pistol now lay harmless and smoldering on the gravel at Showalter's feet.

I looked at Caedmon, found him whole and unhurt. I turned back to Showalter. He was gaping, stunned, transfixed by the sight of his own blood dripping from the end of a sleeve that used to hold his hand.

And then he began to scream.

Showalter's anguished, terrifying curses filled the air for a brief moment before another sound, smaller and softer than the pistol report, silenced them. The sound of metal connecting with the back of Showalter's head.

Showalter's eyes grew wide and flashed empty for a moment. He teetered there a second longer as the muscles in his face relaxed from their contorted anger and pain, lapsing for a moment back into the soft, shapeless visage of the man I'd known. And then his eyes shut slowly as he collapsed to the ground in a heap, the back of his neck bearing an angry red welt.

Chapter Twenty-four

❧

Caedmon stood over him with the standard still raised. "I haven't killed him, have I?"

I scrambled to my feet. "I don't know."

"I had to do something to stop the screaming. The pistol shot might be blamed on an enthusiastic marksman, but a man screaming is sure to bring all the neighbors out."

"You did the right thing, Caedmon," I said, reaching for him and pointing at the standard with my other hand. "Incantations be damned, there is some power in that thing after all."

He tore his eyes away from Showalter.

"And you're all right?" he asked, pulling his hand away from mine and running it across my face.

I nodded, then explained what I knew about the gun, how I'd gambled it would backfire.

We stood looking at Showalter a moment longer. "What should we do with him?" Caedmon asked as he tucked the standard back into his waistband.

"Leave him," I said. We had no idea if there was another person in his household who knew his secret, who might also wish to do us harm.

We bolted for my garden and crept up to the lower wall bordering the paths. Our gardeners were not about, but Aunt Rachel sat in a chair on the patio, right in front of the trellis to David's room.

"You couldn't make the climb without being seen anyway," Caedmon said, seeing my dismay. "What about that wicket there on the south corner?"

I looked and saw that one of the tall, narrow windows of Father's study was indeed standing open. "But Aunt Rachel?"

"Pity it couldn't have been your Clarisse," Caedmon lamented.

I nodded. "Yes, she'd have cleared the way for the star-crossed secret lovers."

I thought I saw Caedmon smile as he took my hand. "We'll have to rig things ourselves—as always. Come on," he urged me, edging over the wall and stepping onto the lawn.

"Caedmon!" I whispered, but it was too late; he had already let go of my hand and was on the lawn and striding toward the house.

I hastened to his side. "Excuse me?" he called out to my chaperone.

She turned and surveyed the two strangers coming up the lawn from the river.

"My brother and I were out rowing this morning, and our

scull seems to have broken an oarlock. D'you mind terribly if we leave her tied up on the bank down there while we bring a rowboat upstream to tow it home?"

Aunt Rachel eyed us dubiously. "It isn't right for young men to come calling at this time of morning."

"We don't mean to trouble you," Caedmon said, confused.

"Some of these careless chaperones may let young men come traipsing under the windows of their charges, but I take my duties to Miss Agnes's reputation quite seriously."

I couldn't fight the giggle that bubbled up.

"And to laugh at an old woman, at the face of tradition!" She threw back her shoulders. "Shame!"

"But our boat—," Caedmon began before she cut him off again.

"The river is too low this season to row. I know you're up to nothing good," she said, and then turned for the house, shouting, "Mrs. Brewster! Come quick, there are vagrants in the garden!"

"Run!" I whispered to Caedmon as we hurried around to the side of the house. Aunt Rachel couldn't follow, but she was raising the household—if not the neighborhood—with her cries.

"Well done," I panted to Caedmon as we ducked into the shrubbery beside the open window. The threshold hovered two feet above the lamb's ear planted in the bed below. I peeked inside and found Father's desk unoccupied, the room still.

"How was I to know your chaperone was an even greater saucebox than you?" he asked.

"Seems we're all full of surprises this morning," I said, reaching up to grab the edge of the window. I could hear the shouts as the servants responded to Aunt Rachel's cries. It would be a miracle if I made it up the steps undetected.

"I'm going to tear across the garden and lead everyone away," he said. "It doesn't matter if I get caught, but you can't be found looking like that."

"Fine," I said. "Let's have the standard. I'll give it to Father."

Caedmon nodded, and placed the standard in my free hand.

I stepped over the threshold softly onto the wide plank floor of the study. I turned to face Caedmon again, finding that for once, what with the advantage of the height of the floor, I was actually a little taller than he was. He looked up at me. We had no time, Aunt Rachel would have the entire household stirred to chase away the intruders. But standing there, staring at him, knowing that for the moment at least the worst was behind us at last, I couldn't make myself hurry.

"I believe this is the part in the story where Clarisse would expect me to thank you for a lovely evening," I said.

He laughed and looked away. At the sound of men's voices joining Aunt Rachel's in the back garden, I smiled and turned to go. Caedmon's hand on mine stopped me.

I turned back to him.

"In the garden before," he said, keeping my fingers bound up in his, "I meant what I said. About you being the most extraordinary—"

"You said marvelous," I corrected him quickly. I was rather tired of being extraordinary and plucky and whatever else he'd called me. Marvelous would do nicely for a change.

"Both," he said in surrender. "I was wondering . . . hoping . . . that perhaps you felt something like that for me."

"I do find myself unexpectedly short a suitor," I whispered.

"You mean—"

"I mean," I inched closer, "that Clarisse, when she presses me for details of my pretend love affair," I said with mock gravity, "will be expecting a report on something else."

He looked confused, then brightened. "Oh! Well," he said, nervously wringing my hand. "I suppose it wouldn't do for us to shirk that duty."

I shook my head. "Wouldn't do at all," I said, leaning toward, letting his arms pull me the rest of the way into the embrace.

The kiss might have taken a bit longer than was prudent for a girl needing to slip upstairs unnoticed and a young man on the run from an angry chaperone. Might have taken longer than was absolutely necessary to satisfy the curiosity of an overly romantic Clarisse. And it might have taken even longer were it not for the fact that I heard someone behind me clear his throat.

I straightened and whirled toward the sound. "Father!"

His eyes bore a flash of surprise before he collected himself.

"Daughter," he said, adding, "Daughter in my son's clothing consorting with someone at my window . . ."

"Mother said you wouldn't return until this afternoon," I stammered.

"Sorry to have inconvenienced you," my father said.

I struggled to speak. I'd counted on a few hours to prepare my story for Father.

"Now would someone like to explain this to me?" Father asked after too long a silence.

I reached for his hand, turned it over, and placed the bronze standard into his palm. "Miles Deacon said you'd know what to do with this."

"Is this—," he began before I cut him off.

"Yes. And Showalter is a villain and lying incapacitated in his garden."

Father looked at the heft of bronze in his hand, then back to me. "But how?"

"My associate, Mr. Stowe," I said, gesturing toward Caedmon, "will be happy to explain if you should like to invite him in. But I really must change. Mother's about to have a very strange day, and I shan't compound it by turning up in David's old things."

I didn't wait for a response. Instead I sprinted across the room, cracked the door a bit, and turned back to find both my father and Caedmon staring at me in confusion. Finding the hall deserted—the house emptied of servants searching for the two young interlopers who'd so disturbed Aunt Rachel—I bolted up the stairs to my room. As I closed the door to my chamber and slid into an exhausted heap on the floor, I wondered if there were any better circumstances for the man I loved and the father I adored to meet.

I had a suspicion there were not.

Chapter Twenty-five

❧

A month passed.

An entire month wherein I did not see Caedmon.

But what a month it was. On June 18—just three days after we recovered Wepwawet's standard—Napoleon suffered his first debilitating defeat at Waterloo.

All of London was wild with the news that the war had ended, that we would know peace at last. Fireworks that were usually reserved for other seasons erupted at all times of day and night in celebration.

Two skirmishes later, Wellington and the combined powers of the English and Prussian forces sent the tyrant packing. Napoleon signed abdication orders in Paris and was exiled once again. His defeat was so complete, and his armies so devastated, that the heavy guard posted around his prison was—according to every paper, politician, and letter from David—a redundancy. Bonaparte had been defeated before, but this time, he'd been *humiliated*.

But there were no fireworks for me. Nor for Caedmon. No one would ever know the service we'd performed for our country. Perhaps that's what it meant to be a servant. Only if you failed or performed sloppily did people pay attention. When you were successful, you were invisible.

The celebrations continued. And the season and the pending debuts took on even greater significance. But I found very little to celebrate. Chiefly because aside from a single cryptic note from Caedmon reading *I'll see you soon*, we'd had no contact at all since I left him in the study that morning.

"He's bound to be busy with filing reports and things," my father said evasively when I asked if he'd heard from Caedmon. "I'm sure he'll turn up."

I wasn't convinced. In fact, I was beginning to worry that some danger had befallen Caedmon.

But slipping off to see him was out of the question.

After Father learned of how I'd taken advantage of Aunt Rachel and my lack of a proper chaperone, he remedied the situation accordingly. The morning after our adventure concluded, a Miss Dimslow appeared at the breakfast table. She explained that she'd been engaged by my father to serve as chaperone. I would have protested had he not also hired a new coachman to serve as my exclusive driver. And ultimately it was their startling similarities that made me doubt their real purpose in our household. There was none of the humility or subservience about them common to the other servants.

Instead there was a vigilant awareness that bordered at times on protectiveness.

So eager were they to screen anyone approaching me that after a few failed attempts to visit Caedmon at the museum— the last trip resulting in the news that he had left the institution for a different position—I gave up trying to go out at all. I half worried that since we'd secured the standard, perhaps the affection and emotion we'd felt might evaporate. This thought and his absence so depressed me that I found myself moping about the house, unable to read or work or study. I wondered if love was always so troubling, if the kind of love you grew into was as fraught with potential for disappointment as the kind you fell into.

Mother, of course, misinterpreted the cause of my heartache.

Showalter had disappeared.

On one of the rare occasions that I had spoken to my father, he'd disclosed to me that men had been dispatched to collect Showalter within an hour of my arrival home, but found him gone. His servants and household staff were as bewildered as could be expected of people who'd lost both their *raison d'etre* and positions in one fell swoop.

His disappearance was a blow of sorts, but Tanner was collected from his sarcophagus at the museum, swearing and cursing upon his release before buttoning up and refusing to speak to interrogators. From what I'd gleaned as the weeks passed, he at last had begun to reveal his mission and connections, and confirmed Showalter's true identity as a spy.

Father had also revealed to me that Lady Blalock had been implicated as an accomplice of Showalter and an agent of the French. Apparently the invention of his history and introduction into our society was entirely her work, and had been her primary achievement in the twenty years of service she'd given to France. She'd even colluded with Tanner and Showalter in organizing the attack on her own lady's maid to make it seem as if her home too had been beset by the mummy's curse.

Of course, the public would never know any of it. The explanations for Showalter's disappearance ran the gamut from some torrid affair to the more fantastical version that held him as the last victim of the mummy's curse. Lady Blalock was reported to have retired to a country estate in Wales to calm her nerves. Such a bizarre turn of events provided sufficient grist to keep London's rumor mill spinning.

Whether I was jilted or tragic in London's eyes, I did not care. I was pleased it meant I could be left alone and expected to be sour without consequence. Even Mother trod a wide and cautious path around me unless a dress fitting or other matter for the debut was absolutely necessary. And Rupert, in his way, offered his condolences. Chiefly this meant that he made some comment about the loss of all that lovely money, but beneath it, I chose to believe he felt some semblance of pity for his sister.

No one pitied me enough to spare me the presentation,

however. Though after a month of being sequestered in my room, enduring Mother's concern and Miss Dimslow's ever-vigilant presence, I actually found myself looking forward to the event we'd been preparing for. I'd never been to the palace, and I'd never seen the prince regent, so though it wasn't half as exciting as what I'd been doing a few weeks ago, it was at least something.

So at the appointed time, I found myself in my presentation gown, lined up with so much other silk and lace just outside a ballroom at the palace.

"You look remarkably well, Agnes," Julia said to me as we gathered in the hallway outside the grand room.

I wasn't sure if she meant in spite of my ordeal or if she was simply paying me a compliment. "Thank you, Julia. And so do you." We did look beautiful, and under different circumstances, I'd have been thrilled to be here, to be sharing this moment with her, to be as perfect as Mother had been preparing me to be in a dress that was made in every detail for me. . . .

But it all felt a bit hollow. A bit like it was missing something. As if the story I was about to settle into would always pale next to the memory of the brief, wonderful chapter I'd just concluded. Would there ever be that kind of adventure? That feeling of partnership? That . . . love?

"I'm so sorry about Showalter," Julia said quietly, nervously fingering the gold pendant at her neck.

I leaned in close and whispered into her ear. "I'm not."

She drew back wide-eyed in shock at my words. But when I smiled and winked, she relaxed and began to giggle. "Is it speaking ill of the missing or whatever he is to say that I never thought him your equal?"

Father had sworn me to secrecy on Showalter's true nature, but this once, I couldn't resist. "Nothing you say about him could be too unkind."

At that, Julia shook her head. "I should be upset with you for making it harder for the rest of us again."

"You'll find someone perfect," I said to her. "And Rupert will let himself be caught soon enough if you'll consent to have him. Besides, I'm beginning to wonder if I'll marry at all."

"Agnes Wilkins! Don't say such things!"

I laughed. But the doors opened and I saw the porter whisper to someone standing inside the room, who then turned and announced the first girl in our procession.

"Miss Emily Woodhouse!" he shouted, as a terrified and glamorous young woman stepped forward into the ballroom and passed from our sight.

"I'm so glad I didn't have to go first," Julia said after a long silence in which we imagined the girl making her way through the room.

I nodded. "Suddenly I just want to remain out here—"

"Miss Agnes Wilkins!" the voice boomed.

Oh dear.

I stepped out of my place in line and shot a nervous

backward glance at Julia. She smiled encouragingly and clapped her gloved hands silently.

And it began. Faces of every age stared as I did my best to sail down the open pathway in the center of the ballroom. I caught Mother beaming in the crowd about halfway down. Rupert stood behind her, and I daresay even *he* looked a bit proud.

Father was nowhere to be seen.

Most of the other faces I saw as I moved toward the prince seated at the far end of the room belonged to strangers. My train glided on the polished marble floor behind me, and I was glad that Mother had relented on the longer one, glad that I didn't add to the spectacle of the moment by requiring someone else to come along behind me to carry the end of my dress.

And then there were the faces of the young men and other chaperones. They bore the same appraising looks I'd seen when Father had let me accompany him to a horse auction when I was small. The feel of their eyes and the thought of the judgments they formed in their minds made me want to turn and bolt from the hall, leaving every one of them behind.

But this was the life I was born to. The one I'd prepared for. And aside from my recent adventure, it would be the only one I'd ever know.

I told myself I should feel blessed to have an audience with the prince regent. Not every debutante enjoyed such a privilege. But as I drew nearer and my nerves grew more frayed, my anger grew warmer at the injustice of it all. I was having very little fun by the time I curtsied deeply just a few feet from where the prince stood.

I studied the gleaming floor below. Saw my face and the width of my dress reflected back at me and waited. Waited for the prince regent, the sovereign of England, to dismiss me and commend me into adulthood, marriage, children . . . duty.

But instead of merely nodding and smiling as I was told he would do, the prince moved toward me.

A current rippled through the crowd behind me.

But still His Excellency moved forward. I kept my eyes down, staring at the gleaming leather of his fine boots as whispers grew to murmurs.

And suddenly the prince spoke low in my ear.

"Well done, Miss Wilkins," he said simply. "Extremely well done."

I was so confused that I forced myself to look up at his face. His expression remained that royal mix of stoicism and superiority, but his eyes sparkled. He gave a slight nod, and then leaned in again.

"There's someone eager to meet you in the salon. An escort is awaiting you through the door to your left. There will be a distraction. Take your opportunity to exit then."

I nodded, unsure of what else to do but rise from my curtsy. He took two steps backward as I retreated slowly away and moved to join the first girl, who was now positioned against a bank of open doors lining the west wall. I could feel her staring at me, wondering what I'd done to merit the breach in the evening's prescribed events.

I avoided her gaze and the stares of the rest of the room. The porter announced another girl, but half the eyes in the room stayed fixed on me. How was I ever to slip out?

Four more girls were announced and entered until we were standing in a cluster at the side of the room. I made sure to position myself in the rear of this small pack, my back to the door. But still I felt the stares of the crowd, even the sideways glances of the other girls, all wondering what the prince had said to me, why he'd singled me out.

And still I waited for the promised distraction. Just when I was sure I had missed it, the porter announced the next girl. I looked up to see her standing in the doorway, saw her take her first steps into the room.

But I saw something else. I saw the poor girl's train find its way beneath the foot of the porter, saw the girl lurch when the fabric held fast, pinned against the floor, her arms flying out as she fell into the crowd of onlookers.

And I couldn't be sure, but I thought I saw the porter wink.

Certainly I couldn't hope for a greater opportunity. All eyes were now on the unfortunate girl, which meant that no one observed my exit.

I slipped as quietly as I could through the doorway. It was more difficult than usual owing to that infernal train, but I managed without being seen. And if I had been, I hoped anyone paying attention would chalk it up to nerves at my strange preferential treatment by the prince regent.

"This way," Miss Dimslow said, taking my elbow.

"You?"

"I'm the relay," she said. "There's someone you need to talk to."

"You're not really just a chaperone, are you?" I asked. And then I saw Miss Dimslow smile for the first time.

"No more than you're just a debutante."

She escorted me down the hall, the music from the ballroom fading. We stopped in front of a closed oak door.

"I'll wait out here," she said, reaching for the knob and pushing it open.

"Thank you," I began as she thrust me inside and shut the door, barely avoiding sealing it on my skirts in her haste.

The room was dark, only a pair of lamps lit in a corner beyond the table.

"So sorry to steal you away like this, Agnes, but it was the only way to arrange a meeting without raising suspicions."

"Father!" I cried, running toward him.

He nodded, took my hands, and raised them to his mouth for a kiss. Then he pulled back and studied me at arm's length. "You are stunning, daughter," he said. "Absolutely stunning."

Someone else cleared his throat.

I turned and was surprised to find two more men standing in front of their chairs by the hearth. The first commanded my attention at once—because it was impossible to ignore the high military dress, starched collar, and decorated jacket. He seemed to take up far more room and space than just his simple form allowed. He was no broader than my father, and certainly no taller, but all the same, he seemed to carry with him the confidence and spirit of ten men.

Before I could inquire as to his name, I noticed his companion. I broke into a broad smile and walked briskly over. "Deacon!"

He returned my smile, accepted my embrace, and laughed quietly. "Miss Wilkins," he replied.

"Deacon, I tried to write to you at the hospital, but my letter was returned. They claimed you'd been released, but they had no way to forward it to you, and when I sent a note with a messenger to your lodgings near the Tower—"

He raised a hand to silence me. "I'm sorry to have worried you. But you should know that your adventures of late have left a great many of us scrambling to keep up. I've been very busy filing reports on your and Caedmon's behalf," he said, patting my hand gently. The bandage from his head had been removed, a raised pink scar curving over his eyebrow the only visible remnant of his interview with Tanner.

"Are you well?"

"Quite, miss, quite," he said.

"And Caedmon? You've heard from Caedmon, then?"

"Patience, Miss Wilkins. We've very little time before you're missed at court, and there are much more important things to discuss at present. Allow me to introduce you to Sir Arthur Wellesley, the Duke of—"

"Wellington," I whispered. I turned to face the man credited with the strategic genius of defeating Napoleon at Waterloo. The man whose name I'd heard spoken in reverent hushed tones through Father's grate. The hero of all England.

I bent my knees, afraid they might fail beneath me, and managed a semblance of a curtsy. Wellington accepted it, allowing a tight smile. "Miss Wilkins."

Father led us to the sitting area clustered around an ebony table, where a tray bearing a bottle of port and four glasses sat. I perched on the edge of the small sofa next to my father, opposite Deacon and Lord Wellington as they settled into winged chairs.

Wellington's eyes fixed on me for a long moment before anyone spoke again. Finally he said simply, "Extraordinary."

I looked nervously to my father, fearful I'd done something wrong. But my father looked at ease, smiling as if I'd just played him a tricky piece on the forte.

"Pardon, sir?" I asked.

"How many years have you?" Wellington asked, the Irish accent in his voice like one of Deacon's scars—all but gone.

"Seventeen, sir," I said quietly.

"And how many languages?"

"Pardon, sir?"

"Languages you speak? How many?"

I was confused. "Ten, sir."

He nodded. "You've learned some of them on your own?"

"Yes, sir."

Now he looked to Deacon. "When you told me what this girl had done . . . I don't know . . . I suppose I expected her to at least look a bit *older*."

Deacon smiled, the same proud smile my father wore.

"Tell me it all again," Wellington commanded, in a way that made me know what it might mean to be in his service and receive an order. I did so, relating how I found the key, how I stumbled on Caedmon, and how together we recovered the standard and delivered it safely to my father.

"How very fortunate she happens to be your daughter," Wellington said as I concluded.

"None so fortunate as I for that," my father said so softly he might have been talking to himself.

Wellington nodded his assent, and then surveyed me again. "Extraordinary," he repeated. "Do you know how many men have tried and failed to do what you and Mr. Stowe have accomplished?"

"I'm sure I only did my duty, sir," I said, starting to feel embarrassed at his praise.

"But few mortals enjoy a duty that allows them to save the lives of thousands of others, to have a hand in the defeat of the world's greatest tyrant, to preserve the crown and glory of England herself."

"I'm sure my contribution pales in comparison to those who fought at Waterloo, or sail with the navy like my brother, or any who know their duties as patriots—," I began before he cut me off.

"My dear," he said. "You've something singularly rare. Something far less common than mere duty."

I couldn't speak as I looked to Father. He merely nodded and smiled.

"Did you enjoy searching for the standard?" Wellington asked.

I glanced at Deacon quickly before turning back to my father, afraid of embarrassing him with my response. But lying to Wellington felt a bit like lying to God Almighty himself. "I did, sir," I said. "Even the dangerous bits."

He nodded. "I suspected as much. And don't for a moment believe that your contributions were not vital in that damned Frog's defeat. If he'd had that standard, I can't begin to think what might have happened. Certainly his men would have fought like animals even more than they did. And if it could do what it is rumored to be able to . . ." He trailed off, all of us imagining that grim possibility.

"But we'll never know. England won't use it, won't trifle with things of that sort. England will win her battles on the conviction of its principles, the justness of our cause, and the favor of the Lord, nothing more," he promised.

"Hear, hear," my father said.

"Of course, sir," I said meekly, realizing that even Wellington believed in the power of the standard, in the possibility of the supernatural. "Then the standard has been hidden again?"

He nodded, studying me, those stern, dark eyes looking down the considerable length of his elegant hooked nose.

"If I had my way, we'd melt it down for cannon shot, but I'm satisfied it is as secure as it can be."

"I'm relieved to hear it."

"Then you'll be relieved to learn that all traces of its former whereabouts have been erased," Deacon said. "The obelisk from Showalter's garden has been destroyed. They've even amended the Rosetta Stone so that partial glyph that led to your and Caedmon's breakthrough is no longer visible. Even the Ptolemy references have been, well, taken care of."

"You've altered the Stone?" I said, aghast.

"Not so much that it matters. And not so much that any of the rubbings that exist won't look like they simply missed a few marks here and there," Deacon said apologetically.

"Allow me to return to an earlier point," Wellington interrupted. "You seem to have some passion for languages; your father tells me you are inclined to travel, and you have demonstrated and admitted to an appetite for the sort of intrigue that led you to do what you call your simple duty in England's service."

I nodded.

"Miss Wilkins," he said, leaning forward in his chair, his

brown eyes finding a kinship in mine, "you have discovered the rarest of gifts among men. For when duty and passion align, they produce a *calling*. And I submit to you, that your calling has found you."

I thought of David's words regarding his own service. Tears stung at my eyes.

"Sir, I appreciate your confidence, but I cannot imagine what this might mean for a young woman in my position."

"If I may?" Deacon interrupted, looking to the duke for permission. He nodded his assent.

"I believe what Sir Wellesley is saying is that England might have use for someone of your unique abilities. A place where the calling he speaks of might be fully realized, should you be so inclined to exercise those gifts in further service to the Crown."

I turned to Father. Now his eyes were rimmed with tears, but the smile remained.

"I don't understand. . . ."

"We'd like to engage your services," Wellington said. "Deacon's been pressing me for years that women could play a more active role in intelligence, and after what you've done, I'm inclined to allow him to expand our ranks. Besides, that damned Blalock woman had half of London fooled, so there's something to be said for the fairer sex dabbling in the game. Not to mention the indispensable Miss Dimslow."

"Miss Dimslow?" I said.

Deacon nodded. "Uncommonly resourceful, that one.

Does frightening things with knitting needles. You'll learn a great deal from her."

"You mean . . ." I couldn't finish.

"Nothing untoward, you understand, but we feel your talents and disposition make you an ideal candidate for the kind of work we find we need done," Wellington explained.

"Intelligence?" I whispered. "You want me to be a *spy*?"

"It's far more complicated than all that, but in short, yes. We believe there are ways for you to continue making the kinds of contributions you have made of late," Deacon said.

I looked at him, narrowing my eyes. "Does this mean that you've been reinstated?"

He smiled and cast his eyes down. "In a manner of speaking. Seems your adventure resulted in my redemption as well."

"But how would I manage to explain to Mother or our friends and neighbors my unlikely choice of vocation?"

"Oh, you'd explain nothing to anyone!" Wellington thundered. "And in any event, the terms of this conversation are to be guarded with the utmost secrecy. As far as explaining, your recent . . . *misfortunes* . . . regarding your intended actually prove quite fortuitous."

"He wasn't my intended. We'd no private or public understanding—"

Deacon interjected. "What my lord means is that your abandonment in the eyes of your peers gives you leave to make a change of lifestyle. We've already discussed this all with your father. If you choose to accept our proposal, for all anyone else knows, you'll be residing in a convent in the Swiss Alps, recovering from the scandal and heartache brought about by these recent events. That should give us ample time to train you at least, though you'll enjoy regular visits back home as any ranked officer might."

"You mean, I'll travel?" I asked, barely able to contain my anticipation.

"Probably far more than you'd like," Wellington said. "I'd wager you'll have cause to see more of the world than the three of us combined."

I turned to Father. "You would allow it?"

He took my hand. "I've argued with these two valiantly for the past week, but they've worn me down enough to make me see what I should have admitted years ago—you're too special a girl to waste on parties and balls. At least for a time. And Deacon assures me that you'll encounter nothing so dangerous as what you've found here in London."

I was almost disappointed.

"And I will miss you, more than I can say, but I can mitigate such longing by knowing you'll acquit yourself with all the valor and composure that David has," he said.

"And I'll be along with you, of course," Deacon said. "Wellington has insisted that I chaperone you both, mentoring you in the craft—"

"Both?" I asked.

At that, the latch clicked open softly behind me and I turned round to catch Miss Dimslow's face for a brief moment as she held open the door and slid aside to admit the tall figure standing behind her. A figure whose deep brown eyes found mine and banished every other thought.

"Caedmon!" I cried, bouncing to my feet.

He hurried to my side and took my hand.

"Miss Wilkins," he said, though he couldn't contain his smile either.

"But where have you been? Why have you left the museum?"

"I've been busier than I expected," he said, motioning for me to sit.

"We convinced Caedmon that keeping secret his progress with the Stone would in the end serve Britain's ends far more than publishing his work," Deacon explained.

"And his silence toward you was our doing, I'm afraid. In the interests of providing a suitable cover story, we thought it best to keep you both separated until your deployment."

Now Caedmon spoke. "They've persuaded me there is pressing need for my experience as a—"

"Paranormal antiquities specialist," Deacon supplied, managing to keep from laughing as he did so.

"A title?" I said, raising an eyebrow.

"Well, one of them," Deacon admitted.

"Mr. Stowe is now Caedmon Deveraux, Esquire," my

father supplied. "He's the son of a foreign service diplomat, reared in North Africa."

"They've concocted an alias for you," I said, staring at him, noticing for the first time the finely tailored new suit he wore.

"An alias that will allow him entry to certain social circles should the need arise," my father said, adding, "I daresay he may even fool your mother at some point in the future."

My heart leaped.

Miss Dimslow popped her head back into the room. "Two girls left," she said. "You might have three minutes before she'll be needed back."

Wellington nodded. "You can plan your future together later," he huffed. "Now we've little time to sort this out."

I tore my eyes away from Caedmon's and focused on the general.

"Your associate has tentatively accepted our invitation to join our work as a field agent and cryptographer," Lord Wellington said.

"Tentatively?"

"Quite. His acceptance is conditional on your own."

"Then we would—I mean to say that—," I stuttered, afraid of seeming too eager on this point.

"You would continue working with your friend," my father said, adding, "under the watchful eye of Deacon, of course."

"It's far too valuable and productive a pairing to ignore the possibilities of future contributions," Deacon said. "But I think you'll find me an uncompromising chaperone. And I won't be alone in keeping eyes on you. Miss Dimslow will be along for extra security."

"When do we go?" I asked, finding it impossible and unnecessary to hide my joy. There would be Caedmon. And Deacon. And something to do with knitting needles.

"We'd like you to begin as soon as possible," Deacon said.

I looked to Father, his head bowed as he studied the glasses on the low table. I sank to my knees in front of him. "Are you sure this is all right with you?"

He sighed. "I can't think of any man who is happy about sending his daughter into a potentially dangerous situation."

I nodded.

"But I also can't think of anyone I'd trust more to do the work than you, darling," he said. "Besides, it will save me having to shut the flue every time I mean to have a sensitive conversation in my study."

I blushed, but felt far too excited to be properly ashamed.

"Then I have your blessing?"

"And my admiration, my affection, and my love," he said, one tear escaping as his voice trembled.

After a long silence in which I held my father, Deacon cleared his throat. I broke off the embrace and turned to face the others.

"Forgive me," I said, wiping at my eyes. "I find the social rules governing a young lady's call to military service a bit fuzzy. I forget myself."

Everyone laughed. I smiled as Father squeezed my hand.

Wellington stood, signaling that the interview had drawn to a close. "Well, Miss Wilkins, I salute your fortitude and courage. I've no doubt that the four of you will make quick work of this trouble in Egypt."

"Egypt?" I whispered, looking quickly to Caedmon's broad smile.

Wellington nodded. "I assume you've no objection. . . ."

He launched into a hurried description of some problem besetting the empire in Cairo. I nodded and tried to appear attentive, gazing at him as he spoke, but I confess I heard precious little. In my mind's eye, I was already riding camelback beside Caedmon, covered head to toe in a veil. But in my vision, even that veil couldn't hide the joy I felt as it radiated from me, like the heat shimmering from the desert sands.

And I was sure A Lady could not have crafted a happier ending.

Author's Note

❧

        While Agnes's adventure is fiction, the seeds for the story sprout from historical events and places. The hundred days, Napoleon's interest in Egyptology, and even the existence of spies—the British version of which were often known as "Wellington's Men"—are all part of the historical record. Even the use of heat-sensitive invisible ink—often lemon juice later activated by holding the paper close to a flame—has been widely employed for various military and espionage pursuits since the first century. And though there are tales of cunning female spies and operatives throughout history—from Rahab in the Bible to Mata Hari during the first World War—there are countless women lost to history who engaged in espionage on behalf of their countries. I prefer to think of Agnes like one of these women—a girl whose contributions to her country go unnoticed precisely because she was so effective.

        In spite of my efforts to ground the story in historical detail, there are two liberties I have taken that I feel compelled to point out.

The British Museum established its collection of Egyptian antiquities after routing Napoleon's forces from Egypt in 1798. Several mummies and the Rosetta Stone were among the items the French were forced to surrender to the British—an indignity some scholars say Napoleon never forgave. A great many of these became part of the collection at the British Museum, where they were featured in the exhibits of the Townley Gallery, which opened in 1808 and began fascinating visitors from all over the world. In fact, the Rosetta Stone has been continuously displayed in the British Museum since 1802. The fact that I have the Stone off display for cleaning in my story is, I hope, both forgivable and believable. The Stone was open to the air and the hands of visitors for most of its time in the museum; only recently has it been placed under protective glass. The Stone did require cleaning—even once to remove a bit of graffiti painted on the side by an overzealous British soldier.

Second, mummy unwrapping parties *were* in vogue in England and in other parts of Europe in the nineteenth century. Mummies were in such plentiful supply that they were processed and reborn (perhaps not quite what the ancient Egyptians had in mind) as paper, paint, railroad fuel, and even medicines. And for the adventurous (and wealthy) European traveling in Egypt, the souvenir of choice was often a mummy—one that might find its way into an entryway as a showpiece.

The practice of mummy unwrapping parties, however, didn't become widespread until a bit later than this story's setting—nearer the late 1840s. I hope that historians can forgive me this liberty and will imagine with me what might have transpired if a mummy unwrapping happened as early as 1815, and concede that a man of Showalter's means and motives might have hosted such an event as the one I describe in the story.

When I began writing *Wrapped*, I set out to write a book that combined my loves for the Regency period, Egyptian mythology and history, and stories featuring spies and secret agents. I've been pleased and spurred along by the way the history provided details for me on which to hang Agnes's story, and delighted by the space left between the facts to do what all writers love: make stuff up.